THE LAST JULY

BREANNA MOUNCE

ISBN: 978-0-615-93477-8

Stardust Romance

Goshen, KY 40026

www.hydrapublications.com

To my s'mores lovers and stargazers:
thanks for the memories.

ONE

"Bug spray?"

"Check."

"Sunscreen?"

"Spray on and lotion, check."

"Picture of your favorite person in the entire world?"

I grab the list from my best friend's hand and roll my eyes. "I'm only going to be gone for two and a half months. Besides, it's only Tennessee, I'm not even leaving the country."

Janine flops back on the bed. "But you're not going to have any cell service most of the time, so you might as well be on another planet! Do they even speak English in Tennessee?"

"Think you're being a bit too dramatic?" I ask, going over my list by myself now. This is my third time checking everything. I'm pretty sure I've packed up my whole summer wardrobe and purchased every bottle of sunscreen I could find at Wal-Mart.

"No, I thought you grew out of summer camp! I figured this would be our last summer together before college, and we'd have one last hoorah." She grabs my photo album off my nightstand, the one I keep there year-round from past summers at Camp Arthur, my home away from home.

"You'll be fine. We have a week once I get back to hang

out before we go to college, and I'll be coming home a few times to do laundry and see my parents. I can see you then," I explain.

Janine grabs one of my folded blankets and tosses it at me. I thank her because it's the one I was planning on taking with me anyway, a ratty old pink one that my grandma gave me when I was eight. I re-fold it and place it on top of my clothes and try to zip up the bag. It takes some force, but finally seals all the way shut after a few tries. I put it on the floor next to my sleeping bag, and my backpack full of leisure stuff like books on my summer reading list I haven't gotten to and some nail polishes just in case my campers want to have a spa night. Spa nights at camp are some of the best nights at camp.

"Yuck, what the heck is this?" Janine asks, disgust written all over her face as she points to a picture in my scrapbook.

I jump on the bed and lean over her shoulder to see the picture. The memory brings a smile to my face.

"Leftover mashed potato mohawks," I say proudly. My hair was so long last summer I won the contest for my cabin. Four days after the game, I was still finding dried up potatoes in my hair. So worth it though.

"That doesn't seem childish to you at all?" Janine asks, flipping the page.

"No, nothing is childish at camp. That's the point, to have fun and do things you never get to do."

"I would never put food in my hair," Janine remarks, flipping through more photos. "What other 'kid things' do you do at this 'camp' place?"

"Rock climb, crafts, archery, swimming… there's plenty to do, trust me. You're really missing out," I tell her, moving off of the bed to place all my stuff by the door. "There's never a dull moment at camp."

"Sounds strenuous. What about the boys? There has to be a handful of cute boys," she asks, closing the photo album with a thud. Each page is so laden with photographs that the book weighs several pounds.

"Ha, I grew up with most of the guys there. No way would I ever be interested in them."

She places the album back where it's supposed to be and grabs her purse. "I wasn't talking about you, I meant for me," she says with a laugh.

She smiles mischievously before grabbing my sleeping bag and heading for the stairs. I shake my head, grab my other two bags, and head for the stairs.

When we hit the landing my mom comes out of the kitchen drying her hands on a towel. "Oh hey girls. I was just coming to make sure you were leaving on time, Penny."

I love my mom dearly, but I hate when she calls me by my childhood nickname. *Penny.* It sounds cheap, whereas my full name, the name she gave me, *Penelope*, sounds ten times more mature. Typically, I ignore most people who shorten my name. It used to drive my high school teachers nuts, but lucky for them, I graduated. Once I'm in college, I can make damn sure no one calls me Penny - that cheap, easy excuse of a nickname.

"Am I never *not* on time?" I tease my mom, just as my phone alarm goes off telling me I need to head out to my car and get going.

She pulls me in for a hug. "Are you sure you can't wait for your dad to get home? He wanted to see you off," she says.

I pull back from her and put on my backpack. "I can't. I need to get there by three so I can get settled in before we have our first staff dinner. I'm required to be there."

If I hadn't added on the *requirement* part, there's no

doubt mom would have made me wait for dad to get home from work, but she finally releases her hold on me and kisses my forehead.

"Be careful," she tells me. "Check in with us when you can."

"Don't hold your breath for a phone call," I tell her, and before she can scold me, I pull out my package of stationery and stamps.

"What the heck is that?" Janine asks, feigning offense.

"If the campers can't use phones, I'm not using mine either. I'm going old-school, snail mail."

My mom smiles and pulls me in for another hug. "Have fun honey, we'll miss you. And remember, you were a camper once, don't try and scare the young ones with ghost stories," she says.

"I would never!" I gasp, trying to keep the laughter from my voice for dramatic effect. "I would be the one trying to soothe them in the middle of the night if I did!"

"Alright, get out of here," she says, smiling and swatting at me with her damp dishtowel.

"Oh, and mom," I say, stopping at the front door. "If anything comes from Maryville, you'll let me know, right?"

"Of course," she says with a smile.

I thought I would have heard from Maryville a long time ago, while all my other friends were getting their own acceptance letters, but I guess that's what I get for applying late. Now I'll be waiting and cutting things close this summer with my school plans. It's been Maryville or I'll wait another semester to apply to another school, I chose Maryville because it's just a short drive from camp, where I'd like to work every summer. Though, the next few months are the deciding factor for everything. I probably should have thought this through last summer.

Once Janine and I are at my car with all three of my

bags loaded, she hugs me tightly too, almost tighter than my mom.

"Don't do anything that I wouldn't, Pen," she says, pulling back and putting on her huge bug-eye sunglasses. Her bikini strings peek out of her tank top straps. Janine lives in swimsuits in the summer, whereas I live in hiking boots, gym shorts and old Camp Arthur tees.

"So, everything is fair game then?" I tease. Janine isn't a prude by any means. Not even close.

"Way to add fuel to the fire, betch," she fires back. I know Janine means well. She gets defensive when she's trying to hold back her real emotions. I just shake my head and tell her not to get into any trouble without me. She flips me the bird as I get into my car and pull out of the driveway. She keeps up the act until the last second and then waves a sad goodbye. I might just miss her more than she'll miss me.

It's a three-hour drive from home to camp, one of those hours used to be pure hell because it's all curvy back roads. It's easy to get to the camp, once you're off the exit, there's two right turns and you're there. My mom made me bring an extra Sprite and some crackers just in case I feel nauseous during the final part of my drive. Between my dad's poor driving and being a backseat driver when I was a kid, I would always get sick the second we started on the dirt road. My mom liked to say it was early homesickness. I would let her believe what she wanted.

Every July since I was ten, I've gone to Camp Arthur. I know the place like the back of my hand. I could probably navigate the twisting and turning gravel pathways with a blindfold if I had to.

This year is different than all the others, and not just because I'm not an actual camper. This year, I'm in between, I'm a camper *and* a junior counselor. This year, I'll be here for the whole summer. When I finally turn down the road for camp, I notice other things have changed too. A lot of the old gravel roads have been black-topped, and they've put in a pool to compliment the lake. The subtle differences are all needed upgrades, but they take away some of Camp Arthur's rustic charm.

I don't like change. Summer camps aren't supposed to change. They're supposed to look as they did when they were first built. Camp Arthur always made me feel like we were in the sixties or seventies, especially considering how old some of the furniture is in the common areas, parts of the cabins, and the bathrooms. Most bunks are made from wood and have names from previous campers carved in them too. If I look hard enough, I can probably find my name on six different bunks.

It's strange being here without my parents dropping me off, I admit.

My parents were always the clingy type that insisted they come with me to my cabin to make up my bunk and make sure I got settled in. They would always talk my counselors' heads off about the things I shouldn't do and which activities I love. Why they thought a college-aged counselor cared about my sleeping habits and that I will refuse to eat on taco night was way beyond me.

As I readjust my duffel bag over my shoulder and walk toward the registration area to get my cabin assignment, I notice they've built a new welcome center that looks too modern next to the woods. I liked the old rustic one built long before I was born. I should have been prepared for the change though. When my parents and I received the promotional pamphlet in the mail, we were told the camp was being run under new ownership.

Have the owners even been to a real summer camp? I wonder, taking in some of the more modern sights.

A new wooden sign hangs below the awning of the welcome center proclaiming, *'Camp Arthur Est. 1974. Mountains of Possibilities'.*

I just need to enjoy my final summer here as a CIT, a 'counselor in training'. Who knows if I can come back next summer as a legitimate counselor? The next two and a half months will decide that.

I walk inside the welcome center, the air conditioner on full blast and find a receptionist at a desk behind an open window like we're in a doctor's office. She looks bored out of her mind, flipping through *Cosmopolitan.* The front cover reads, *"How to please a man, when you're not on your knees."*

I clear my throat to get her attention.

She doesn't look up from her magazine. "What's up?" she asks tiredly.

Well, aren't we a happy camper? "I need to check in, I'm a junior counselor here for training," I tell her.

"Aren't you a little early?" she asks, finally putting her magazine down to check on the time.

"Just by 28 minutes."

She lets out an exaggerated breath and looks through the papers on her desk, clearly not ready for the other ten or so people that should be showing up for training. "What's your name, kid?"

"Penelope. I'm probably the only Penelope on your list," I say, trying to get her to smile.

She doesn't smile. She's testing my patience as she continues to search the desk. Finally, she finds the paper she's looking for. It appears that a coffee cup was sitting on it at one point because there's a brown ring stain on it.

"Penelope… Penelope…. Ah, here you are," says the worst receptionist ever hired, seems like she could use more training. "Cabin 6. Lucky you. You've got one of the new ones on the other side of camp. Air conditioning and everything. Enjoy."

If the new owners of Camp Arthur are anything like this girl, I'm not sure I can survive two months working here for minimum wage. Growing up, I envied the employees here at Camp Arthur. They were all so kind and pleasant to be around. They treated me like a friend, not an incompetent child.

"Lucky me…" I sigh, ignoring that my old cabin didn't have air conditioning. I loved having the windows open and listening to the crickets and other animals at night. There's something peaceful about a cabin with only four walls, a ceiling, and a floor, out in the middle of the woods. They always put the older girls further into the woods because the younger kids are too terrified of what goes bump in the night.

Miss Stickupmybum hands over my information, and I'm thankful I shouldn't have to be around her much longer. I take the packet quickly and walk away, but she stops me. My heart hammers in my chest at her tone that says, 'I'm in charge.' I hold my bag a little tighter.

"Don't you need help finding it?" she asks. "I can walkie someone to take you there. You're a bit too early, so everyone's out doing their own thing. I think they're all at the pool."

"No, I'm good," I tell her, not even bothering to look back when I open the door, and set off for the dirt path that leads to the wooden bridge. To be honest, I have no idea where my newly built cabin might be, but I want time to check things out before a counselor has full reign over me.

I cross the rickety bridge and walk by the mess hall, glancing in to see if it's the same. Thankfully, it is, from what I can see. I walk toward the trail that leads to the nature center, looking at a freshly painted sign that points to cabins six through ten. I'm glad Camp Arthur is expanding, but I worry it won't have the same camp feel to it when I become a counselor here. People come to camp to get away from the city and learn how to handle being without cell service or their normal daily routine, not to live in a luxurious cabin the size of a small house. Camp Arthur certainly does not *need* air conditioning or cell towers. Luckily, I haven't seen a cell tower yet, though it wouldn't surprise me to find one disguised as a tree.

"Hey!" shouts a friendly male voice. A guy wearing a pair of camo cargo shorts and a tie-dye t-shirt jogs over to me. Janine would shake her head in disgust at his mismatched patterns. His hair is shaggy brown and it almost curls into his eyes. It looks like he hasn't had a haircut for a year, but it fits him. He's wearing a headband with daisies poorly glued onto it, but something about it screams adorable and friendly. Adorable and not for me, because when he stands in front of me, I see he's wearing a Counselor ID badge attached to his Camp Arthur lanyard, not a CIT. I can't let myself get distracted by anyone. If I want to work here after this summer, I need to keep my eyes on my goal.

"Uh, hi," I say when he finishes catching his breath, he will probably yell at me for walking through camp alone. I glance around to see if anyone else is coming or if it is just him. I've never seen him here in the summer's prior as camper nor counselor; most counselors are repeats for at least four years, long enough for them to have a summer job through college and then move off to a job in the psychology or social work fields. Apparently, jobs like that love seeing 'camp counselor' on your resume.

"You lost? I can help you find your cabin," he asks, his voice deeper than I anticipated.

"No, I'm fine. I've been here before," I tell him as I continue onto the trail, not actually knowing if I'm heading in the right direction for once in my camp life, but I refuse to actually admit that out loud.

"Are you one of the new trainees?" he asks, catching up with me again, which is easy for him because his legs are so long. He's literally the tall, dark, and handsome type.

"Yeah." *Why else would I be here?* I want to add, but I'm pretty sure I'm still just a little upset from my experience with the camp receptionist. She makes the saying, misery loves company, a real thing.

"Cool, so I'll see you later then?" he asks, coming to a stop and turning to head back to where he came from. A slight breeze ruffles his hair and he pushes it out of his eyes.

I smile at him. "Yeah, totally," I reply. I'm glad he doesn't question me further. My frustration from the annoyed receptionist is wearing off as I encounter more of camp life from a non-camper perspective.

The boy walks back up the steep, dirt trail but turns around and my stomach does somersaults from the huge smile he gives me. "I'm so sorry, I didn't get your name," he says.

"Penelope," I tell him quietly. He doesn't hear so I try again a little louder and with more courage. "I'm Penelope."

Something in his eyes brightens up, like I've told him the secret to living. "Penelope," he repeats. "Nice to meet you! Glad to have you at Camp Arthur. I'm Sampson."

I finally find the cabin I'll be assigned to for the rest of the summer some time later. To my surprise, it matches the other cabins in the original part of camp, but it looks brand new. The grass hasn't even grown around it yet. That means many muddy footprints will be tracked through the cabin. When I open the door, it's quiet. One of the bottom bunks is made up with a pink and green comforter and sheet set, so I know the counselor who's training me is already settled in.

"Hello?" I ask into the empty cabin, dropping my bags off on another bunk. "Anyone here?"

"Shh," I hear faintly from another room followed by a chuckle.

I creep toward the voice and glance in another room with an extra bunk covered in clothes, extra toiletries, and other items spread out around the room and...

"Holy crap, I'm sorry. I'm sorry, I'm early." I say, covering my eyes when I see a guy and girl quickly pulling their clothes on in the corner of the small room. The girl fumbles with the buttons on her polo, blushing while the guy looks smugly pleased. He doesn't bother speeding up his dressing routine.

"I'll just... go wait outside." I say, practically running out of the cabin. I hear the guy laugh followed by the sound of skin slapping skin hard, the girl scolding the guy I assume.

Five minutes later, the guy exits the cabin, a huge grin on his face. Even I want to smack that smug look off. "Welcome to camp, newbie," he laughs.

"Thanks," I mutter.

Once he's out of sight, I hop off the picnic table and head back into the cabin, bracing myself for an even more awkward introduction. This time though, I knock hard on the main door before actually going in.

"Hey," I say. "My name's Penelope, I'm your junior counselor."

She doesn't look up at me, just keeps digging through her duffle bag. "You're early," the girl says coldly.

"Yeah, so I've been told," I say. "Sorry about that. I wasn't expecting to find that… whatever it was."

"And I wasn't expecting you, so we're even," she tells me, finally looking up. "My name's Viv. Welcome to camp. Let me give you a tour of our humble abode.

"This is my bunk, you can have the one over there. That way we can each have a side of campers to concentrate on. I let them pick their bunks, first come, first serve. As long as they keep their stuff under the bunks and out of the walkway, we're fine. Windows stay closed, I don't want any bugs in here," she explains.

I follow her up the small ramp and into the next room. "This is obviously the bathroom. I try to break up shower times, half volunteer for morning showers, the other half get night and they can swap the next week, ten-minute showers per girl.

"And this room," she continues, turning me around and gently pushing me into the room where I found her and Mr. Shirtless. "Is the *privacy* room. You can keep extra items in here, extra clothes, that sort of thing. If you need a moment to yourself, you can come in this room to escape the campers, or if you have a guest…"

"Guest?" I ask. "I thought we couldn't have outside guests stay or visit."

Viv smiles a wicked smile and winks at me. "I didn't say outside visitors. There's always a lonely co-worker to hang out with. It's going to be one long summer away from civilization and you'll be surprised by how sexy a sweaty frat boy in a camp shirt can be."

"I'm only seventeen, I…"

"Sweetie, no one cares. You're almost a college girl, right? All the guys want is a piece of ass. You'll have to grow up in a few months anyway. Just think of this as college but with boot camp and babysitting as your full-time job," she says.

Before my jaw has the chance to drop, I walk away from my new least favorite person to organize my bunk. Is this what camp is always like for the employees? Am I just finally seeing the behind-the-scenes drama? I unroll my sleeping bag on top of the fitted sheet I put over the small dingy mattress, I hear the main door swing open and closed. I head over to see where Viv is going and she rolls her eyes when she looks at me.

"I'm going to go for a trail run. When I get back we'll head over for dinner," she says, and before I can object, she's gone, leaving me alone in the cabin.

I sit on my bunk, looking around at all the empty bunks that will be filled up with campers in a couple days. Campers that I'll be in charge of. Campers that will be under my watch twenty-four hours a day, for the next three months. Maybe I'm in a bit over my head…

After waiting an hour for Viv to get back, I'm already bored. I've read thirty pages of a book I brought that's supposed to last me two weeks, and I've finished organizing all of my things. Out of boredom, I decide I want to walk around camp. I head for the lake, halfway across camp, one of my favorite spots in the whole camp. As I head there, other co-workers are making their way around camp. A few are playing a game of 2 on 2 soccer, while I see some are soaking up the sun at the pool.

The lake dock is usually crawling with campers fishing or canoeing. I never told anyone, but once, when I couldn't sleep, I snuck out to the lake at four in the morning before anyone else got up. That's my favorite memory of camp, but when asked, I have to make something up, like the time I actually climbed to the top of the rock wall to ring the bell or the first time I passed my swim test. In my mind, nothing compares to sneaking off to the lake right before dawn.

Right now, I want to be alone for a little bit. Once dinner is served, my official training will begin. That's when they make us do team games, exploring nature, and discussing anything the counselors deem fitting. Viv strikes me as a counselor that's not too concerned about camper feelings. Sometimes I think the counselors use campers as test subjects for their college courses, especially the ones wanting to be shrinks one day. I'm all about loving nature and sharing my feelings, but I don't want to be forced to do it at seven in the morning during the summer. I'm sure that'll change now that I'm a CIT.

A twig breaks behind me and when I turn, I assume it'll be a bear or another vicious animal coming to maul me. It's actually Sampson, with his backpack and a water bottle in his hand, and that trademark friendly smile on his lips.

"Fancy seeing you here," he says as he joins me on the dock, his forehead glistening with sweat. We both sit there with our feet hanging over the edge. Mine hover, but his are covered in water up to his ankles. I notice his flip-flops buckled to the back of his pack. Camp usually bans flip-flops, or at least they do for the campers. It's apparently too dangerous for them to walk around in such wound-inducing footwear. Maybe that's why they blacktopped most of the gravel areas. Everything is just too dangerous for campers.

"Were you following me?" I ask, trying to say it in a flirty way I think my prettier friends back home would use to lure a boy in. Janine is always good at that. When I try, my throat tightens, and the words come out all wonky.

His cheeks blush, and it's the cutest thing I have ever seen, well aside from newborn kittens learning to walk. "Yeah, that's not weird, right? I just thought it would be cool to hang out before we have to start babysitting."

Babysitting? Does he not realize how cool this job is?

I try my best to keep my tone under control because I'm annoyed that he thinks his job is babysitting. "Not all of them are kids, you know? Some of them are already preparing for college and working toward their dreams."

"Sorry," he says, his blush getting deeper. "I just meant the younger ones. They make me nervous. I'm always afraid they'll get into poison ivy or go missing. Pool time is a very stressful situation for me. Too much can go wrong. I don't care how much lifeguard training I've had, I don't know what I'd do if I had a child's life in my hands."

Before I realize it, I'm playfully bumping my shoulder against his. "It's okay," I say. "I just really love this place, and not many people give the campers enough credit. Some of them are probably more responsible than the counselors."

"I never thought of it that way, but it's probably true, well aside from the boys," he jokes.

A few minutes of silence pass between us. I swing my legs back and forth, watching our reflections shimmer in the water. I look at his reflection next to mine and wonder how it's even possible for him to be this nice to me. Everyone else seems to have an attitude problem.

I wonder how old he is since I've never seen him before. I look like a child beside him, with my fat baby cheeks and braided pigtails.

"I'd like to spend some time with you," Sampson says breaking the silence. "Maybe later after lights out, we could have a late-night snack. Me and some other people are having a bonfire. They just lifted the burn ban yesterday."

I smile at his eagerness because I've never met a no-nonsense guy that will just speak up about what he wants. I don't answer though, I'm not sure I can sneak away as easily as he can or if I'm ready to get close to a guy.

"We should get back," I say, scooting away from the water and standing up. He reaches for my hand so I can pull him up, and I struggle because he's so much taller than me, and our bodies collide. His hand rubs my back, and I feel like an electric current has gone right through my spine. I've actually never had the opportunity to be one-on-one with a guy. My parents have always been the no-boys-allowed-in-room type of parents, my dates have always been chaperoned.

"Yeah," he agrees with a hint of sadness lacing his otherwise cheerful voice.

We walk back, and I have this odd urge to reach out and hold his hand, but I just fold my arms across my chest, not knowing what to do. He makes small talk with me until we cross the bridge. As soon as we're by the dining hall, I see Viv with a pissed off look on her face.

"Where have you been?" she asks like some sort of stereotypical babysitter.

I start to speak, but Sampson does first. "Hanging out

by the lake. Where have you been? I haven't seen you all day."

Her face drains, but then she's back to the Viv I met two hours ago. "I wasn't talking to you, Sam. I was talking to her," she clarifies.

She says *her* like I'm not even here or worse, like I'm a dog that just urinated on a rug.

"I waited on you for an hour, Viv. When you didn't come back to the cabin I figured you forgot about me, so I thought I'd explore before dinner," I tell her.

Her hair is wet like she just took a shower. Her t-shirt has a turtle on it saying she's a 'Kappa Little'. Clearly, she wasn't too worried about me if she had time to shower and change clothes.

"Whatever, let's just go eat dinner," she says.

She walks in first, me and Sampson following behind like puppies with our tails between our legs.

"God, I feel bad for her boyfriend," I whisper to him. He says nothing, just fakes a smile. In that moment, I realize I'm no longer in the presence of the care-free and happy Sampson I encountered twice today.

"I'd like to take this time to give a warm Camp Arthur welcome to our new counselors in training!" A tall man in khakis and a button down shirt with the sleeves rolled up says at the head of the dining hall. His armpits leaving two giant sweat stains, he's *not* dressed for camp. "My name is Mr. Garreth and I'm the new owner of the camp. Please stand up if you're a CIT."

So, this is the schmuk that's ruining my favorite place?

Me and the other trainee's stand up while the head counselors give a bored clap. I quickly sit back down, bracing for them to haze us the second this business man goes back to wherever he lives while everyone else runs his camp for him.

"As you all know, we'll be evaluating you over the next few months to see if you have what it takes to be a counselor here next summer. Every two weeks, me, you, and your trainer will sit down to discuss how you're progressing. We only take the best here," he continues. "Once camp is over, I'll take a week or two to deliberate with the other counselors and employees to see if you'll be hired on for next summer. You will have an answer before you leave here at the end of July. Any questions?"

No one raises their hand. I'm tempted to ask how in the world Viv still works here if they only take the best, because I've been around her for less than a day, and I'm already dreading spending every minute for the rest of summer with her.

"Alright, let's get dinner going," he says with a cheesy clap of his hands.

"You heard him, Penelope. Go grab some of the food," Viv says, nudging my leg with hers. We're sitting in the employee meeting room, so me and the other CIT's have to walk into the empty mess hall and go to the kitchen. There's about twelve plates already made up, and I can see the kitchen staff taking a smoke break outside.

"If I knew I was going to be a waiter this summer, I would have just worked at McDonald's," a guy says beside me.

I laugh, handing him two plates and then grabbing two for myself to take to the table. "This has to be better than working fast food, right?"

"Ask me again in a month and I'll let you know," he

says. I recognize him from my previous years at camp. He was always kind of a hell raiser. It's hard to imagine him working here.

"Kenny, right?" I ask. "You used to chase me around the lake with a worm in your hand."

"Oh no, did I?" he asks, shaking his head. "I'm sorry. I was kind of a prick when I was a kid. My parents were going through a divorce. I had some issues."

"That's fine," I say. "It's Penelope, by the way."

"Nice to meet you, again," he says, a little embarrassed. "Let's try and help each other get through this summer in one piece. I've already goofed up once."

"Just be glad you didn't walk in on your trainer having sex," I say.

Kenny almost drops his plates. "Really? That must have been... *interesting*," he says with a smile.

I nod. "Pretty sure I'm now on her hit list."

"It's going to be an interesting summer, isn't it?" he asks.

"Sure is, and it's barely even started."

TWO

"You two, go get some wood," Viv says, pointing at Kenny and me. The twenty of us counselors and CIT's are having a bonfire. We're supposed to be learning how to start a fire, keep it going, and put it out safely. The sun is setting and lightning bugs are joining us in the field.

Kenny offers Viv a mock salute before we both head off in the direction she pointed.

"So, what brought you back to camp, Kenny?" I ask.

He stops to pick up the first log he finds. "My parents told me to get off my butt and find a job. This was the closest thing to home, that and the little ice cream store you pass to get here. I don't have a car yet, so it needed to be close enough for me to ride my bike. Figured me being a camper here previously might help out. Besides, it is kind of fun."

"So you're local?" I never knew he actually lived close to camp. I thought the whole part of sleep-away camp was to be *away* from home, not a couple blocks down the street.

"Yep, lived here all my life. What about you?" he asks.

I find two more logs and instead of me carrying them, Kenny offers to take them for me. I gladly hand them over. "I actually live about three hours away," I reply. "I've always wanted to work here though. Free food and board while also getting paid to do something I've dreamed of, you know? I couldn't pass the opportunity up."

Spotting the perfect log under some green shrubs, I bend down to pull it out but just as I am, Kenny yells at me to leave it. I jump back, terrified that he saw a snake or spider that I didn't.

"That's poison ivy next to it, just leave that one," he says.

I look at him confused. "How'd you know that's poison ivy?" I ask.

He shrugs his shoulders. "I was a boy scout, I've been covered in that stuff too many times to not know what it is by now. Trust me, you do not want to touch the ones with three leaves," he explains.

"It can't be that bad," I tease.

"It is, trust me. Not as bad as itching from chicken pox, but you would be miserable for the next two weeks," he explains.

"Well," I say. "Thanks for saving me."

He smiles at me and points to a few more sticks and tree limbs to pick up before we head back.

"You know," he starts to say, but then stops and shakes his head.

"What? Tell me," I say, as we get closer to the fire's location.

"I honestly thought this summer was going to suck, but you seem like a cool person to hang out with. Way better than that Viv girl. God, I feel bad for you. Living with her is going to suck," he says. His voice sounds honest and oddly comforting.

"Gee thanks," I say. "Promise not to chase me with snakes or any other creepy crawlers this year?"

He nods and smiles. "I didn't mean it like that," he jokes. "I meant that you seem to actually know how to treat a person and like you're going to enjoy what you're doing this summer. Viv seems like someone jammed one of these logs up her ass. And I swear I won't chase you with anything this summer."

"I totally get what you're saying, kill them with kindness, right?"

"Something like that," he says. When we get back to Viv and the other counselors, he drops the wood and does an exaggerated curtsy. "Here are your logs, ma'am, as requested." He snaps off another mock salute.

I laugh and drop the kindling next to his pile and walk away before I can see the snotty look on Viv's face. *Note to self, that girl has no sense of humor.*

"HEY, WHERE ARE YOU GOING?" Sampson asks as I get up to leave the bonfire.

The older counselors started drinking shortly after the fire was started, and I'm sure most are already four or more beers deep. Kenny stuck around for a little bit, but left because he needed to run home and pick something up.

It seemed obvious the bonfire exercise had less to do with learning fire safety than it had with getting the CITs to do free labor for the official counselors.

"I'm not old enough to partake in the camp games currently going on," I tell Sampson. He glances down at his beer bottle, and I notice him hold it behind his back like he's suddenly embarrassed to be involved.

"Oh yeah, but hey. What about that snack? Or I can walk you back to your cabin?" he asks.

"Nah, I'm fine," I reply. We both glance back to the fire where someone is yelling for Sampson to get back over there. "You go have fun. I don't want to be the odd person out."

One of his friends comes over and without saying anything, grabs us both by the wrist and pulls us back over to the fire. I awkwardly take a seat on one log and look down at my tennis shoes.

"Here, newbie," his friend says as he twists off the cap of a beer bottle. "Drink! Join in the fun!"

"Oh, no. I'm fine," I say, but he hands me the beer anyway and walks away, handing out more beer to the others. I sit and stare at the cold drink, wondering why I'm so terrified of liquid in a bottle.

"You don't have to drink it," Sampson says, coming up behind me and sitting down.

"Or you could, you know, not be a total narc," Viv says, glaring at me though the fire. A few people chuckle but go back to their own conversations quickly. I take a swig of the beer and immediately want to spit it out. *How do people enjoy this?* I stare at Viv as I take a second sip, and she shakes her head before going back to whatever she has pulled up on her phone. It's almost too dark to see anyone, the fire casts odd shadows over everyone's faces.

"You really don't have to drink that," Sampson says. Nudging my knee with his own. "I can get you a bottle of water or something."

"The taste grows on you I hear," I tell him. I look at the label and it claims to be a hard apple cider. "This tastes nothing like apple cider though."

Sampson laughs, "Because it's not."

"At least make sure I don't pull any 'placebo effect' stuff. Like you guys actually didn't give me alcohol, but I go about the night thinking I'm drunk. That would be highly embarrassing." I can imagine the stories that would circulate among the counselors if I was tricked by such a ridiculous ploy.

"I can't make any of those promises. Usually the placebo dunks are the most entertaining," he says with a laugh.

"Gee, thanks," I say, sipping more.

"Let's play a game!" shouts one of the other female counselors. "Truth or dare?"

"Lame," Shouts Viv, chugging down the rest of her beer. "Five-finger, Never Have I Ever."

"Yes!" slurs the drunk girl who recommended truth or dare, not fazed by the 'lame' comment from Viv. When I get a better look at the drunk girl, I realize it's Miss Stick-upmybum from earlier. Clearly, she found a way not to have such a sour attitude. *Perhaps she should drink more often.*

Everyone gathers around the firepit, holding a beer in one hand and holding their other hand up, five fingers ready. I've never played Never Have I Ever with alcohol, but I assume you just put down a finger and drink if you've done whatever gets said.

"Alright," says Viv as she opens up another beer. "Never have I ever… had a crush on a camper."

Everyone looks at me, and I blush as I put a finger down and take a sip. "Never have *I* ever had sex on camp property."

Viv glares at me, but doesn't take a sip of her drink, nor does she put a finger down. The guy I caught her with however, he takes a huge swig and smiles at her the whole time. To my surprise, half of the other counselors put their fingers down and take a sip. I don't look over at Sampson, because I don't want to know.

Someone else keeps the game going. "Never have I ever thought about doing this job because I actually like it," the boy says.

My finger goes down, along with four others from other counselors.

"Never have I ever been drunk...?" I say shyly. I knock six people out of the game. Only a few remain, most of whom have only one finger still up.

"We'll change that," snickers a guy sitting near me, opening a bottle of beer with the opener on his keychain.

The game goes on for only a few more turns, and finally it's down to me and Sampson. He doesn't look at me, just idly swishing the remnants of his beer around in his bottle.

"End it already!" yells a girl who is having her neck sucked on by another guy. "Newbie goes first!"

I sigh, knowing I can't use something dumb like 'never have I ever used the guys restroom', so I go for it even though I know I'll be teased a bit. "Never have I ever had sex."

Sampson finishes his beer and closes his hand around another bottle. "You win. New champion!" he announces.

"Who was the original champion?" I ask as he gets up to give me another drink.

"You're looking at him," Viv says, wrapping her arms around his waist and kissing him on the ear lobe. "My little goodie-goodie! He might have knocked you out of the game if this were three weeks earlier."

She gives me a sinister smile and pulls him back over to the log. She Kisses him deeply, and I know it's all a show for me. Viv seems to be the type of girl that doesn't feel comfortable with herself unless she's getting everyone's attention.

I saw her half-naked with another guy just a few hours ago. Now she's making out with Sampson in front of the same guy... He doesn't even pay attention to the fact that her hands are sliding up Sampson's shirt, or that their tongues have been entwined for nearly a full minute. Are they in some weird, open relationship? Why didn't Sampson say something? Clearly, he's into someone willing to give it up.

Sex has never been on my radar. My friends don't even talk about it. Well, Janine does, but she lost her virginity after junior prom. Which in high school years is eternity, according to her and some of my other friends back home. All my other friends are more boy crazy than anything. I grew up with parents who raised me not to discuss S-E-X in public, my dad gets upset when I even say the word, but here I am playing a game with people far more experienced than I am. I was taught to not be embarrassed of my body, but right now I want to melt into the earth because I'm so young and naive.

The only thing left to do now is sit and drink and try not to make a bigger loser of myself. If Janine were here, we would laugh this whole thing off together. She'd tell me how cool and awesome I am by not going along with the crowd, and I would smile and tell her how bad of a liar she is but thank her anyway. She would also give Viv a run for her money in the business of being a mean girl.

"She's a bit hard to get along with, eh?" someone says sitting down next to me. "I'm Dora," she adds.

Dora holds her hand out to shake mine. She's wearing Bermuda shorts and an orange shirt that says 'Tennessee' across the chest in white bulky letters. Her hair is cropped short, and a few piercings dot her ears.

"Penelope," I tell her. "And yes, I'm not sure how I will survive the summer with her as my mentor."

"Yikes, good luck with that," she tells me, taking a sip from a silver can with a blue ribbon on it. "If it makes you feel any better, you won't have to do *all* the activities with her."

I take a drink from my bottle and almost spit it out. "Geez, this is gross. Tastes like urine."

Dora chuckles and takes the bottle from me, handing it off to someone already too drunk to care about my germs on the rim. She brings me back a glass bottle with mostly clear liquid in it. "You'll probably like this better, almost no alcohol in it," she tells me, twisting off the cap with ease and handing it over.

I take a hesitant sip, bracing myself for the flat taste, but then realize this girl knows how to recommend a drink. "Wow, this does taste good. What is it?"

"Hard lemonade," she explains. "Be careful though, for a new drinker like you, three or four of those and you'll be sleeping out under the stars. Then you'll wake up covered in bug bites."

"That will probably happen no matter what," I say, drinking more.

Before I know it, I finish that bottle and half of another while making new friends. They laugh at my corny jokes, and for the first time in the entire day, I finally feel like I'm starting to fit in as a CIT.

"Rise and shine," a familiar voice says.

I can already see the bright sun through my eyelids. I drape my arm across my eyes and moan a weak protest.

"Come on, I have Tylenol and water. You're going to love me for this," the voice says.

"What happened last night?" I ask, squinting one eye open and seeing Sampson staring down at me. The light is painfully bright. "Where am I?"

"You passed out in the middle of the field. I was walking back to my cabin last night and saw you frolicking around with other counselors. You guys were cackling like hyenas and staring up at the stars."

"Oh. God," I say, and then feel my head throb. I sit up slowly and take the Tylenol and water bottle from Sampson without protest. My first hangover. Oh, joy. "Where did everyone else go?"

"They left about thirty minutes ago," Sampson says. "You were out cold."

"Did I do anything stupid last night?"

Sampson says something, stops and then starts again. "Not at all," he finally says with a devilish smile.

"You're a crappy liar, has anyone ever told you that?"

He chuckles. "Don't worry about it, everyone gets drunk and says dumb things. Let's get you back to your cabin before the boss wakes up and sees that you were drinking. We'd all be screwed then."

Sampson walks me halfway back to my cabin, but he stops at the mess hall because he's on breakfast set up duty today and I continue alone, bracing myself for Viv's incoming ire. When I walk in, I find her in the bathroom, pulling her hair up into a messy top bun. She smiles wickedly at me, and I go to the second sink to splash water on my face.

"Morning!" she says, friendlier than yesterday by far.

"Morning," I tell her in return, drying my face with my hand towel.

"Last night was fun, right?" she asks.

I smile and step into the bathroom stall, realizing I have to pee *really* badly. "Yeah, tons," I tell her. "Who knew that's how the counselors spend their free time?"

"You haven't seen anything yet," she says. "We leave in

fifteen minutes for breakfast. Hurry up and get yourself together. Try not to throw up on anything."

Did I throw up yesterday?

And she's back to her normal snarky, unpleasant self. That didn't take long. Luckily, I'm good about getting ready in the morning. I brush my teeth quickly and toss on some gym shorts, a t-shirt, and tennis shoes. I grab my backpack just as Viv opens the door and says that it's time to go. Judging by her expression, I think she's disappointed that I won't be late.

Almost all the counselors are already in the mess hall when we get there, and as I'm walking into our meeting room, Viv pulls me to the side. "Do me a favor and don't embarrass me. If you do, it'll end up worse for you," she says quietly.

I stand there in awe, wondering why she would feel the need to say such a thing. She's known me for one day. We've only spent about three hours together. If anyone should be embarrassed, it's me.

And once I walk through the door, I am humiliated.

"There she is!" shouts one of the guys from last night. I vaguely remember him telling me his name was Keith or something. "You were hilarious last night, newbie."

I blush and find an empty seat next to Kenny, who doesn't look up at me from his plate full of eggs and bacon. I reach out with a shaky hand for the plastic pitcher of orange juice and pour myself a glass. My arm protests, a good indication I must have slept on top of it last night.

"How was your night?" I ask Kenny, trying to ignore all the snickering from everyone else.

"Good, not as eventful as yours though," he tells me, taking a bite of bacon. He seems upset with me, but I have no clue why. *Why does he even have the right to be mad at me? I did nothing wrong.*

"Yeah, I probably should have gone back to my cabin last night…"

He looks at me and lowers his voice. "You're right. I just want you to watch your back. If the director knew you were out there drinking underage, you would be kicked out of here in an instant. I know you've always wanted to work here. Don't let any of them take that from you," he says.

I look at him and then reach for some bacon, knowing that might be the only thing I can stomach this morning. "Um, thanks? I didn't realize you cared."

"I'm just looking out for you. That's what friends do."

"Thanks," I say more sincerely, feeling like I've been scolded by a teacher or my mother.

The camp director shows up a few minutes later and briefs us on what we'll be doing for the day. I sneak a glance in Sampson's direction and find he was looking my way too. A moment passes between us, but I don't know how to judge it. Confused and embarrassed, I return to my bacon in silence.

THREE

I'm paired up with Dora, one of the only people I remember talking to last night, along with two other counselors in training and two random counselors. Luckily, I didn't get put in the group with Viv, though her group has more people I know and like, namely Kenny and Sampson.

"Alright, here's what we need to go over today: CPR, which I'm assuming everyone already has their certification for, a few camp songs that you need to know, and some basic rules to follow," says Dora, taking charge since she's the oldest in the group. "Where do we want to start first?"

No one speaks up, so Dora looks at her clipboard and suggests we begin with the basic rules first. Everyone else groans.

"Rule number one, be a mentor and friend to everyone you come in contact with here at Camp Arthur," she begins.

Clearly Viv needs work on this one.

"Rule number two, no canoodling with the campers. This should be obvious, and remember dating or intimacy in front of the kids is frowned upon. This means you, Casanova," Dora looks toward the guy I saw half naked in my cabin on day one. He has that smug expression that I'm thinking this is a permanent fixture on his face. I'm also going to assume his name isn't actually Casanova, though it feels fitting.

"Don't hate," he says, leaning back in his chair and

crossing his arms over his chest. "What can I say? The ladies like me."

So, Casanova is kind of an over-confident prick. *Perfect.*

"Rule number three, and I shouldn't have to say this, but please do not create any unnecessary drama. Everyone should act and behave like an adult. This is your job. Be respectful of everyone, and we'll all survive the summer. I know so-and-so might have looked at your boyfriend the wrong way or you heard that this person and that person were hooking up, but keep it to yourself. You're not in high school anymore." Her voice rings authority as she speaks.

Dora drones on about the rest of the rules at camp which most everyone knows already: don't buy sweets for the campers unless given approval in advance because of allergies, don't let a camper go off on their own once camp officially begins, report any issues you come across, no boys in girl cabins and vice versa, and so on.

"And last but not least, make sure everyone is accounted for when you arrive and leave somewhere. If a camper wonders off, say 'Code Houdini' over your walkie-talkie, and everyone will be on the look-out. Occasionally, we'll have a kid whose parents are going through a divorce, and the parent who doesn't have custody tries to see the child. That's happened a few times," she says.

One girl who is also training raises her hand to ask a question. "What about a counselor in training? Can they date another co-worker?"

There's a few snickers from the people in the group and the girl pretends like this is a legit question she needs an answer to.

"Are they both over eighteen?" asks Dora. I can hear annoyance in her voice, and I'm wondering how we got back to the dating rule.

"No...?" the girls says hesitantly. I wish I were better at

remembering names, but I suck. *There are twelve of us! How do I not remember her name?* How am I ever going to remember all of my campers' names?

"Then no. And a CIT cannot date a camper either. If you're over eighteen, you can basically do whatever you like as long as you don't let it get in the way of your job," Dora says. "I get it, it's going to be a long, hot summer, but rules are rules and laws are laws. The last thing we need is to get sued for sexual harassment on a minor. Treat this place like school. You wouldn't hook up with your teacher would you? This is your job this summer, you're not here to flirt and goof off. If you wanted that, you should have gone on a beach vacation instead."

The girl tries to hold back a smile but doesn't answer the question.

Dora smacks the palm of her hand against her forehead. "Okay, whatever, just please stay out of trouble."

"CPR time?" asks Casanova, jumping up out of his chair and popping his knuckles in preparation.

Dora sighs and tosses her clipboard down on her backpack. "Yeah sure. Put on your bathing suits and head to the pool for CPR and water safety. I'll see everyone there in thirty minutes. If you haven't had any lifeguard training prior to camp, you're meeting Sid in the dining hall for some games you may want to play with your campers."

While everyone files out, I wait around for Dora.

"Do you need any help?" I ask, swinging my backpack over my shoulder.

"No, I'm fine," she tells me as she does the same. "How are you hanging in there? I heard about the rest of your evening."

I cover my face with my hand. "Jesus, does everyone but me know what happened?"

"First time you've been blackout drunk?"

"First time I've been drunk," I correct her.

She smiles. "Happens to the best of us."

"Or the dumbest. It won't happen again."

"Don't be too hard on yourself, no one should hold drunken words against someone."

I shrug. "I thought the saying was, 'Drunk words, sober thoughts.' I just wish I knew what happened or what I said."

"Don't beat yourself up. Usually you end up piecing together the evening and if you don't, it's for the best," she says.

"I hope you're right," I tell her, heading off to get ready for the pool.

Thankfully, the cabin is empty when I get back. I don't walk in on Viv with whoever she's screwing around with, and I don't have to deal with any of her snarky remarks. I can finally be alone, at least for ten minutes, while I try to cram my pudgy body into my one-piece swimsuit.

I show up with only a minute to spare, but surprisingly, I'm the first to arrive. Everyone else in my group trails in shortly after me. We all gather under the shelter, everyone except the ditzy girl who grabs a lawn chair and spreads her towel out on it. She puts on a little show of taking her shorts and shirt off, presenting an American flag in the form of two pieces of fabric that some might consider a bikini.

"Get it, girl," hollers Casanova, of course.

"Pig," I say under my breath. How in the world have

these two had lifeguard training and certification? I wouldn't trust them with my backpack, much less my life.

He hears me, which was kind of my plan.

"Well show us what you've got if you're so jealous," he teases.

I cross my arms over my chest. "Eww, no thanks."

"Suit yourself," he says and then also proceeds to do a little strip tease down to his board shorts.

Are you kidding me? Who thought it would be a good idea to put these people in charge of children?

I almost vomit when he struts around the pool, his hairy torso matted down with sweat and his pasty white skin showing where his farmer tan begins. He heads down to the deep end and cannonballs into its depths, which is actually only ten feet deep.

"And Josh has just demonstrated the first pool violation," says Sampson as he strolls in wearing red swim trunks and a whistle around his neck. "Can anyone tell us what rule that is?"

I glance around and nobody's paying attention, they're all laughing as Josh aka Casanova resurfaces with a loud whooping noise coming from his mouth.

I raise my hand but don't wait to be called on. "Everyone must shower before entering the pool."

"Shower?" ditzy girl asks. "I can't shower, I just did my hair!"

Why are you even at camp?

"Everyone must shower," agrees Sampson. "Also, no running or horseplay around the pool. Jumping in is acceptable, but campers are not allowed to dive. Feet first, always. Most of the rules are posted on the wall behind me. If a camper has to be told three times that they've broken a rule, they have to sit out for the remainder of pool time."

Casanova gets out of the pool pulls his swim trunks up where they slipped down his torso. I gag again, but it seems ditzy girl gets a kick out of him. They would probably be good together - both seem to want a ton of attention.

"Alright, who wants to be my test dummy?" Sampson asks, dropping his backpack down on a plastic chair.

Ditzy raises her hand. Dora and I just roll our eyes.

Sampson sighs. "You have to get in the pool and get your hair wet."

Her face falls, along with her raised hand. "Nevermind."

"I'll help you," I tell Sampson as I get up and head over to the shower to rinse off. I try to ignore Casanova and the two other guys who are snickering about me taking off my shirt and shorts to reveal my one-piece, the one-piece that camp recommends you bring instead of a bikini.

"Okay, go jump in the deep end and back. We're going to demonstrate a drowning body," he announces.

I slide into the pool and suck in a gulp of air because it's so cold, then wait for him to begin his rescue before I actually play the victim role. He gives a small talk on drowning victims and then has Dora start the stopwatch to see how long he takes to pull me out of the water.

Sampson starts at the lifeguard stand, grabs his yellow life preserver, and dives in. I flinch away from his splash, then float on my belly with my head in and he comes over to me within seconds. He pulls my head out of the water and then props my body up on the life preserve before quickly pulling me to the side of the pool.

"Be dead wait," he tells me when we get to the side and I wonder exactly how he will get me out. Sure enough, two strong arms are pulling me out by my torso. To my dismay, I realize Casanova owns the second arm.

Dora stops the watch and declares that it took 30 seconds.

"Alright, let's review," Sampson says, laying a towel down on the ground for me. "Once you hear a lifeguard blow the whistle, be on alert. It's either a warning or to tell that someone's in serious trouble. He or she will dive in with the rescue preserver, and then once we get to the side, another lifeguard should be there to help retrieve the person. Next we assess the situation…"

I lay there playing victim, zoning in and out of what he's telling me. I know all the normal training; active victim rescue, passive victim, spinal rescue, CPR and so on. I took a refresher course a month ago knowing I wanted to become a lifeguard here or at least make myself known so everyone knows I can help if we're short on staff.

"Penelope?" Sampson asks, and I realize he's been trying to get my attention.

"Yes?" I ask, looking up from where I'm laying down on the cement.

He smiles, and I watch as some water falls from his hair. "I was asking if I have permission to give an example of CPR on you. Didn't want to scare you when I do fake chest compressions."

"Oh yeah, sure," I say, going back to pretending to be an unconscious victim.

Sampson demonstrates pinching my nose, tilting my head back and blowing in my mouth. I tense when he's an inch from my mouth, but he doesn't actually do the mouth breathing, of course. He then shows the chest compressions with his hands just above my breastbone.

"Um, Sampson?" says the ditzy girl and I open one eye to look up at her. "I think it would be beneficial if you actually show us how to breath in the victim's mouth."

Someone in the group snickers and Sampson just rolls his eyes. *It's not a kiss*, I tell myself, *it's just CPR training.*

"I'm sure you get the point," says Sampson. "Besides, I'm sure Penelope doesn't feel comfortable with that."

I shake my head a bit too eagerly. "No, it's fine. You can do that, it's just training. Who knows, it might save a camper's life this summer."

Sampson leans down next to me again, "Are you sure? You don't have to do this. I have a feeling the group is just trying to get a rise out of us."

I nod and close my eyes. "I'm sure, now if you don't mind me, I need to go back to pretending like I'm unconscious."

Sampson places his hand over my nose and tilts my head back. Even though my eyes are closed, all my other senses are on high alert. I can smell the chlorine in the air, I can hear ditzy blonde popping her bubble gum, and I can feel the hair on my arms standing at attention.

When his lips meet mine, I hear Dora explaining the actions that Sampson is doing. I try so hard to act like this isn't happening, to keep my tongue at the back of my mouth, but a small sigh slips from my mouth and into Sampson's. I squeeze my eyes shut, hoping no one else heard it, but I know Sampson has because I feel him hesitate when he pulls away from me quickly to start some fake chest compressions. Thank God I brushed my teeth after breakfast this morning. I'm mortified, I just want to keep pretending I'm dead.

"And look at that, our victim is rescued by Sampson the Hero!" I sit up and look to see Viv standing right there, slow clapping with her own group of training counselors. Surely, almost the whole camp staff is now watching us.

"Oh hey, Viv. Glad you showed up for your Pool Safety

refresher. Better late than never," Dora says, crossing her arms across her chest.

Viv glares at her, and then smiles at Sampson. "I was just coming over to swap groups with you. Looks like things got a little out of hand here."

"Viv, it was just--" Sampson starts to explain.

"Alright, nothing to see here," Dora says, shooing everyone off. "Go to the mess hall and get something to eat and then we'll finish this after lunch."

I stand up and gather my towel and clothes, sliding my sandals on. I don't even glance up at Sampson because I'm afraid of what I'll see in his eyes. Everyone has cleared out and I'm almost out of Viv's firing range when I hear her and Sampson arguing.

"Viv, just let her go. She didn't do anything," I hear him say.

"Hey, new girl," she calls. My stomach jerks. "Not so fast."

I turn around, but don't look up at her. I just concentrate on not letting the tears fall from embarrassment. I haven't cried at camp since I was ten, and I won't cry now.

"Don't you ever think about doing that again," she says through her teeth.

"I didn't do anything," I say, and I didn't. Sampson chose me to be the helper for CPR training.

"He's mine, he'll never fall for you. You're a kid. Find your place and stay there," she commands.

I finally get the nerve to look her in the eye. "I'm not a kid, and maybe if you didn't want someone else to take him from you, you shouldn't be hooking up with other guys behind his back," I retort.

I make sure not to say the last part too loudly no matter how much I want to out her in front of the entire staff. I will not be the one to get in the middle of their lovers' quarrel. All I want is a peaceful summer at camp - a guy is the last thing I need on my mind.

She stares me down, fire in her eyes. "If you ever tell him, I'll get you kicked out of this camp quicker than you could even imagine. Mind your own business."

I chuckle and shake my head, turning to walk away. "Whatever, you're not going to scare me. The only thing you can hold over my head is the fact that you're my mentor for the next three months."

I turn back around one more time. "And you're kind of doing a crappy job at that, so if anyone has a job to worry about, it's you."

She doesn't say a word, but I can see her whole body tighten in what appears to be hatred. If anything, I'll learn how to not behave as a counselor, so this pairing won't be such a waste of time. Sampson joins her by her side, pulling his backpack on and smiling over at me.

"Pool's all clear. We can head out," he says. "Want to walk with us?"

I smile and shake my head. "Nah, I'll give you two some alone time. I'm going to take the long way back to the cabin. See ya later," I say, heading off toward the woods.

Viv says nothing, but I can feel her eyes trying to burn a hole in the back of my head. What does he even see in her? Guys don't enjoy being in hostile relationships, right?

FOUR

The woods behind all the cabins is creepier than I remember. Or maybe they're just creepy because this is the first time I've ever walked them by myself. Campers are usually never allowed on the trails unless they're headed to one of the amphitheaters, but it hasn't been used in years. I honestly can't remember the last time I was on this trail. It seems they don't maintain it as much as they used to. The grass is breaking through the dirt in most places and there are a ton of tree limbs down.

Why did they let me take this trail if it was this bad?

Well, I know why Viv allowed it.

I kick off what branches I can, trying my best to restore the trail since no one else has. I pick up an old, ripped grocery bag that's stuck to the thorns on a bush and carefully bundle it up to fit in the side pocket of my backpack.

"Cleaning up after some litter bugs?" a voice asks, stopping me in my trail.

"Oh my gosh!" I scream, my hand pressed against my chest. Kenny is walking toward me on the trail. "Why would you do that? You can't just sneak up on someone!"

He puts his hands up and laughs. "Sorry, I thought you heard me coming this way."

"No! What are you doing out here anyway? No one walks this way," I tell him.

"Except you, apparently. I could ask you the same thing," he shoots back.

I pull my water bottle out and take a sip before

responding. "I needed an excuse not to walk with Viv. She's a… firecracker."

Kenny smiles. "She's kind of bitchy, isn't she? From what I've heard, everyone feels bad that you have her as a mentor for the whole summer."

"Why does she even have a job here?" I ask, throwing my arms up. "She doesn't seem to like anyone, and she probably isn't good with children either. Who knows, maybe she's just snotty toward females. She seems to *love* the guys."

"I heard she only got the job because of Sampson. Since his parents are the new owners, she scored the summer job. She probably didn't like the idea of him working so closely all summer with the other female counselors, so she pretended like she wanted the job. She seems pretty clingy to me," he explains.

"And we haven't even been here for a week yet," I say. "So, Sampson's parents own camp now?"

All of Viv's threats seem to fall into place at once. She has connections. Would she actually be able to get me fired without a reason though? I think not. Still, the prospect is a little frightening.

A loud clap of thunder jolts me from my thoughts, and I practically jump out of my skin. Kenny and I both look up at the sky through the greenery. Sure enough, the sun has been replaced with a dark grey sky.

"I should go before it starts raining," I say, looking back at Kenny.

"Let me walk you," he says sweetly, but then switches to a friendly smile when I hesitate. "Wouldn't want you getting hit by lightning and no one know you're out here."

"Well, since you mentioned it. I am terribly afraid of thunderstorms."

He smiles and gestures in the direction I was walking, the direction he had come from. "Shall we?"

"We shall," I say smiling. "And you can't make fun of me if I jump from the thunder again. I'm allowed to be afraid of loud things."

He puts his hands up in a surrender. "Fair enough."

By the time we make it back to my cabin, it's pouring and our clothes are soaked. I don't even think about it, I just pull Kenny inside with me. Not wanting him to have to walk all the way back across camp to his cabin.

"Let me grab some towels," I say, ruffling through my duffle bag. "You can stay here until the rain calms down."

"Thanks," he says, and I hand him one of my towels. He ruffles his hair dry with one and then wraps it around his shoulders.

I kneel down and go through my bag again in search of some dry clothes and pull out a pair of sweats and a t-shirt. "I'll be back, I'm going to go change real quick. I hate wet clothes more than anything in the world."

Kenny chuckles and sits down on an empty bunk as I scamper off to the bathroom. I place my clothes on the sink and look at myself in the mirror.

It's been a long while since I've looked at my reflection. I've never been the type of girl to spend hours doing her makeup and hair, perfecting her image. My cheeks are flushed and my hair is dripping wet, my eyes look wild. I'm almost afraid of the girl standing in front of me because of those wild eyes. I look away, close the bathroom door and change quickly, eager to be dry once more.

When I come back out, Kenny is standing by my bunk holding onto my teddy bear I brought from home. He must have slipped out of my duffle when I was looking for clothes as I hadn't found time to fully unpack yet.

"Who's this?" Kenny asks with a teasing smile, holding my teddy bear in one hand.

I calmly walk over to him and take the bear back, gently sitting him on my bunk. "Mister Moose. He's a gentleman that doesn't like to be mocked," I tell him.

"Moose? But he's a bear," Kenny says, confused. He gives me one of those looks that makes me think I've gone insane.

"You don't know how he identifies!" I say, pretending to be appalled.

"Note taken," he laughs. "So, does this Mr. Moose have an origin? What's his story?"

I sit down on my bunk and pick my teddy bear back up, touching his soft white fur. "An ex-boyfriend got him for me. He's just one of those items you can't let go of because of the memories. I know it sounds silly, but it was one of the first things I got from a guy, and I just like it. Don't judge me."

"I'm not judging," he says with sincerity in his voice. "So what happened between you and the boyfriend?"

I put the bear back down. "We decided it would be best to break up. He started college last year. I didn't want to be the high school girlfriend he left behind. I think it was for the best. All of my friends had boyfriends going off to college and they were miserable. They waited for calls and texts and always got upset when their boyfriends couldn't come home for homecoming or football games."

I stop talking because I feel like I'm saying too much and boring Kenny.

"Well, sorry things didn't work out. Breakups are hard

no matter what." He seems mature beyond his years, which is something I think I'm naturally drawn toward.

I chuckle and roll my eyes. "Nah, it wasn't bad. It was a long time ago anyway. Well… long time ago in my eyes. I just wish we could have stayed friends."

When I look up at Kenny, he's just about to sit down next to me when the door to the cabin slams open and we both jump at the sound.

Viv is giggling and has her arms wrapped around Sampson's neck, enveloping him in a kiss. She glances over at me and her eyes look sinister.

"Oh hey, you two. Sorry for barging in, we'll be down the hall if you need us."

When I glance to Sampson, his cheeks are red and he appears to be trying to remove himself from Viv's clutch. She ignores his efforts and pulls him down the hall by the hem of his camp polo.

Once the door closes to Viv's chamber of lust, Kenny and I look at each other. His face is just as red as Sampson's, as if he was just caught doing something that he wasn't supposed to be doing.

"I should get going, sounds like the storm has calmed down," Kenny says, rubbing unseen tension out of his neck.

I nod. "Yeah, I'll see you around then."

Kenny smiles and waves good-bye, leaving me to sit and try to ignore the whispers and unmentionable sounds coming from the cabin's designated private room. I try not to think about Sampson's lips on mine at the pool, especially now that they're back on hers.

I'm startled awake, finding I've taken an unplanned nap while trying to ignore Viv and Sampson. When I jump up, I almost hit my head on the bunk above me and quickly lay back down.

Sampson is kneeling next to my bunk, and I reach down to pull my cover over my head in embarrassment. "Jesus, haven't you ever heard of the phrase 'don't wake a sleeping bear?'" I scold him.

"Sorry," he whispers. "I just wanted to apologize for earlier."

I pull the blanket down so just my eyes are peeking out. "Which part? When your crazy girlfriend threatened me or when she stormed in and made my friend uncomfortable?"

"All of it. I know she's a bit much, but she'll grow on you."

To me, it sounds like he says the same thing to a ton of people because I don't see Viv 'growing on me' at any point in my life, but I won't say that to Sampson.

"Where is she right now? I'm sure you'll get in trouble for speaking to me," I mumble under the blanket.

"In the shower. I was just heading out to get ready for dinner."

He stands up and fiddles with the collar on his polo. I notice a small bruise on his neck, along with some smudged pink lipstick.

"Hey, I'm probably in the wrong for saying this, but keep your guard up with her. I know I just met the both of you, but make sure she is who you think she is before things go too far," I say, and I mean it.

He glances back toward the hall where we both hear the shower turn off and then looks at me with understanding in his eyes.

"Do you know something?" he whispers. "You would tell me if something was going on right?"

I want to tell him what I saw the first day when I got here, how I saw her with Mr. Casanova, but I'm also terrified of her following through with her threats. She's turning my happy place into hell on earth.

"All I'm saying is to keep your guard up. I'm not looking to get in between you two and start any drama. I'm just saying that you might not be seeing what everyone else is seeing," I try to explain.

The hair dryer turns on and Sampson gives me a simple nod before he turns away and heads out the door, just as a lingering peal of thunder sounds.

FIVE

After five more days of training and hazing from Viv, I'm in need of a day off. I just want to be alone for a while. Most of my fellow counselors got away from camp while they still could. The parking lot only held about five cars, mine included. I spent most of the morning not running into anyone, not even the cooks because they got the day off.

After I make myself some toast in the kitchen, I head off for the small lake hoping to have it to myself so I can relax. I already feel so much better considering Viv left last night after dinner. She said she was going to a college party and she'd be back late Sunday.

Not that I care.

The lake is empty when I get to it, fog rising from the water, creating an eerie feel. All the paddle boats, canoes, and kayaks are still propped up alongside the shed where we keep life jackets. I search for a life jacket that fits me, pull it off the clothes line, and pick my kayak and an oar out of the bin. Every noise I make breaks the silence.

I drag it over and gently slide it into the lake, making ripples across the calm surface, the tadpoles hanging around the dock quickly swim away. Once I'm situated, I push off with my oar. A few ducks swim by hoping for some bread crumbs, but I finished my breakfast on the way over. Once they realize I have nothing to offer, they move along.

I paddle around slowly, in no rush to be anywhere, just

enjoying the peace and solitude. The shed doors slam closed behind me, and I almost tip over in a panic to see what's happening. I try to stay calm and assume a deer bumped into it in confusion.

Turning around, I see Sampson coming over to the observation deck with a fishing pole and some bait, a tackle box already sitting opened and ready to be rifled through.

"Sorry, mind if I fish for a bit? The fish bite more in the morning," he asks.

"Just you?" I respond.

He nods.

"Sure, that's fine," I say, and turn away pretending like I have somewhere to go, but the lake isn't big at all. You can only put about six canoes on it at once before it feels crowded and everyone's bumping into each other. To call it a lake is honestly an over exaggeration. It's so small that any fish caught has to be released.

Sampson and I say nothing else for a few moments that feel like an eternity, but when I look at my watch, it's been only thirty minutes. Thirty minutes of me paddling in a circle and him not catching a fish. Not that I was paying attention.

"You're a crappy fisherman," I comment as I paddle over to him. "If you were in the apocalypse, I'm sure you wouldn't make it long."

He smiles down at me. "Maybe you're just scaring them away with your terrible paddling."

"If anything, I'm helping by pushing them toward you."

"I'm not sure that's how it works."

"Meh, I haven't studied the life of fish, so I wouldn't know," I start paddling back to the loading deck.

"You done?" he asks.

"Yeah, figured I'd find something else to do. No one's here, I've never had the camp all to myself."

He meets me over at the smaller deck and sits down to hold the kayak with his feet as I pull myself out and up. He also pulls the kayak out of the murky water for me, and I slide the life jacket off and take it back over to the line.

"Want to get lunch later? There's a nice bar back in town..." he asks, pulling the kayak back to its resting spot.

I hesitate at the word bar. "I'm not sure I can get in," I say, feeling embarrassed by my age.

"It's more of a bar and grill. Kids go there all the time... not that you're a kid. It's just not a normal bar until late. Under 18 is allowed in until 10, I think." It's kind of cute when Sampson stammers on, but I scold myself for even thinking such things.

"Yeah, sure. When and where?" I ask.

"I'll drive, it's easy to miss. Just meet me at my car at noon. It's the blue Ranger," he says with a smile.

"Kay, sounds good. I'll see you then."

Lunch is fine, I tell myself. What Viv doesn't know won't kill her, right? I just hope she doesn't kill *me.*

After changing my outfit five times in an attempt to look nice, I'm running about five minutes late. All I brought to camp was about two weeks' worth of t-shirts and gym shorts. I finally settle on a plain black tank top and a pair of khaki shorts that somehow made it into my bag, then make a note to bring back nicer stuff the next time I go home to visit.

After running all the way from my cabin to the parking

lot by the welcome center, I'm out of breath and can feel the dry dirt covering my toes. I cough and can practically taste the dirt in my mouth. Everything in the camp is dusty, especially if it hasn't rained in a few days.

Sampson is patiently waiting at his Ford, leaning against the bumper. Then he sees me, and his face brightens up a bit.

"Sorry, I'm late," I say when I make it to him. "Lost track of time."

"You're fine, hop in. Hope you're hungry. They have fantastic food," he says.

I smile and climb in the passenger side and pull my seatbelt across my chest to fasten it. Sampson has already put the top down, and I'm thankful I kept my hair in a ponytail instead of fussing with it.

Sampson and I are both quiet on the drive. I just enjoy checking out the countryside and listening to the music he selected. I'm a strong believer that lyrics can say so much about a person. I recognize the song and it makes me relax a little.

"Here we are," he says, turning the music down as he turns into a small parking lot and into one of the open spots.

"Irene's," I say reading the sign. "So, does Irene actually work here?"

"Not anymore. She opened this bar before I was even born, but passed away a few years ago. It's family owned and almost all of the employees are relatives," Sampson says, sliding out of the Ranger

I slide out and follow him inside the dark bar. I'm expecting to be hit with a huge cloud of cigarette smoke when I walk in, but the air is actually easy to breathe. There's a bartender cleaning drinking glasses at the bar where only three people are sitting, and a waitress comes out from what looks like the kitchen just as we're sitting down at a booth in the far corner.

"Hey darlins'," she says as she lays two drink napkins in front of us and hands each of us a menu. "What can I get you to drink?"

"I'll just have a Guinness," Sampson says easily.

"I'll have a Sprite," I say, feeling lame for not ordering a beer.

The waitress nods and heads over to the bar to get our drinks. I look over the menu, trying to find something that I like other than chicken nuggets. Kids eat chicken nuggets. Boneless wings are the same thing but more grown up, right?

"They have amazing sandwiches and burgers here," Sampson says. "I usually get the Reuben."

The waitress comes back with his beer and my pop. "You guys know what you want?" she asks with a thick southern accent.

Sampson nods and tells me to go first, so I glance back down at the menu and order the first thing I see under the pasta header. He orders the Reuben with a side of wings and the waitress heads off to the kitchen.

"So…" Sampson says, not followed by anything.

"So…" I say too. "What's on your schedule for the rest of the weekend?"

He takes a sip of his beer and then puts it back down, licking the foam off his lips. "Not much, just planning on hanging out. You?"

"Same, can't go home. It's not worth it because of the drive. Are you planning on going home?"

Sampson hesitates before he answers. "I might tomorrow for lunch. Want to join me?"

Two dates in two days? But… are they dates?

Viv's face comes to mind and the thought of what she

would do if she knew I was spending the evening with Sampson and his parents, what she'd do if she walked into this bar right now, flashes through my mind. Her recent threats on getting me fired seem legit, but I agree to go for lunch at his parents anyway.

"Awesome, I can just pick you up at your cabin."

"How far of a drive is it?" I ask, wondering if we'll have time to get back before Viv questions why either of us disappeared.

He takes another sip of his beer and I'm thinking he does that to give himself time to think. "Not far at all, actually. We'll be back to camp before you know it."

"Someone said your parents bought Camp Arthur, is that true?" I ask, sipping my Sprite.

He blushes. "Yeah, I should have told you, but it just never came up and I don't like telling people. They'll end up thinking I get special treatment because of it."

"Aren't you…" I say, but I'm not sure about how to phrase it so I just let the words tumble from my mouth. "Aren't you afraid of what Viv will say if she finds out that we're hanging out two days in a row? I don't want to get between the two of you. I'm not looking for drama this summer…"

Before he can respond, the waitress comes by and drops off our food. I thank her and wait for her to walk away before turning back to Sampson for an answer.

"She won't be back until late Sunday," he says. "When she's not required to be here, she doesn't return until she's needed. You honestly probably won't see her until Monday afternoon."

"How reliable," I say under my breath before taking a bite of my food.

"I'm sorry for how she's treated you so far," Sampson says, taking a bite of one of his fries. "I've never seen her be this shitty to a person. She can be a bit snobby normally, but this is a new level. I'll talk to her, I'm not sure what has gotten into her."

In that moment, I know I should probably tell him what I saw that first day when I walked in our cabin. How she's probably treating me like crap because I saw her hooking up with someone that's not her boyfriend, someone who isn't Sampson.

I've spent the last week going over ways I could tell him and trying to predict his possible reactions, some ending up with Viv cornering me in the bathroom and beating the crap out of me like a bully in an 80's teen movie to Sampson telling me I'm a liar and me getting kicked out of camp for 'starting drama'.

I twirl pasta onto my fork and just shrug my shoulders, not wanting to tell him. "You don't need to say anything. I'll accept being her punching bag for the time being."

"You shouldn't though," he says. "No one deserves to be treated the way she's treating you."

I shrug and twirl another section of my pasta, not making eye contact with Sampson. "So tell me, why are you with her? What makes Viv so... *desirable*?"

When Sampson doesn't respond, I look up to see if there's any sign of me upsetting him with my question. He's glancing away and chewing on a bite of his Reuben. A bit of thousand island dressing has escaped to the corner of his mouth. When he finally swallows and looks at me, I see hesitation in his eyes.

"Honestly, I'm not sure. I guess it's because we met in college, at orientation actually. No one was talking to either of us, so we banded together. See, Viv wasn't always a social butterfly, she was pretty chill before college started. By the second semester though, she had joined a sorority and we only had time to hang out on Sundays. I finally got up the nerve to ask her out when she dragged me out of my dorm to go shopping for a dress to wear to her first formal.

"She was complaining because none of the Sigma guys were available, and she didn't want to go alone, but she was required to go. She heard one of her pledge sisters talk about how 'if you didn't show up with a date, it was social suicide' so I told her I would go."

"And she agreed?" I ask.

He laughs and shakes his head. "Hell no! She told me if I ever wanted to go with her to a sorority party, I had to be in a frat. I ended up doing what any man with 'puppy dog syndrome' would do…"

"No," I say, my jaw dropping and slamming my hand on the table. "Tell me you didn't join a frat just for a girl."

He smiles. "But, of course, I did."

"So, you got the girl. Are you still in the frat?"

"You're looking at the VP," He tells me, wiping his hands on his napkin.

I stare at him in awe. "You don't even look like a frat boy though, where are your dockers, your boat shoes, and your Greek shirt? Do you have your letters tattooed down your neck?"

"Whoa, hey," he says putting his hands up in a playful surrender. "Stereotype much?"

"Sorry, but seriously, you don't fit the mold. I mean, you have the possessive, psychotic girlfriend…"

"Don't let Vivian represent the whole Greek system. We actually do a ton of charity and community activities. She's pretty good at helping her sorority be more involved around town, even during the summer. She works hard…"

"Why do I feel like you're always making excuses for her?"

Sampson pushes his plate away and laces his fingers

together, putting them in front of him. "Let's forget about her right now. Let's hear more about you, Miss Secretive."

"What do you want to know? I'm an open book." I say, taking a sip of my drink and looking at him through my eyelashes.

"The first night, you know you don't have to try and impress anyone, right? Most of these people are secret train wrecks anyway," he says.

Ah, I was hoping we would never have to speak of that night again, but it was bound to come up sooner or later. "Live and learn, right? I never do that by the way… that was a big mistake," I tell him.

"No harm done," he says. "We all have our moments."

I nod and finish my lunch as we banter back and forth about home life, friends, school, and what we're hoping to get out of this summer. I feel the anxiety of Viv's threats slide away the more Sampson and I talk. I almost wish that Viv wasn't in the picture so he and I could at least have a friendship.

SIX

"I can't believe you've only been at camp for like, a week, and you're already meeting your new boyfriend's parents," Janine says from my cell phone speaker. Her voice fills the empty cabin, making me feel like she's actually here, which is a good thing. It's calming my nerves.

"I told you," I say as a roll my eyes. "He's not my boyfriend, he has a girlfriend."

"Speaking of Satan, where is she?" Janine began calling Viv Satan the second I texted her about the whole situation with Casanova and threatening me to stay away from Sampson.

I sigh and stare at the wood grain on the bunk above me. "Most of the other staff members are gone until later today, early tomorrow. It's been pretty nice and quiet around here, the calm before the storm."

"Whoah, wait! Hold up!" Janine says and I can practically see her stopping in the middle of whatever mall store she's in with the excitement in her voice. "You mean to tell me it's just been you and Sampson alone at camp all weekend and nothing has happened between you?"

"Janine, what did you expect to happen? I won't steal another girl's boyfriend no matter how horrible she is or what she's done wrong. Sampson and I are just friends... he's too old for me anyway."

"So... what you're saying is that if he weren't taken," she says, her voice drifting off to let me draw the sinister conclusion myself.

I glance at my watch and realize it's already time for me to be ready. Sampson will be here in ten minutes and I haven't bothered to get out of my sweat pants.

"Drop it, just help me figure out what to wear. I think all I packed are gym shorts and t-shirts."

I can hear the smile in Janine's voice. "Bottom of your duffel, I packed you that cute little sun dress you wore to the senior class dinner," she says.

"Have I told you lately how much I love you?" I ask, finding the dress exactly where she said it would be along with a pair of wedges that I've seen Janine where on a ton of summer dates.

"You can repay me by promising to take off the last weekend in the month to come with me to the bonfire bash. Maybe by then Satan will be out of the picture and you can bring Sammy boy."

"Wishful thinking, eh?" I ask, just as someone knocks on the cabin door. "Hey, I gotta go. Sounds like Sampson is here!"

Before I can hang up she screams over the speaker, "Don't forget to get off for the bonfire! I'll make it worth your time!"

I hang up without responding just as another knock comes from the door. I answer it, my heart pounding because I know it's Sampson. Sure enough, he's standing there with a smile on his face. He looks me up and down and shakes his head chuckling.

"What?" I ask.

"Staying in your pajamas all day?" he asks smiling. "Don't get me wrong, I'm all for comfort but you might want to change."

I glance down and realize I was so distracted by my conversation with Janine I completely forgot to get dressed in real clothes. My cheeks burn with embarrassment.

"This is awkward, sorry. I was busy all morning actually unpacking and organizing my stuff, I lost track of time," I tell him as I open the door. "Come on in, it'll only take me about five minutes to become presentable."

Sampson follows me in and plops down on an empty bunk, "No worries. My parents don't live far anyway."

I grab my dress and wedges off the bed and head into the bathroom. The dress is now one size too small, and I remember it didn't actually fit me when I wore it a few months ago. It had been the only size left when I bought it. Thank God Janine and I wear the same size shoes though. The last thing I would want to do is go back out there and trade out wedges for my gym shoes.

I look at myself in the full length mirror hanging on the door, my hair laying limp on my shoulders, zero volume, I run a hand through it trying to fluff it up. Sucking in my gut, I head back out to where Sampson is. It's still hard for me to actually get used to seeing a guy in a girls cabin. When campers are here, it's forbidden. A male counselor can't even step foot in a cabin even if he just needs to talk to a female counselor or vice versa.

Sampson stands up and smiles. "You look nice."

"Thanks, but don't get used to it," I say shyly, grabbing my backpack out of habit and putting the straps over my shoulder. "Ready?"

"Yeah, let's get going."

We leave the cabin, walking up the tree root covered trail to where his golf cart is sitting. Sampson hops into the driver's side and pats the spot next to him.

"Where's your car?" I ask, sliding onto the cart and making sure my dress is tucked under my thighs. The seat burns under my legs from the summer heat, it's almost too painful to sit down.

He releases the emergency brake and we roll back a

few inches before he presses his foot on the gas and we move forward, heading in the direction opposite of the camp entrance.

"Don't need it, told you we're not going too far."

"Oh God," I say, clutching the little dash. "You're not taking me to the very back of camp to murder me, are you?"

"We are going to the back of camp, but there won't be any murdering... today..." Sampson teases.

"Sure, that's what all murderers say before they slash the pretty girl's throat."

"Well, I can't argue with the pretty part."

We're both quiet and I blush, but the sound of the gravel crunching under the wheels of the golf cart slice through the silence.

"You can't say things like that," I say bashfully. Part of me hopes he doesn't hear.

"I'll stop," he says, but when I shake my head he continues. "I promise. You're right. Friends?"

I turn to look at him and his smile seems sincere, but the words sounded slightly too painful to even say. "Friends. So, really, where are we going? There's nothing back this way but the old farm."

"Yep," Sampson says just as we pass by the old log cabin. "And a huge Victorian house."

"Really?" I ask, sitting up straighter hoping to get a quick glimpse of the house. "I've never been any further than the cabin."

"Yeah, that's pretty much where the camp property ends, then the rest of the land belongs to the owners."

"I thought your parents were the owners," I say confused, and then it makes sense. "Wait, you live at Camp Arthur, you and your parents?"

"Ah, took you long enough to figure it out!" Sampson

puts the golf cart in park in front of the most gorgeous ivory colored colonial house that I've ever seen. A spacious porch wraps around the entire house with a few porch swings and some patio furniture.

"How long have you been living here?" I ask, staring at the house in awe.

"I haven't been living here too much. I have a room, but I either stay in my cabin or during the school year, I'm in a dorm. We've only owned the place since last Christmas." I follow Sampson up the rock sidewalk to the front porch.

The smell of freshly baked cookies sneaks through the screened windows of the kitchen. Sampson opens the squeaky screen door and holds it open for me to follow him through.

"Mom," Sampson calls as we walk through the foyer and into the kitchen. "We're here."

"Oh, good. Is Viv with you?" his mom asks, but she doesn't turn away from the stove to look at us, a pot of boiling water in front of her.

"No, she hasn't gotten back. It's just me and one of my friends, Penelope. She just started working here."

His mom turns around and wipes her hands off on a towel. She smiles brightly at me and comes over to shake my hand, "Penelope, what a pretty name. It's so nice to meet you."

"It's nice to meet you too, Mrs..." I say, realizing I don't even know their last name. I've heard it once, from his dad on the first day, before I even knew it was his dad.

"Mrs. Garreth, but you can call me Molly. You guys ready for your campers to get here?" she asks.

"Ready as I'll ever be," I say. "I'm used to the other way around. I've been a camper here for years."

Molly claps her hands together once, a smile growing

across her face. "That's great to hear! Maybe Sam, my husband, would love to hear some of your stories. This is our first year running Camp Arthur. We want to make sure the kids keep coming back for all the things they love. You've met Sam, right?"

I remember back to my first day here earlier in the week. "Yeah, he introduced himself to me and the other CIT's."

"Well he should be here in about an hour. He had to run to the store. Sampson, why don't you take Penelope out and show her some of the farm?" Mrs. Garreth says. "I just started lunch. Should be done in about 45 minutes."

"You don't need any help?" I ask.

She smiles, her eyes crinkling in the corners. "You're our guest, go enjoy yourself and have fun. You'll have your hands full for the next two and a half months."

She reaches into a jar next to her and pulls out two cookies and hands them to us.

"Shouldn't you warn us about spoiling our appetite?" Sampson asks, but I take the cookies anyway.

"It's the weekend," Mrs. Garreth says simply. "You can have cookies whenever, besides, they're fresh right now."

Sampson taps me on the shoulder and I follow him out the back door, my cookie already in my mouth and chewed up. I try to hand him his but he smiles and shakes his head so I shrug and pop the other one in my mouth also.

The wrap around deck opens in the back of the house to some land with a vegetable garden and a larger lake, bigger than the one in front of camp. Sampson sits down on the steps and I walk down them to take in the scenery.

"She likes you," says Sampson. "My mom, she seemed to like you a ton."

"How can you tell?" I ask. "We just met, she doesn't even know me."

Sampson shrugs. "She's a good judge of character. So what do you want to do?"

"What do the owners of camp normally do? I've never paid attention to what they do."

"Well, we have some farm animals," Sampson says. "And some trails that lead into camp. There's not much, we can just walk around the lake."

"Sure," I say but then glance down at my shoes clearly made for aesthetic and not walking.

"Take 'em off," Sampson says sliding his own sandals off. "Who needs shoes?"

"I don't think so," I tell him. "I did that once and got stung by a bee."

He slides his shoes back on. "Alright, if you're feet start to hurt, I'll carry you. Problem solved, but just promise you never force yourself to wear uncomfortable shoes again. I hate when girls do that."

I smile and nod my head. "Promise."

"Sampson, honey, can you clear the table?" Molly asks her son as we walk back in from outside. "You're dad said he's about 10 minutes away."

Sampson and I take our shoes off by the back door and something about having my bare feet on the floor of his family's house seems very intimate. I tiptoe across the wood floors, over to the island where four plates are sitting with silverware on top.

"I can set the table if you'd like," I offer to Mrs. Garreth.

"Thank you, sweetie," Molly responds. "Sampson, you

need to bring her around more often. You're too sweet, Penelope."

"It's no big deal," I smile back. "I just like to pull my own weight wherever I go, and it's the least I can do since you're having me over."

I carefully grab the plates and silverware and head over to the dining room table where Sampson is closing a few textbooks and notebooks. I place a plate on each of the four place mats and put a fork, knife, and spoon at every spot.

"Taking summer classes?" I ask Sampson as he slides his books into a backpack.

"Yeah, one a month for the summer. It's more expensive," he says. "But I'm a semester behind."

"Where do you go to college?" I ask, finishing setting the table.

"Maryville."

I slap my hand on his chest. "No way! That's where I'm going! I start in August. Well...hopefully. I applied a little late."

"Really?" he asks, smiling. "Why'd you choose Maryville of all schools?"

"It's kind of stupid. I was planning on keeping a summer job here and then going to school at MC since it's so close. I'm kind of over the town I grew up in. Figure I'll live in the cabins while camp is going on and the dorms during the semester."

"That's not stupid, sounds like you have a plan."

The front door opens then and a man's voice travels down the hall and into the kitchen. "Something smells fantastic."

"You're just in time," says Molly. "We're getting ready to put lunch on the table."

"Ah, I see we have company," says the man as he takes

off his baseball hat. The camp director from my first day, Sampson's dad, Sam Garreth, I try to wrap my head around this. How am I ever going to think of him as the same person?

"Sam Garreth," he says holding out his hand to shake. "Nice to meet you."

"Penelope," I say, shaking his hand. "We met last week... sort of. I'm one of the CITs."

Mr. Garreth gives Sampson an odd look, but then turns his attention back to me. "Ah, so are you excited to be working for us this summer?"

"Yes actually," I start to say, but he cuts me off.

"Oh, no you're not. You can be honest with me, I'm always looking for suggestions on how to make Camp Arthur a better, more enjoyable place."

"No, no," I say, shaking my head. "What I was going to say was, working here has always been a dream of mine. I've been coming here every summer, this was always my home away from home."

"Yeah?" Mr. Garreth asks. "That's so nice to hear. I knew we had some former campers. So what is it that keeps you coming back every summer?"

Mrs. Garreth motions for all of us to sit down and she brings over a plate full of chicken breasts, along with some sides. As Sampson's parents pass around the food, I try to impress my boss with my answer while also giving him my honest opinion on my previous Camp Arthur experiences.

"It's not one specific thing," I say as Sampson hands me a bowl of roasted potatoes. "The first year I didn't like camp and my mom told me to try it again the next summer and if I didn't like it, then I wouldn't have to go back.

"The next year things were a lot better. I had fantastic counselors, I made a ton of friends, and I didn't want to leave when the summer was over. I guess I just love that it's a break from reality. I assume it'll be different as a counselor, but I'm still excited to be here and try it out."

"We're happy to have you with us," Mr. Garreth says as I hand him the potatoes in exchange for the chicken. "Who's training you this summer?"

Sampson beats me to the answer, "Viv, actually."

"That so?" replies his mom, and I'm not sure if I imagined it or not, but her tone didn't sound pleased.

"Yeah," I say, picking up my fork and knife to slice through my chicken. "I haven't had too much time around her, but I'm sure that'll change once the campers arrive."

"Well if she gives you any trouble, let us know," says his dad in a joking manner. "Speaking of Viv, what's she up to, son? Haven't seen her around lately."

I zone out the rest of the conversation between Sampson and his father and only glance up from my plate once. Mrs. Garreth gives me a sad but somehow reassuring smile.

Did I miss something?

Once the conversation about Viv is over, Mr. and Mrs. Garreth ask about where I'm from, my plans for college, what my parents do, and so on. Part of me treats it as if this is my interview for a full time summer counselor position, but the other part of me is just enjoying the warm embrace I feel from sitting around this family. That's what camp is supposed to feel like: like you're around family. Friends that turn into family.

I feel homesick suddenly and wonder if I will be able to handle moving my whole life here, year-round, away from my family and away from my friends. Of course, I would go off to college in a different state, but working in a different state too? Packing up all my stuff and only coming home for the holidays?

"You okay, dear?" Mrs. Garreth asks.

I nod, getting way ahead of myself. "Yeah, sorry. I was just thinking."

"What I was saying," Mrs. Garreth continues. "Was if you ever need a place to go, you can come here. You're always welcome. It must be hard to be so far away from your parents."

"Yeah, harder than I thought," I say honestly. "My dad is probably taking it harder."

"You and your dad are close?" Mr. Garreth asks smiling.

"Super close. I've always been a daddy's girl," I smile back.

"I've always said if we had a daughter, she would have me wrapped around her tiny little finger."

"You would lose your mind," Mrs. Garreth chuckles, pointing her fork at her husband. "You'd be worried sick about her anytime she left the house. Always critiquing her outfits to make sure she didn't have too much skin showing."

Sampson laughs. "I couldn't imagine you having a daughter, dad."

"Alright, I want you to make a goal this summer," Mr. Garreth says, folding his hands together and resting his elbows on the table. "Take a few campers under your watch, not just the ones in your cabin. Pick two or three campers outside your cabin and pay special attention to them."

Mr. Garreth looks between the two of us. "You too, Penelope. You guys might not think these kids look up to you, but some of them will. You'll be their friends while away from home, an older sibling, a role model, a parental figure. Always remember that they're watching."

"Totally," I say bursting with excitement. "That's actually why I have my heart set on working here! I had some counselors that impacted my life, and I would love to be a role model for the campers. I feel like there would be nothing better than being a CIT this year and then coming back full on next year, where I have a camper or two glad to come back to see me."

"That's what I need here at Camp Arthur!" Mr. Garreth says. "I love when counselors take interest in getting to know their campers. Watch out Sampson, this one might snag your job next year."

Just then, Sampson's phone rings from his pocket and he excuses himself from the table to step outside and take it.

Mrs. Garreth grabs her plate and her husband's, and I help her clear the table. I stack Sampson's plate on top of mine and stack the other empty bowls from dinner and bring them into the kitchen.

"That was really good, Mrs… Molly, thanks for having me over," I say.

"Any time, dear," she says, taking the plates from me and placing them in the sink. "If you ever need someone to talk to, I'm here. Being so far away from home for the first time can be tough."

"I appreciate that."

"Believe it or not, Sampson had a hard time his first semester at college when he moved out on his own," she says. "I remember him calling me every day for the first month. That's why we decided to buy Camp Arthur, we wanted to be closer to him and my husband wanted out of the city. It was perfect."

I smile at her story, not being able to picture Sampson ever being the needy type.

Sampson comes in then and puts his shoes on. "Hate

to eat and run, but I need to get going. You ready, Penelope?"

"Sure," I say, walking over to put my shoes on.

As we head to the door, Mrs. Garreth grabs two sandwich bags and fills them both up with something and hands a bag to each of us, "For when you need a little treat."

I glance at the bag and see the freshly made cookies. I thank Mrs. Garreth and follow Sampson out the front door and back to the golf cart. On the short drive back to my cabin, I can't get the smile off my face. For the first time since I got here this summer, camp is feeling like home again.

Dinner rolls around and I'm practically on cloud nine with happiness. I almost have a skip in my step as I'm walking up to the mess hall to get dinner. Getting to know Sampson as a friend, with no one else around and just enjoying camp, was possibly the best weekend I could ask for.

All of my co-workers are making their way back to camp, filling up the employee parking lot with their dust covered cars and walking back to their cabins with fresh laundry and bags of snacks. A few people are in the mess hall when I get there sipping on some coffee while reading a book or scrolling through their social media feed on their cellphones.

I grab a bowl and make a small salad since that's the only thing the cooking staff has ready since the campers aren't here yet.

Part of me is tempted to go sit by one of my other counselors and try to make friends, but I don't want to be too eager or annoy anyone. After all, this is the last chance for alone time before the real work begins.

I choose to go sit toward the back of the mess hall, wishing I had brought my cell phone to dinner or a book to read so I have something else to do to occupy my time. For ten minutes I stare at my salad like it's the most interesting and entertaining thing since the election last year.

"Earth to Penelope," says a voice next to me.

"Shit," I say, looking up as Kenny is sitting down beside me. "You scared the crap out of me, you jerk. Why do you always do that?"

He ignores my comment and pulls some food out of a plastic bag.

"That looks so good," I say, staring at his dinner. Fast food. Junk food. "I'm so hungry. All they had was salad."

"Well," he says, continuing to pull out food from his two bottomless bags. "You'll be happy to know, I was thinking about you when I was sitting in the super long drive-thru and I thought I would share. Don't know what you like or don't like, so take what you want and I'll finish the rest."

"Kenny," I say, gripping his arm. "You're a lifesaver."

He blushes and I pull back my hand, reaching for some chicken nuggets and fries.

"How was your weekend? Go anywhere?" he asks, stuffing his mouth with a burrito.

How many fast food places did he hit up? I think to myself.

"Just hung out," I say. "Went out for lunch but stayed close to camp."

"I totally forgot you live a bit of a distance away, don't you?"

"Yeah," I say. "Wasn't worth going home since we just got here last weekend."

"I'm such a moron, I should have invited you out or something. Kind of just assumed you were doing your own thing," he says.

I shake my head, wondering just how different my weekend would have been had Kenny invited me out with his friends. "It's fine, maybe next time."

"So, are you excited for camp to officially begin?" Kenny asks.

"Yeah, I honestly can't believe we're not campers this year though. It's going to be weird."

"I can't believe people are putting *me* in charge of their kids!" he says laughing, some cheese falling from his mouth and landing on his shorts. He wipes them off with a greasy napkin.

I almost spit out my food in a fit of laughter, but grab my own napkin before my dinner covers the table. "Well they haven't met you yet, so they might change their minds."

"True, I didn't really think about that."

The door behind us swings open and I don't have to turn around to know that the voice belongs to Viv, and she's speaking to Sampson. That must have been why our lunch earlier was cut short. She says jump, he says how high.

She's back earlier than we thought.

"Sampson! Sup?" Kenny asks, waving them over.

Neither of them take a seat at our table. I take a quick glance at Sampson, but his attention is on Kenny. "Not much," he answers.

"How was your weekend?" Kenny asks pounding fists with Sampson. I never viewed Sampson as the type of guy who 'fist bumps'. But I also didn't think he was a frat guy or a momma's boy.

"Good. How about you guys? Do anything fun?" Sampson's eyes linger on mine, but I notice Viv's grip on his hand tighten.

"Not too bad. Just chilled out," Kenny says, chewing off the tip of a fry.

I nod my head along with Kenny and snatch a chicken nugget so I have an excuse to not say anything.

"I need you to put together the welcome bags for the kids tonight. I left all the stuff in boxes on your bunk," says Viv, trying to show off her power over me.

"I'll get it done," I reassure her.

"What are you guys up to tonight?" Kenny asks.

"Don't worry about it," Viv almost snaps but catches herself. She leans her head on Sampson's shoulder. "Just spending some time together before things get hectic."

"So while you two…" I start to say and then realize I'm speaking out loud. "So, while you two spend time together, why don't you come over and help me with bags, Kenny? I'm sure Sampson needs help with your camper bags too. It's the least we could do for them."

"Um, yeah. Sure," Kenny says as he jumps up from the bench and starts gathering up our trash. "I'll go throw this stuff away and meet you outside?"

I slowly get up from the bench with a smile on my face. "Stay out as long as you need tonight. I'll handle all the camper preparations."

"Awesome," Viv says, that horrible edge to her voice.

"See you tomorrow, guys," I say heading for the door. "Oh, and thanks for keeping me company this weekend, Sampson. I don't know what I would have done without you. Would have been bored out of my mind."

He tells me it was a pleasure and I smile as I watch Viv

go rigid with anger. I know it was childish of me to mention Sampson hanging out with me while everyone was gone, but I know Viv won't have time to corner me about it because we'll be too busy tomorrow preparing for campers. I'm tired of her pushing me. It's time for me to stand up for myself.

That may have been the stupidest thing I've ever done.

"Can you hand me a small shirt?" I ask Kenny.

We've been packing goodie bags for our campers for two hours now. We're sitting on the cold concrete floor of my cabin, empty granola bar boxes surrounding us and a large pile of drawstring bags already completed off to one side.

Kenny checks the tags on the insides of the shirts and tosses one in my direction. "That might be the last small. Everything else looks like mediums and larges."

"Only ten more camper bags to go. Why Viv thought this was a one-person job, I have no idea," I say, stretching out after adding another completed bag to the pile. "If I didn't have you, this would have taken all night."

"Teamwork," he laughs. "How has she not acquired that skill in life yet?"

I shrug my shoulders and toss him a granola bar and open one for myself. "Thanks for helping me. I really appreciate it."

"Yeah, no problem," Kenny says, counting out ten granola bars and then opening up one leftover and taking a bite out of it.

I let out a yawn, not even realizing how tired I am. "What time is it?" I ask.

Kenny glances down at his watch. "Almost midnight."

"I thought Viv would be back by now," I say. "It's kind of crappy of her to ditch me the night before we get our first campers."

Kenny pulls his phone out of his pocket. "I have a text from Sampson. Looks like she's staying at our cabin," he says with a sigh.

"Of course she is," I say, rolling my eyes. I go sit down on my bunk, staring down at the mess we need to clean up.

"Can I ask you a question?"

"Sure, what's up?" I ask. A few crazy things run through my head, but most of them are good.

Kenny stares down at one of the bags and plays with the drawstring. "I don't want this to sound bad, and you don't have to tell me. I just… there's not something going on with you and Sampson, right?"

"What, no! That's crazy! Why would you even think that?"

His laugh sounds nervous. "I know, it's silly. I must have just been imagining things."

"Things like what?" I ask, trying to smile my best innocent smile.

"He just looks at you differently. When he's around Viv, whether you're there or not, he looks terrified. I've seen him when it's just the two of you though and he seems happier," he explains.

"Well, nothing's going on as far as I know."

"It was stupid. Forget I even said anything. I mean, he's like super whipped by Viv. Why would he even think about getting away?"

"Exactly!" I say. "Besides, I won't be a home wrecker. I'm not that kind of girl."

"No, you're right. I feel like an idiot for even thinking that way." He looks down intently at the floor.

After a moment passes between us, I place a bag on each bunk with their name tags. Kenny grabs his campers' bags and places them in one of the t-shirt boxes to take back to his cabin.

"Well, I guess I should be going. We have a busy first week ahead of us," he says, holding his box over his head.

"Yeah, let me get the door for you." I walk in front of him and push it open.

"And thanks for your company."

"Anytime," I say smiling.

I watch him pull out a mini flashlight from his pocket to light his way. *When did Kenny, the kid who I used to despise being here at Camp Arthur, turn into such a gentlemen?*

SEVEN

The door to the cabin swings open and I jump out of bed, reaching for a weapon but only finding one of my flip flops. It takes me a minute to realize it's just Viv returning from the previous night. I crawl back into my bunk and pull my blanket over my head, trying to shut out the sun coming in through the windows.

"Good morning," Viv sings, her mood completely changed.

"What's up with you?" I grumble, only pulling the blanket down enough to show my eyes.

"It's a new day, my sweet, sweet, Penelope," she says. "What's up with you? I gave you the cabin to yourself last night and you didn't snag your opportunity?"

"Opportunity for what?"

"Um, you and Kenny. Hello! He's so into you!" she exclaims.

I pull the blanket down to my neck. "Kenny and I are just friends."

"Doesn't mean you can't do more than friendly things."

"I don't get what you're trying to say."

She smiles and shakes her head. "So young and naive. You'll grow up quickly this summer. Don't worry."

I watch as Viv grabs clothes from our storage room and heads to the bathroom, wondering what exactly happened last night to get her in such a good mood. I try to accept reality, but there's no way someone can go from hating you for a week and then trying to be your best friend or at least nice to you.

I slide my legs out of my sleeping bag and place my feet on the floor, leaning down to reach into my duffle bag for a pair of athletic shorts and my green staff t-shirt that says 'Camp Arthur' across the chest, with our motto, 'Mountains of Possibilities' across the bottom.

Hopefully that motto stands true this summer.

After heading to the mess hall to grab a quick bowl of cereal and some coffee, I fill up my water bottle and set off toward the welcome center. When I get there, Kenny's already setting up the table and chairs for us. He smiles and waves when he sees me, and he places the binder full of the campers' names, addresses, and special instructions on the table.

"Reporting for check-in duty," I say, dropping my backpack under the table and placing my drink on the ground next to my chair. "Sorry I'm late."

"It's fine, not much for us to do just yet. Campers shouldn't start showing up for about forty-five minutes," he says, glancing over a list of our duties.

"So, what do we do?"

"Says here that we're just supposed to find the camper's name in the binder, have the parents sign next to their name, and then we send them into the welcome center to get checked for lice and to drop off meds if they have any. It appears our job is pretty simple," he says. "Bring anything to do?"

"I can go snag some supplies from the art center," I say

nodding. "We can make the first friendship bracelet of the thousands we'll be making this summer."

"Sounds good. You should probably show me how to make them so I know for later. I'll call over the walkie for someone to cart us a cooler and some cups over. It's supposed to be super hot out today." He runs a hand through his shaggy brown hair to keep it off his ears.

I nod in agreement and head over to the art building. Inside, it's the cleanest I've ever seen it. Usually the tables are covered in lace, string, beads, macaroni noodles, glue, and other items used to make crafts. Looking at the blue walls covered in various colored handprints, I feel nostalgic. I spot my yellow handprint from three years ago when they repainted the building. I was fourteen. I place my hand over it and smile, my fingertips only covering it by a tiny bit.

They'll probably paint over these handprints again soon, but hopefully I'll be here to leave my mark on Camp Arthur once more. I remove my hand from the wall and go over to the storage cabinet in search of the thin string for bracelet making. I find a wide assortment and just grab about six colors with a pair of scissors, some tape and a piece of cardboard.

When I get back to Kenny, he's just finishing up on the request for the water cooler. "They said it will be about an hour. They're filling them right now and loading them up on the golf cart, dropping them off at the cabins first."

"Then we have plenty of time to do a friendship bracelet tutorial?" I ask, smiling, putting down the items from the art building.

"What's the cardboard for?" Kenny asks.

"You," I laugh. "It's easier to teach on cardboard. That's what the counselors used to do for us instead of just taping the strings down."

Kenny just stares at me, clearly not understanding.

"Trust me, it'll be a lot easier for you. By the end of the summer, you probably won't need it anymore."

"If you say so," Kenny says.

I take the scissors and make a slit at the top of the cardboard and then six slits at the bottom for the thread to fit through. Kenny picks out six of the colors, and I cut off equal amounts, tie them together at the end to slide into the top cardboard slit, and then place one strand of each through the other openings.

My setup is different, though a little easier. I tie off three colors and then tape it onto the table. I show Kenny how to make knot after knot, though I make progress quicker than he does. I've made these bracelets a lot more than he probably has. Whenever it rained in the past at camp most girls, including myself, would stay in the cabin and make bracelets to exchange with each other.

By the time the first camper shows up, I've already finished a bracelet and started on a second one. I glance over to see how far Kenny had made it, and he only finished about an inch.

We stop what we're doing as the camper and her parents walk over to our table, dragging along two rolling suitcases behind them. The girl looks to be about eight years old, but that's all I can get from her because she hides behind her parents' legs.

"Hello," I say in my cheeriest voice. "Welcome to Camp Arthur, can I have the camper's first and last name, please?"

"Daisy Miller," says the mom. She doesn't seem thrilled to be here. I imagine they might have suitcases of their own packed up and be ready to head out on their own vacation.

"Miller comma Daisy," I say looking over the list of

female campers. "Ah, here we are. Look at that, you're my first camper!"

I hand them over a temporary name tag with Daisy's name on it and her cabin assignment. They sign by her name and I initial beside it, then give them the directions on where to go from here.

"After you finish inside, you can grab one of the counselors waiting on the patio and they'll help you with her luggage and finding the cabin," Kenny says, offering a smile.

Once they walk away I turn back to Kenny. "One down."

I look out into the parking lot as another girl climbs out of a cherry red Benz convertible, her parents trail behind her with three rolling suitcases, the mother chatters on a cell phone, while the father appears to talk aimlessly.

"Can I get your name?" I ask when the girl comes up to the table.

"Morgan," the little girl says as her mom covers the mouthpiece of her cell phone to add her last name.

"Morgan Meyers, and she's on a strict diet plan. Vegan. I already sent in her papers so if we could speed this process up a little bit that would be fabulous."

Kenny and I exchange a look before I look down my list of campers and place a checkmark next to her name.

"You're in my cabin too," I say, and notice her dad is talking into his Bluetooth headset and Morgan's mom is half listening but concentrating more on the conversation in her phone.

"Hold on," she tells the person and then looks at me. "So, *you'll* be her counselor this summer?"

"Counselor in training," I say and she glances over me. "There will be a main counselor in our cabin also. She'll be meeting you at the cabin."

Mrs. Meyers gives a nod. "You need to make sure to keep an eye on Morgan. Don't let her have any junk food, she's on a strict diet. She has ballet in the fall."

"Mom," Morgan groans as her face turns red.

"Morgan, ladies don't wine. Now come on, let's get you to your cabin, dad and I have a flight to make tonight."

As Morgan follows her mom and dad into the welcome center, I shake my head.

"Are you kidding me?" I whisper.

"I hope campers' my parents aren't like that," Kenny says. "I think the clingers might be better, the ones that try to call and check on their kids once a week."

"Agreed." I say, tapping my pen against the clipboard holding the campers cabin assignments.

"Where the heck is that water? It feels like it's already ninety out here," he says, squinting up at the sun and then wiping some sweat off his forehead with the collar of his staff shirt.

"Here it comes," I say, seeing someone driving the golf cart and holding onto the giant cooler in the passenger seat. When the cart gets closer, I realize Sampson is the one behind the wheel.

"Sorry guys," he says, unloading the cooler for us and sitting it on the table with some plastic cups. Some of the other staff come over to fill a glass too. "How's check-in going?"

"Fine," I say. "Only two so far."

"I'm sure it'll get busier soon," he replies. "If you guys need anything else, let me know. We'll be coming around with some sandwiches for lunch soon."

"Thanks," Kenny says. "Do I need to be back at the cabin once our campers start coming in?"

"Nah," Sampson answers. "Once they drop their stuff off at the cabin, they're directed to either hang out with their parents for a bit or head to the pavilion and fields to hang out with other campers until check-in is over."

"Gotcha," Kenny says. "I'll see you back at the cabin to get ready for dinner around four thirty?"

"Yeah, dinner is at five. I'll grab our campers from the field and bring them back to the cabin."

Sampson hops back onto the golf cart and peals out, heading in the direction he came from. I feel a pang in my stomach because he didn't say bye. I shut it out though, because six more cars with campers show up and I need to concentrate on them, not Sampson.

"Oh my God!" I say, standing up from the table. "Kelsey?"

"Penelope!" she yells, jogging over to give me a tight embrace.

"How did it slip my mind that you were coming back this year? I guess I just assumed you were too old to return as a camper!" I say, releasing her from the hug. Her parents come up behind her and Kenny helps sign her in.

I lean over and glance at the book where Kenny is making a check next to her name. "You're in my cabin!"

"No way! This is going to be awesome!" she says. "How's the other counselor?"

I shake my head. "She's something."

"We only have five campers left to check in," Kenny says. "Why don't you guys go hang out and catch up? I'll finish check ins."

"Are you sure?" I ask.

"Yeah, go for it. There's only thirty minutes left anyway."

"Thanks," I say, turning to Kelsey and her parents. "Head on in and see the nurse for your super fun lice check, and then I'll meet you out here."

"Yuck, sounds like *loads* of fun," Kelsey says as she walks away and into the welcome center with her parents.

I take her bags over to one of the final people still transporting campers' bags and load it onto the golf cart. "Goes to cabin six, please."

"I'm on it," says one guy.

"Hey, I'll take it." Ah, Casanova at it again. He comes walking over and hops on the golf cart before the CIT can take off. "I have some business to attend to in those parts anyway."

He winks at me before he takes off, and I just stand there frustrated. What can he possibly do, anyway? With campers here, his little games with Viv must end, right?

Once Kelsey has completed her check-in, we both wave goodbye to her parents as they drive away. She grins mischievously at me. "Let the fun begin."

"Safe fun," I clarify. "Remember, I'm working this summer. I can't let you get away with too much. I'm your counselor."

"You're such a party-pooper," she says, pouting but brightening up within seconds. "So, how many cute guys have you seen so far? Is it slim pickings?"

"I don't know!" I tell her, my voice rising in shock. "Geez, I'm technically an adult this summer, I can't be looking at other campers."

"I'm not talking about campers! I'm talking about the guy counselors! Remember when we used to always crush on them? They were always so hot, and now that you're one of them, you totally have a chance!"

"I'd rather not get involved with… wait… I shouldn't be discussing this with you, you're my camper!"

"Technically, I'm not your camper for another forty-five minutes, and then I'm under your control," she winks. "Oh my God, speaking of hot. Did you know Lain was returning this summer?"

She points over to the soccer field and sure enough, there's Lain with his Kool-Aid-blue mohawk. Every year he comes back with different color hair, it's kind of his thing. Last year his hair was down to his shoulders and bleach blonde, almost white. I have to admit that he's always been one of the hottest guys here, but it has always been 'slim pickings' at Camp Arthur. And, of course, the hottest guy must pair up with the hottest female camper for the summer.

"I think this is my year," Kelsey says. "I will talk to him."

"Now?" I ask.

"A great man once said, 'If not now, when' or something like that."

I shake my head. "That's an album by Incubus."

"Huh, really? Then he's a smart man."

"He's a band," I say, but she's already halfway across the field.

At first, the interaction is awkward between Lain and Kelsey. She's twirling her hair around her finger and when he says something that I assume is funny, she places her hand on his chest for a second.

I stand there for about five minutes before finally leaving to head back to the cabin. It's going to take time to adjust to my life as a counselor versus my previous years as a camper. If I were a camper, I would have followed Kelsey over like a lost puppy dog. Now, I have responsibilities.

It's going to be an interesting summer.

Back at the cabin, Viv puts me in charge of helping the girls make their bunk name tags while she's off learning a skit all the main counselors should learn before the opening bonfire.

I'm not good at remembering names. Thankfully, we're having the girls label their bunks and they have to wear lanyards with their names on them. We do, however, get a list with the names of our cabin mates, ages ranging from eight to sixteen.

Daisy, Kelsey, Lauren, Morgan, Annie, Ronnie, Katrina who likes to go by Kat, Chelle (don't you dare call her *Michelle*), Brittany, Olive, and Jenn with two N's. Luckily, we're supposed to play name games every day for the first two weeks. I've already started one with the girls.

"My name is pondering Penelope and my favorite animal that starts with a P is a platypus." I don't actually like platypuses.

One of the younger girls giggles, "That's silly!"

"Well, then you come up with something better for your name!" I say, faking hurt.

"My name is Chelle," ah, *not* Michelle. "Crazy Chelle and I like cats!"

"Girl," I smile. "You and me both! Alright, who's next?"

"My name's kinky Kelsey and I like…"

"Kelsey, shhh!" I say, my face turning blood red.

The other three older girls laugh with Kelsey and I just shake my head.

"What does kink-e mean?" asks Daisy. I only remember her name because I checked her in first.

"It's not a real word, don't worry about ever needing to use it," I suggest. "Kelsey is just kidding. Kidding Kelsey."

"My name's original Olive, and I like making origami," says another girl from her bunk. She seems like she might be one of my favorite campers for the summer. She quietly did her bunk tag when she got here and then relaxed in her bunk and read a book. Kelsey on the other hand, she might be the death of me this summer.

"Alright," I say, checking my watch. "Looks like it's time to get ready to head to dinner. Afterwards we have a bonfire, so wear closed-toed shoes and pack some bug spray."

Some girls rummage through their bags in search of their gym shoes, and the others don't make a move at all. How am I possibly supposed to get over ten girls ready to go by myself?

"Alright, meet me at the door when you're ready to go," I say, and then an idea pops into my head. "We're sitting as a cabin at dinner tonight. Last two people in line have to be the helpers who run and get food for us."

That does the trick. Everyone puts socks and shoes on in a hurry. Daisy is the first one in line and she smiles up at me, quickly followed by four more. Finally, Kelsey and Chelle take up the back of the line.

"You set me up for failure, Penelope," she says. "You know I can't get ready that quickly."

"Better luck next time," I say. "Alright, let's go to dinner!"

EIGHT

I've come to realize that pool time is the only time I can fully relax. With the lifeguards taking over the pool, I can just sit on the sidelines, read a book, and enjoy myself. It's only day three with campers, and I'm already pumped to have two off days at the end of the week. I didn't realize how much effort counselors put into this job.

After taking a quick dip in the pool to cool off, I go over to where Kelsey is trying to get a tan.

"I just don't get it," Kelsey says. I can't tell if she's looking at me because her huge black sunglasses are too tinted. Kelsey hardly ever swims at camp, so me and her took over two of the lawn chairs.

"Don't get what?" I ask, drying my arms off and wrapping my body up with my towel when I notice some of the boys from the other cabins ogling me, or possibly ogling Kelsey in her revealing bikini. I'm pretty sure the camp pre-registration packet says no two-piece bathing suits, but Kelsey has the body and wants to flaunt it, just like always.

"Lain," she states. "I don't get why he doesn't remember me. We've practically grown up together every summer."

I lie back into my chair and look toward the guys; Lain is over there with his dyed hair laughing with them. He catches me looking at him and waves.

Kelsey squeezes my arm before I can lift it to wave back. "Oh my God, he saw us looking at him. Don't wave back. I'm so mad at him."

"Why don't you just go over there and say hi?" I ask. "Try to talk to him again. I'm sure he wants to talk to you if he's waving and smiling."

"Should I? What if he laughs at me? Or the guys won't go away so we can talk?"

"So be it," I tell her. "You'll never know if you don't try."

Kelsey adjusts her bikini for maximum cleavage and stands up with an air of authority I wish I had myself. She has so much confidence she looks regal, like a princess about to tell off a poor servant. I'll never be as strong as she is.

I'm about to reach into my pool bag and pull out my copy of The Scarlet Letter when a shadow spills over my legs.

"This seat taken?" asks someone standing by the chair Kelsey was in.

"No, she's busy. You can have it," I say, assuming they just want to move it somewhere else.

To my surprise it's Sampson, and he sits down next to me. At first, he says nothing, and I have no idea how much time passes. It feels like an eternity. All I know is that I could sit here forever and not say a word to him. That would be perfect.

"Why aren't you swimming?" he asks, not looking at me, but at least we're on speaking terms again. One minute he's avoiding me because of Viv, and the next we're friends again.

I shrug my shoulders. "I took a dip earlier. I just like that I don't have to be in charge of anything right now. This is my time to just chill out. What about you? Shouldn't you be guarding some lives?"

"I'm off duty today," he says, pulling on his grey board shorts. "We alternate. I get Mondays and Wednesdays."

"Gotcha," I say as I glance to one of the three lifeguard stands where Viv is sitting. She has her legs crossed, whistle in her mouth, and she's staring at me. "How's Viv?"

He looks over at her and then back to me. "You spend more time with her. Shouldn't I be asking you?"

I chuckle, but I don't find it funny. "She's not around much," I say. "Figured she was always sneaking off to be with you."

"Really?" he asks, shaking his head and letting my words float around in his mind. "Not really. I mean, she has her own activities to do. Probably busy with that."

I want so badly to shake him and tell him to see Viv for who she really is, but I don't, I can't. I shake my head instead and open my book to where I left off. Instead of taking the hint that I want to be alone, he picks a new topic to discuss.

"So," he starts. "How long have you been coming here?"

I sigh and place my book back into my backpack. "Since I was ten. This is my home away from home. My happy place. Some people like the beach, I like camp."

"You really want to work here again next summer?"

"Yeah, it's been my dream job since about five years ago," I tell him simply. I look at him and watch as he relaxes a little. Something makes me look around to see if anyone is in listening distance. Why does it feel like I'm doing something wrong, when I'm not?

Our eyes meet. Until this moment, we were looking anywhere but at each other. He brushes his hair out of his eyes and I smile.

"I'm going to say something I shouldn't," he says as he looks away from me. "I'd like to get to know you Penelope. I still do even under these circumstances."

"Same goes to you," I whisper back. "I mean, you seem really cool. But Viv... she's so possessive. I can practically feel her burning a hole in my chest right now."

"Viv's a bit scary, isn't she?" he asks, scrunching up his nose.

"A bit," I say. "Has she always been weird about you having friends that are girls? Or is this a new personality trait?"

He runs a hand through his hair in frustration. "Eh, not really. I've never had friends that were girls though. She doesn't get weird when we go to parties and I talk to other girls. It's actually pretty strange, she sort of encourages it..."

"Do you let her talk to other guys?" I ask.

"Of course," he says. "I'm not going to be that over protective boyfriend who freaks out whenever she gets a text from a Jack or a Matt."

"But a Zach is uncalled for, right?" I tease.

"No, Zachs. Hell no. Have you ever met a nice, trustworthy Zach?" I shake my head and he continues. "Exactly."

I almost mention the name Josh, aka Casanova, but I decide now's not the time.

"You know," Sampson says. "Kenny seems smitten by you."

Sure enough, Kenny is sitting on the side of the pool and waves at me. I wave back and tighten my towel around my torso.

"We're friends. We actually went to camp together when we were younger," I say.

"Yeah?"

I look him in the eyes. "Yeah, nothing more. I don't know why you and Viv think we should be together."

I raised my voice a little, but I instantly feel bad about it. My cheeks blush and I cross my arms over my chest.

"Sorry, I just thought it might pass the summer by a little quicker," he says.

"I don't want the summer to pass by fast," I say. "Don't you get it? I love this place. You don't realize how lucky you are that your parents own this camp. You get to live at my happy place year round while I have to go back to the real world in August. I've planned the next four years around Camp Arthur."

"Miss. Penelope!" calls Daisy, running over to me in her little Elsa swimsuit. "I need to go tinkle!"

I get up and slide my flip flops on and turn to Sampson. "Sorry, I have to go."

"Nature calls," he says, and as I'm about to escort Daisy to the restroom he grabs my wrist. "I'm sorry if I upset you."

"It's okay," I say, shaking my head. "Sorry if I got bent out of shape."

He nods. "It happens."

I guess he should be used to it though, dating Viv and all.

After dinner, we were supposed to have a campfire, but storms are rolling in so the camp has been split into three groups, part of them staying in the dining hall for songs and games, the others going to the old barn and then my cabin and two other cabins going to the Welcome Center.

We brought over some board games, one of the male counselors brought over his guitar for some singing and then a few other activities from the overflowing storage closet. It's do what you want to do until the storm passes and we can go to our cabins for the evening.

I've just lost my third game of Candy Land when Daisy comes skipping over to me, her pigtails bouncing. "Penelope!"

"What's up, girlie?" I ask her when she plops down next to me, sitting on her knees.

"Can you help us pull the gymnastics mats out? Morgan wants to show me her cartwheels and stuff!"

The campers playing the game with me have all gotten up to go try something else so, I toss all the pieces back into the box. "Sure can."

I'm happy Morgan is taking the time to actually interact with the younger kids. She seemed very introverted when I first met her, I guess all it took was finding something she loves to do to get her out of her shell.

I take the board game and return it to the table for other campers to play and then go into the storage room to pull the two huge mats out, one at a time. Kelsey comes over to help me set them up for the girls and soon enough, more campers come to watch and try their turn at a cartwheel or tumble.

Morgan's good, no wonder her mom was so stern about her diet. I'm wondering why her parents didn't send her to a specific camp for ballerinas or gymnasts, don't they have those options available? Kelsey has a few campers surrounding her and she's teaching them a cheer with letters to spell out Camp Arthur, but I stay focused on Morgan. She slides her shoes off, to make it easier to spin. Moving to a section of the room without carpet.

She moves into position and I know there's a direct term but I was only in ballet for a year when I was five before I quit because I didn't like being on stage, and then she moves her arms in front of her and spins in six quick circles and returns to her start position. Daisy claps her hands with some younger boys that came to watch, a few get up and try to imitate Morgan's spins, but they just tumble to the floor or stagger looking like tiny drunk humans.

The lights in the building flicker on and off with a loud bang of thunder and a flash of lightning in the windows. Three of the younger kids cling to my legs, shaking from the noise.

Truth be told, thunder and lightning scare me too. It's tornado season here in Tennessee, which makes me even more paranoid. At least we're in one of the more stable buildings.

The electric finally shuts off completely and I usher the kids away from the windows and back into the larger room where some of them are laying on their stomachs around a small laptop screen watching a Disney movie, they're heads propped up on their hands. Me and some of the other counselors grab flashlights, it's almost pitch black in the building, so we can get the rest of the campers in a group to find another activity to keep them busy until we're free to go to our cabins.

Daisy climbs into my lap while Kenny and one of the other male counselors act out a skit, and asks me to braid her hair in pigtails, I separate her soft, thin hair and style it while I let my mind drift off to thoughts of Sampson and things that will never happen between us.

NINE

JUNE

We've only had the campers for a week, but I'm so relieved to finally have two days off where I can go home. I get up around 5 in the morning and grab my bag I packed the night before while the campers were already asleep. Only one of them is up now reading on her Kindle, her back turned away from me.

Mr. Garreth told us that when we're packing up to go home for a day or two we need to do it without the campers there. Supposedly, some campers might grow attached to you because they might have divorced parents and they can't handle seeing another adult figure leave. We're not allowed to tell them where we're going either, and if you're staying and your co-counselor is leaving, you just have to say that the other person will be back some-time soon.

It's silly to me, but I will not argue with the boss.

I quietly open the door to the cabin and close it softly behind me, making sure not to wake up anyone. I turn on my small flashlight because the sun hasn't risen yet. The walk to my car is peaceful with the crickets still chirping, and the birds haven't woken yet.

"Psst!" comes a voice from the welcome center porch as I pass by.

I spin around, drop my laundry bag on the ground, and prepare to use my water bottle as a weapon.

"Jesus, Sampson!" I squeak out. "What the hell are you doing out here?"

"Couldn't sleep," he says shrugging his shoulders. "Came out here because the cabin was stuffy and it already smells like boys going through puberty."

"That's because boys are currently going through puberty in there."

"Heading home?" he asks.

I pick up my laundry bag. "Yeah, figured I needed my own bed for a little bit. I promised my friend at home that I'd go to a bonfire with her."

"Are our bonfires not good enough for you?" he teases.

I blush and thank the Lord he can't see me that well. "They are, but my friend helped me out, so I'm paying her back. Bonfire's tonight, so I figure I should make it home by nine and then I'll have all day to hang out with my parents."

"That should be nice, drive safely. You back on Sunday?"

"Yeah, Sunday evening. After dinner," I say.

"I'll see ya then," he says.

I wave and turn around, heading for my car.

"Mom, dad, I'm home!" I say as I close the front door behind me. I drop my laundry bag off by the stairs and head into the kitchen.

"Honey, you're back!" my mom says. She comes around the kitchen island to hug me. "I've missed you so much."

"I've missed you too. Where's dad?" I ask. I hadn't seen

his truck in the driveway, and he's always had Fridays off from work.

"He's going to meet us for... lunch," she hesitates a little. "How about you go rest up from your drive? I put fresh sheets on your bed. I'll wash your dirty laundry and then we'll go out to lunch. How about that old diner you love, Little Shrimp? You're old favorite."

I smile. "Sounds good. Wake me up in an hour or so."

My bedroom is just the way I left it. My parents haven't turned it into a workout room or storage closet like they teased they would. I kick off my flip flops and crash down on my bed, pulling a blanket over my body. I love camp, but sleeping on a thin mattress you can't really call a twin sized bed doesn't make for the best sleep.

Before I know it, I've fallen asleep. I check my watch to see how long I've been sleeping, and it's already noon. I rub my eyes and stretch out, glad that my feet don't hit the stairs of the bunk bed, just more bed. I get up and walk over to the bathroom, fixing my hair and brushing my teeth. Finally, I get to take as much time as I please, enjoying the quiet.

I go over to my closet and change out of my gym shorts and into a pair or peach colored shorts with a white tank top, happy that I don't have to worry about getting my clothes dirty and stained.

When I go back downstairs, my mom is sitting at the kitchen table sipping on what looks to be tea. "Why didn't you wake me up?"

She turns and smiles at me. "Sorry, I tried but you were knocked out. Figured it would be best to let you sleep some more. You probably don't get much with the campers, do you?"

"Lights out at eleven, wakeup call at seven. I usually get six actual hours of sleep because the girls stay up giggling all night or someone has a nightmare and I have to calm them down."

"That sounds exhausting," mom says. "Why don't you give your dad a call and let him know to meet us and we'll head out. Tell him we'll be there in about twenty minutes."

She gets up from the table and grabs her purse and keys, heading out through the garage. I call dad, and he picks up on the third ring. He seems a little cheerier than mom, but that's not saying much. I'm thinking maybe I shouldn't have come home this weekend.

The garage looks cleaner than I remember it. When I get in the car I buckle my seatbelt and turn to mom. "Did you guys get rid of some stuff?"

"What?" she asks. "Oh, yeah, we had a garage sale. There was a bit too much clutter in here."

Dad already has a table when we get there. He waves me over and pats the seat next to him for me to sit. "How's my little girl doing?"

I hug him tightly. "Fine, tired. I got up at five this morning to drive home."

"How's your first job treating you?"

"It's different than being a camper, but I still get to do most of the cool stuff I enjoyed doing. We have camp games on Monday, so I'm excited for that."

"That's good. Have you made any new friends?" he asks.

"I mean, sort of. Kelsey is there again, but I have to watch over her now instead of hanging out. That kind of sucks. It's different, it kind of feels like I have to keep a distance with everyone now."

"Are you ready to order?" asks the waitress, her pen already poised over her tattered notepad.

"I think we are," says my dad pointing to my mom. "Ladies first."

Mom glances over the menu, not ready to actually order as always, so I go first instead. I order my usual, a plain cheeseburger with a chocolate milkshake.

Dad orders wings and a beer while mom just orders a salad. She never orders a salad while out for lunch or dinner.

"So, have any big plans for your weekend back?" Mom asks.

"Yeah, I'm supposed to go out with Janine tonight. I promised her I'd go to a bonfire."

"That sounds good. It'll do you girls some good to catch up," my mom says, sipping on her water.

"Yeah," I look between my mom and dad, neither of them really looking at each other. "Am I missing something?"

"What do you mean?" my dad asks.

"You two, you're being weird."

My parents finally exchange a look between each other and then they both look off into two different directions. Before I can ask what's going on for the second time, our waitress sets me and dads drinks on the table.

"Your food will be out in a few minutes, holler if you need something," she says with a smile on her face.

The three of us nod our heads and the waitress places the bill on the table upside down. "When you're ready to check out, you can pay at the counter."

Once she walks away my parents go back to avoiding me and each other.

"Tell me what's going on," I demand.

My mom sighs. "We were hoping to leave you out of this. We expected you to be at camp for the whole summer and not be coming home too often."

"Well, sorry," I say, feeling like I'm not wanted around here or anywhere for that matter. "I thought you guys would want to see me. If you didn't want me to come home, you should have just told me. I'm sure I can find a laundromat to do my clothes."

Our food arrives and our waitress must sense the horrible conversation because she's sneaks off quickly without asking if we need anything else.

"Your mother didn't mean it like that," dad says, wiping his hands on a napkin. "What she meant was, we thought you would never have to know. That we could fix this while you were gone."

"Fix what?" I say, still not following along.

"We're currently going through a separation," mom blurts out all at once.

"You mean you're getting a divorce?" I ask, pushing my food away.

"No, that's not what this means, not yet," dad says. *The 'not yet' part hits me like a sledge hammer in my chest.*

I sit back in my chair and cross my arms. "You weren't planning on telling me at all this summer? How long has this been going on?"

"Since April," my mom says. "We're trying to work this out. We figured it would be easier while you were gone all summer."

"Did you move out?" I ask my dad, tears forming, my voice shaking.

"I'm temporarily staying at your grandmother's," my dad says. "Don't worry about us, honey."

"Are you kidding me? My parents tell me they might be

getting a divorce, and I'm not supposed to worry?" I stand up from the table and walk away.

"Where are you going, Penelope?" my mom asks. A few customers have turned to look at the small town drama unfolding in front of them. It wouldn't surprise me if my parents' divorce ends up in the county paper under announcements, next to a cow for sale and an engagement featuring a picture of a couple clad in all camouflage.

"I'm going to Janine's, I'll be home late," I say, walking out the door, heading in the direction of Janine's neighborhood with an empty stomach. Lucky for me, she only lives about a mile away from the restaurant. My parents don't try to stop me. I can only hope they stay and enjoy lunch together, but I know that won't be the case.

By the time I get to the front door of Janine's house, I'm drenched in sweat from the summer heat. My t-shirt sticks to my back and my hair stuck to my neck. I'm a mess. As soon as Janine opens the door, she knows just how much of a mess I am.

"What happened? Where's your car?" she asks, pulling me into a hug, not caring about how gross I smell from the walk here.

"At home."

"How'd you get here?"

I shrug my shoulders. "Walked from the middle of town," I tell her.

She pulls me up the stairs and tells me to go get a shower while she grabs me some better clothes. Thank god we wear the same sizes.

After I shower, I walk into her room and curl up in her bed wearing the Class of 2017 t-shirt and jean shorts she left in the bathroom for me. She's already in the bed, scrolling through something on her phone. I rest my head on her shoulder.

"Do you want to talk about it?" she asks, laying her phone on her bedside table.

Do I? I don't know.

"My parents are thinking about getting a divorce. I've been gone for like, two weeks and my dad has already moved out," I say, feeling a bit emotionally numb.

"That's awful," Janine says, running her fingers through my hair. "I just saw your mom at the store the other day and she seemed fine. How long have they been deciding?"

I scoff. "No clue, I guess a couple months now. They said they were hoping to fix things this summer in the hopes of me not knowing anything was wrong. What? Was I just not supposed to come home and never know what was going on?"

"I'm sure they have reasons," Janine says. "People grow apart, maybe it's for the best."

"For the best?" I ask, sitting up to stare at her. "My parents have been married for twenty-five years, why would anyone throw that away? You know my parents, they've always been happy and perfectly made for each other."

"I know, let's just… how about we forget what's going on with them. Let's go get a mani-pedi before the bonfire tonight, and then buy something new to wear. You have one of their credit cards for emergencies, right? I think this could be considered an emergency. They owe you for keeping you in the dark."

I stare down at my finger nails, dirt and paint from camp under them. "You're right. Let's do it."

A fifty dollar mani-pedi, eight missed calls from my parents, and a seventy-eight dollar shopping spree later, Janine and I are at one of her friend's houses waiting for guests to show up for the bonfire.

My mom's picture flashes up on my phone again and I decline her call, shoving my phone into my pocket. "When is everyone supposed to be here?"

Janine's friend, who I've seen around school but never knew Janine talked to, responds. "Probably in fifteen minutes."

She pours Doritos into a bowl and then goes to grab a two liter off the top of the fridge, her crop top rising way above her belly button, her bra almost showing. I quickly look away, wondering if she will change before people get here, or if I'm possibly the one who should change. Day three of wearing the same gym shorts and all.

"Cool," I say. "So, your parents just let you have parties all the time?"

She laughs. "Sort of. They never really know about it, they're always out of town on trips."

"You don't go with them?"

"They haven't taken me on vacation since I was old enough to stay home by myself," she says as she pulls red plastic cups from the cupboard. "I don't mind though, I'd rather stay here with my friends and drink and party."

"How do you get alcohol," I ask, noticing there's only three 2-liters next to the cups. "I mean, we just graduated high school."

"College boys, duh," she snickers and rolls her eyes.

Janine and I exchange a look and she just smiles and shrugs. The doorbell rings and Janine's friend claps her hands and skips over to the door. As she welcomes in the new guests, Janine comes over and hugs me.

"I know she's a bit much at first, but she's been such a

good friend to me since you've been at camp. Try to have fun tonight," Janine tells me.

Five guys come in, all carrying six packs of beers and wearing Greek letters on their shirts. Another six girls follow in shortly after them with four more guys. I recognize only a few. Everyone grabs a drink and heads out to the backyard to start the bonfire, everyone except me and another guy who lingers behind.

"What's up?" he asks. "My name's Denny."

"Penelope," I say simply, pulling out my phone to pretend like I'm distracted.

He laughs and when I don't laugh with him he takes a sip of the beer he just opened. "Shit, sorry. Thought you were joking about that being your name."

"Why would I joke about that?" I ask, placing my phone on the counter with a thud.

He shrugs and offers me a beer but I shake my head no. "Girls lie."

"So do guys."

"No, guys tell the truth, girls just don't want to hear it."

I roll my eyes. "Let me guess, you're single."

"Why do you want to know, you interested?" he teases, arching his eyebrows at me.

"Nope!"

"Got a boyfriend?" he asks.

"Not really." I say.

"It's a yes or no question, but let me guess: 'it's complicated'," he says, using air quotes on his last two words.

"Fine, no. I don't have a boyfriend," I say.

He smiles at me, and I notice just how handsome he might be under his arrogant demeanor. "Since we established that and you don't want a beer, let me make you a drink."

Non-subtle guy Denny, begins to go through the cabinets looking for what I assume must be alcohol to mix, but I stop him before he can flaunt his bartending skills. "No thanks, really, I'm fine. I don't like drinking."

Denny stops rummaging through the cabinets with a nod and pours me some coke into a cup. I watch to make sure he doesn't slip anything in it, everyone always tells you never to drink a drink from a stranger at a party. He places the cup in front of me and then sits down on the bar stool at my side.

"Thanks," I say, wrapping my hands around the cup. "So, how do you know… I'll be honest, I forget the name of the person who lives here."

He laughs and takes another sip of his drink. "Mindy, she's friends with my little brother who is also here. I just tagged along to make sure he doesn't get in trouble."

"Frat brother?" I ask.

"Real brother," he says. "Who do you know?"

"Janine, she's friends with Mindy. I'm just in town for the weekend."

"Ah," Denny says. "Where are you in town from?"

I can be anyone I want to be with this guy. I'm never going to see him again.

"The Maryville area," I say.

"Do you go to college down there?"

"Yep," I say, not having to lie completely at all. It's not my fault how he fills in the blanks.

We talk for about forty minutes, about college, the things we do in our spare time, my job, and so much more. Denny is really loquacious, I have to look up the term when he uses it to describe his chemistry professor. My mind does get taken off my parents' separation for a little bit, but as I loosen up a little, I notice his body turning into mine and slowly getting closer. When his knee bumps against mine, I get up from my stool and back away.

"We should go hang out with everyone else," I say.

"Do we have to? They're all so much younger," Denny whines.

"I'm only here for the weekend, you can stay inside if you want but I'm going to hang out with Janine."

He pouts but goes outside with me anyway. I walk over to Janine who's talking to one of the guys in the frat.

"Hey friend, how are you? This is Jason!" she says. Clearly, she's already tipsy. Jason has his hand on her thigh, right below the hem of her dress.

"Hey, you sound like you're having fun," I say to Janine, faking a smile.

"I am!" She leans in to whisper into my ear, but it's pretty obvious that Jason can hear her because she's not whispering at all. "Jason's so cute! Isn't he? He's on the baseball team at school."

"That's cool," I say, glancing over at Jason who is pretending like he doesn't hear her as he drinks his beer.

"I saw you talking to *Dennnny*," she blathers on, saying his name over the span of ten painful seconds. "You should so hook up with him. I bet that would make Sammy boy jealous."

"I'm not trying to make him jealous, and I don't want to hook up with anyone," I reply, getting annoyed with this new version of Janine. How has everyone I loved changed so much over a few weeks?

She leans over and tries to whisper to Jason. "She's a virgin."

"I can hear you, Janine," I say, furious.

"It's okay!" she says, patting my leg. "I'm sure one of your suitors will be happy to help out. How many are there now? Denny makes three?"

"Janine, shut up," I demand. "You're being an ass."

She turns to Jason. "Don't you have a name for those

in college? Girls who talk to guys but don't do anything? Tease?"

"What the actual hell, Janine?" I stand up and start to storm off before any of these people can stop me.

I pull my phone out of my pocket and dial the only person I feel would be able to calm me down. He picks up on the third dial and as soon as he says hello, I start to sob.

"Penelope, are you okay? Penelope?"

"I'm here, sorry. I shouldn't have called. You're working," I say through my tears.

"Give me a second, don't hang up." I hear Sampson's campers talking in the background and then the next minute it's quiet. "Are you still there?"

"I'm here," I say, breathing in a deep, shaky breath.

"What's wrong?" he asks.

"Everything. I shouldn't have come home."

"Just talk to me," he says. "Are you in a safe place?"

My house is way further than the walk from the middle of town to this neighborhood. "I don't have my car and I'm at some girl's house that's at least ten miles from home."

"Can you call your mom or dad?" he asks, trying to be helpful.

"They're the reason I'm even out here," I sob.

"Call your parents, tell them where you are and that you need to be picked up. Then call me back and I'll talk to you until they get there."

"Sampson," I whisper. "I'm a bit shook up, it's silly."

"It'll be okay."

And somehow that's all I needed to hear. It. Will. Be. Okay.

My mom is relieved when I call and she swears she's not mad and says she'll be there in a few minutes. I breathe in deeply to calm my nerves and call Sampson back. He picks up immediately.

"She's on her way," I tell him.

"Good, now what's going on?" he asks, sounding just as relieved as my mom did.

"My friend brought me to this party and she was being awful, not herself, and this guy was being weird to me... oh, and my parents are thinking about filing for divorce."

Sampson is quiet, and I feel dumb for dumping all of this on him. This is the stuff you dump on a boyfriend or your best friend or family, not a guy who you just met a month ago.

"Let's handle one topic at a time, okay?" he says. "The guy, he didn't touch you inappropriately, did he?"

"I think he wanted to, but I didn't let him. I walked away before he could. He was drinking..."

"Drinking isn't an excuse. If he tries to approach you, stay on the line and get away from him. Now, what happened with your friend?"

"She was also drinking," I say, explaining the entire thing to him. "She's not normally like that. I thought she'd be there for me, but instead she's trying to impress some college guy and her new friends."

I can tell he's biting his tongue on what he wants to say, but he keeps his words calm. "And your parents?"

"It's a big mess, I just want to come home," I say, shaking my head in defeat.

"Your mom will be there soon to take you home."

"No, I want to come home as in to camp. I regret coming back here, but where else was I supposed to go for two off days?" I ask.

"You know if you ever need a place to go, you're welcome at my house whether I'm there or not. My mom is always there to talk to, and she likes having you around," he says. "She hasn't stopped talking about you."

"I know," I say. "I just feel so stupid right now."

"Don't feel stupid, none of this is your fault."

Headlights illuminate the end of the street. "I think my mom's here."

"Stay on the line until you know for sure," he tells me.

The car comes to a stop and I see my mom sitting in the passenger seat, my dad driving. My mom looks like she just rolled out of bed, her hair up in curlers and her reading glasses on.

"It's both my parents," I say. "They're going to kill me."

"It'll be okay," he says. "Promise me if you need anything, you'll call or text. I don't care if it's three in the morning or any other time."

"Thanks for talking to me, Sampson."

"No problem, text me when you get home."

"Sampson," I start to say but I stop.

"Yeah?"

I muster up some courage, as much as I have left in myself. "You're an amazing person. You deserve so much more…"

I hang up the phone before he can say anything else and then walk over to the car to see just how much trouble I'm in.

"I'm sorry I didn't tell you," my mom says as she rubs my back. "I thought we'd work this out with you gone all summer and when you came home, everything would be back to normal. You would have never known."

"I just don't understand," I say. "I've never seen you and dad have a fight or disagreement."

We've been lying in my bed for a good hour now, my back to my mom's chest. It's three in the morning, and we're both exhausted. When my parents picked me up, they weren't upset, they were just relieved. They told me they were glad I called them and that they understood why I was upset.

"Sometimes people grow apart," she whispers.

"After two decades?" I ask, voice rising.

"I know, it sounds crazy. We sound crazy."

I hate to even think of the next question I ask. "You guys… neither of you cheated, did you?"

"Oh, sweetie, no. I don't think I could have sat in a car with your dad for more than five minutes if that were the case."

"Then why? Was it me?"

She turns me to look at her. "Don't ever blame this on you. It's not your fault at all."

"But I shouldn't have come home…" I protest, turning back around and burying my face in my pillow.

"Honey, you can come home whenever you want, don't let us stop you."

"What happens now?" I ask her, feeling more helpless than I ever have.

She hugs me tightly and presses a kiss to the back of my head. "That's for me and your dad to worry about."

I slowly give in to sleep as my mom plays with my hair, hoping that when I awake, this will all have been a horrible nightmare. That I'll wake up in my bunk at camp.

So my two days off weren't what I had hoped for. My best friend isn't the same person I left a month ago, and my parents aren't together but they're working on it. I texted Sampson an update the next morning, but after that I shut my phone off. When I turned it back on Sunday morning, there were no missed calls or texts from Janine. No apology for her behavior. Nothing from Sampson came in either.

There *was* a text from Kelsey though, which shouldn't be possible because campers aren't supposed to have their cell phones on unless it's an emergency.

Viv is a nutcase, reads her text. *Come back soon. P.S. How can Lain get hotter and hotter every day?*

She ends her text with the two thumbs up emojis and a winky face.

Be back this afternoon, I send back.

I head downstairs to get something to eat before I leave, and I can smell bacon before I even reach the stairs. When I walk into the kitchen, my mom is pouring orange juice into three glasses and my dad's making bacon and scrambled eggs.

"Morning, baby," says my dad. "How'd you sleep?"

"Okay," I say. "What time did you get here?"

Mom's in her pajamas and house coat, but my dad is in jeans and a t-shirt, also wearing his shoes which tells me that he doesn't feel at home here in the moment. It makes me sad, but they both seem to at least be happy on the outside. I guess that's progress.

"About half an hour ago," he explains. "Thought I would surprise you with a Sunday breakfast like we used to have."

"Isn't that nice?" my mom says with a smile, handing me a glass. "I'm pleasantly surprised too. Oh, you're laundry is completely washed, dried, and folded. I tossed a rain jacket and umbrella in there too, you forgot it the first time."

I smile, thinking about getting caught in the rain with Kenny a couple days ago. It seems like years since that happened.

"Thanks, momma," I say. "I have to head out after breakfast. I planned on being back to camp right before dinner."

Dad finishes breakfast and we all sit down at the kitchen table as a family, a family who may or may not be disheveled, but we're still a family. Hopefully my parents do exactly what they planned on this summer and use their time as empty nesters to reconnect and remember why they fell in love in the first place.

I'm relieved to be back at camp four hours later. Part of me would be happy if I didn't have to return to my home town again this summer. If anything, the weekend showed me there's not much left for me there anyway. Just my parents. Even though camp hasn't been like it used to be, I'm still happy to drive under the arch with 'Camp Arthur' carved into it.

According to the schedule, everyone should be finishing up lunch and heading to their afternoon activities. I take the long way around the mess hall so I can go drop my clothes off at my cabin and head down to the archery field where I'm supposed to help supervise with Kenny.

As I trek back across camp, it's mostly quiet. Everyone's already at their activity stations. I pass under the giant ropes course and enter the wooded trail that leads to the archery range. I can hear the instructor demonstrating how to hold the bow and going over the mandatory safety talk. I quietly join the group and realize Kenny isn't here, it's Sampson instead.

My cheeks flame up. I haven't talked to him since early Saturday morning. I know I shouldn't feel this awkward. He nods in my direction and gives me a little smile, just to show that he's glad I'm back or maybe that he feels sorry for me. Who knows?

Once the instruction is finished, the campers line up for their turn to shoot and Sampson takes a seat next to me.

"How are you?" he asks.

I shrug my shoulders. "Feeling better now that I'm back here."

"Has your friend tried to contact you yet?"

"Not a single text," I say, shaking my head. "Part of me just wants to forget any of it happened, but the other part of me wants her to realize how poorly she behaved that night."

"I'm sure she'll come around," he says, bumping his shoulder against mine. "How about your parents?"

"Honestly, I don't want to think about it anymore. That's their problem, not mine."

"Gotcha," he says. "I hope you don't mind, but I told my mom about your situation at home. If you need to talk to anyone, she's there to talk. Don't keep everything to yourself, it'll drive you crazy."

"Thanks," I say. "And thank you for being there for me Friday. I didn't know who else to talk to and I panicked. I shouldn't have bothered you."

"No, it's fine," he says and then goes to a whisper. "If

you ever need anything, don't worry, you can always call me. That's what friends do, they help each other."

"Miss Penelope! You're back!" squeals Daisy, running over to me after her turn at archery. "I missed you so much! Don't ever leave again."

"Aww, but what if my parents miss me?" I ask her.

"Me and Sampson will miss you more."

I look over at Sampson with a smile, still holding onto Daisy. "Is that true, would you miss me more?"

"Of course we would," he says, playfully pinching Daisy's cheek. "You're our BFF."

"No, she's *my* BFF, Sampson," Daisy protests. "Get your own."

Sampson and I both burst into a fit of laughter.

"How about you go take some of your stress out and shoot some hay bales with an arrow?" Sampson suggests.

"That sounds like a fantastic idea," I say.

TEN

Every morning the directors of Camp Arthur give each cabin a schedule of activities for the day along with the names of two to four counselors who are in charge of those events. I look over the list my cabin received trying to figure out what everyone is doing today, and it looks like I have a day hike to Abrams Falls in the Smoky Mountains… it's a tough hike in the middle of summer when the sun is beating down.

Viv and I start writing down who wants to go and do which activity. She's been assigned to rock climbing for the day. I convince most of the younger girls that they don't want to do the hike. Even though it's for the ten and older age group, there's no way a ten-year-old would enjoy the five-hour hike in the heat.

"You should come hiking," I suggest to Kelsey, who is holding up two crop tops, debating between which one she'll wear. Both look to be the same shade of powder puff blue, and neither of them are made for hiking.

"No, no, no. I can't hike," she tells me as she starts searching through her luggage for shoes to match.

That's when I know I need to convince her with something she enjoys. "Will you hike if Lain comes?"

She stops going through her clothes and turns to look my direction. I'm sure she's trying to figure out if I'm serious or not. "You play dirty, but yes, if he goes I will," she says with a devious smile. "It's that or fish and we both know I'm not baiting a hook. I literally just painted my nails."

Thankfully, Lain has his hiking attire on too and is surprised that Kelsey wants to go with us. It wasn't surprising that Kelsey didn't have any hiking shoes, so I let her borrow a pair of my gym shoes, which she also didn't have a pair of. She must have lost her camp packing list or shredded it, avoiding the recommended camp gear in favor of items that show off her figure.

Instead of sitting with our cabin at breakfast, we mingle in with some of the people going on the hike, including Sampson. I fight the urge to sit right next to him, so I pull Kelsey to the other side of the table so Sampson and I are close to talk, but not close enough to make me look desperate.

He smiles at me and I watch as he interacts with the younger kids. It's definitely not the same as how he acted with me the first day, but he's more like a brotherly figure, and he seems great with kids. I stop myself from thinking about how good of a dad he'll be one day. Those are crazy thoughts only girls in relationships can have - girls who have been with their significant other for years.

I pick up my cup and take a small sip of water, that's when I almost spit it back up because his arm is reaching across the table and making me chug the glass.

"Drink up!" he cheers as the campers at our table laugh. "If you want to hike, you need to be fully hydrated!"

Kelsey giggles next to me and once I've finished my glass of water, Sampson starts filling up everyone else's glasses too, filling mine up for a second round. He sends Lain to fill up the now empty pitcher. It's almost like we have our own little college crew, except instead of chugging beer, we're all chugging water and making a game of it.

What if he's one of those guys that's obsessed with partying? I can't keep up with a lifestyle like that. My idea of the perfect Friday night is staying in and binge watching Gilmore Girls on Netflix. What would Rory do? She has been known to be a homewrecker...

I smile at Sampson and he returns it. Even though we're surrounded by everyone at camp, I feel like it's just the two of us. Everything feels and seems so innocent that we might never cross that line. He's with Viv, and I don't want to be known as a girl who steals another girl's boyfriend.

Nothing is going to happen. I won't be that girl.

There's a ninety percent chance that I was in over my head when I signed up to go hiking during camp instead of hanging back and enjoying the ropes course or arts and crafts. I've finished the last drop of my second water bottle that I planned on saving for Kelsey who wasn't prepared for any strenuous activity at summer camp, and we haven't reached the falls yet. I'm not sure if I've even taken my eyes off the trail since the first half mile. I finally look ahead of myself and notice half the group is already turning the corner. The last one I see is a giggly Kelsey holding the hand of Lain, neither of them looking fatigued at all.

Boy, are they moving fast? Both relationship-wise and on this trail.

"Don't worry, I'm still here," says Sampson from behind me without any sign of exhaustion in his voice. Two of the counselors had to hike at the front of the group and the other was supposed to take the back. I almost forgot that he was even near me. All I've been concentrating on is my breathing and trying to not make a fool of myself.

"Aren't you tired?" I ask him, aggravated that he's not breathing as heavily as me. Maybe I should go get tested for asthma.

"I've hiked this trail about ten times in my life. Pretty sure I have calves of steel and lungs of Superman now. And besides, I'm also an Eagle Scout, and we come prepared."

"Show off," I mutter, more attitude in my voice than I wanted.

It's so quiet and peaceful up in the mountains that I just want to stop for a moment to take it all in, even if we're not to the falls yet, and I'm just too exhausted to go on at the moment. Sampson interprets my pause as a warning sign.

"Do you need to turn back? I can tell Ben over the walkie that you're not feeling well," Sampson says. I get butterflies in my stomach from how considerate and protective he's being.

It's tempting to turn back and give up, but I don't want to look like a girly girl, especially when Kelsey is powering through so well. I turn down the offer. "I wanna see the falls, I just need a small break."

I reach into the side pocket for my water bottle, but remember I've been out of water for a long time. Without me even asking, he hands me the rest of his.

"I should have warned you, err, everyone that this was a tough hike and that they need to watch how quickly they drink their water. The worst part is on the way back," he tells me.

I'm baffled that the worst part is on the way down, because it's felt mostly uphill to the falls. This clearly isn't the trail that I remember. "Yeah, I could have used the warning. I'm just surprised Kelsey is pushing through. She's not outdoorsy. I had to beg her to come today."

"Then why does she come to camp?" he wonders. He doesn't ask it in a harsh tone, just curious.

I shrug my shoulders. "She used to love doing this kind of stuff, but I think she's grown out of it since we were kids. Her parents bribe her with a shopping spree every year. Me on the other hand, I doubt I'll ever grow out of this place. Seriously, look at me, I'm wearing a camp shirt from two years ago, and my hair is braided into pigtails. My style screams summer camp. I'd give anything to be here year round. I like it here better than at home. It's relaxing."

He smiles. "If it makes you feel any better, I love your pig-tails."

I look around, making sure no one is near enough to hear. Part of me thinks I didn't hear him correctly, that there's no way he actually said those words. "I don't think you're supposed to say things like that."

He stands up with a sigh. "I know, I can't help it, you're not like the girls that work here, or the girls at college or any girl I've ever encountered for that matter. You're real."

"You have Viv," I remind him and he sits back down, not saying a word.

I'm not sure what to say next, so I do what I do best and change the subject. "How much further?"

"I'd say a mile and a half. The group is probably only half a mile ahead of us now." When he says it, there's a bit of sadness in his tone.

"What's up?" I ask.

He shrugs his shoulders but smiles. "This might be the only time I get to have a chance to get to know you without anyone else around. It feels like this summer is flying by."

The insecure little girl in me panics because when she

hears those words, she assumes he doesn't want to get to know her after camp is over and that breaks her heart, but she refuses to let it show.

"Let's not worry about any of that. I'm sure there will be plenty of other opportunities. We can always go back to Irene's one night and hang out."

He stands up and pulls me up with one of his hands, just like I did when I pulled him up from the dock. We start heading up the trail and for ten seconds he holds my hand and it gives me the boost of energy I need to make it the rest of the way to the falls. Just a small, perfect distraction.

It's beautiful at the falls, but the water is freezing for June. I'm thankful I wore my bathing suit under my clothes and brought my swim shoes, because I feel like I'm overheated from the hike. Kelsey refuses to get in the water until Lain says he's going in. Since she doesn't get her hair wet, I let her borrow one of my pigtail holders. I have to take both of my braids out and my hair is as curly as can be. I try to tame it as best as I can by putting it into a ponytail.

I watch Sampson out of the corner of my eyes as I take off my t-shirt and my shorts. Walking into the water, I panic from the frigid temperature and I'm about to change my mind when I hear Kelsey scream. I turn around and see only her butt and legs. Lain has her hanging over his shoulder and runs right by me, splashing the cold water everywhere. I think I'm safe, but then my feet aren't touching the moss covered rocks any longer. One of the stronger boys is carrying me fireman style and he tosses me into the water once we're deep enough.

I scream, getting mountain water in my mouth, but when I come up all I hear are the guys being scolded by Sampson's booming voice. I'm slightly embarrassed when the rest of our group and some other vacationers turn to look at the scene we're making.

"They chose to come with the boys, if they can't handle a little water, they shouldn't have come hiking," complains one of the other boys.

Sampson's face is turning red and I feel slightly embarrassed at his reaction and the attention it's bringing to us. I never thought I would see him this angry. He seems so reserved most of the time. "Camp is supposed to be a place where everyone feels safe. Both of you bringing the girls into the water isn't promoting safety."

I hear Lain mutter under his breath. "We're not at camp Flower Power," he says.

Some of the other guys start laughing. I glance at Sampson, who pulls his flower headband off, freeing his hair and his curly bangs fall over his eyes. This is the first time I've seen him not act his age.

I turn to see Kelsey ringing out her hair, but she's not mad, she's grinning from ear to ear. Maybe this year will be good for her. It seems like Lain will help her come out of her pretty-girl skin.

Awkwardly, I walk out of the water and cross my arms against my chest. It's even colder outside of the water. I go in search of my towel and when I get there, Sampson wraps me up in it. He lingers a few seconds too long. He reminds me of when I was younger and at the pool or beach my mom would wrap me up so I'd get warm. A simple, innocent act, but I feel weird that it's happening.

"You okay?" he asks.

"Just cold," I say, my teeth chattering together. Thankfully, the sun is already blazing against my skin. I know I'll be warm in a minute or two.

"Boys will be boys," says Ben from a rock he's perched on. "Sorry they don't have manners. We're working on that."

I smile at Ben, remembering him as a counselor from last year and I go sit on a rock next to Sampson as I watch most of our group play in the water. Some of them taking bets to see who can bare to stand under the waterfall the longest. It's obvious Kelsey will come in last place.

"How are things with Viv?" Ben asks Sampson, and I feel a little awkward sitting next to them.

"Okay," he says. "She's been weird the last few weeks. Her temperament is kind of awful lately."

"Why'd she even ask for a job here this summer if she was going to be constantly on your case?"

"I don't know. it's not even that she's on my case," he says. "She's been pretty secretive. I found her phone the other day with a cryptic text from someone named J and when I asked her about it, she got all defensive."

"What did the text say?" I ask. Sampson looks down at his hands.

"Something like, 'can you get away' or something. She jerked the phone away before I could clearly read it," he says. "Maybe I misread it."

J? Josh? Casanova? Did Sampson almost figure it out?

"It's probably nothing, bro," Ben says, clapping Sampson on the back. "Remember how crazy she was over you?"

"*Was*," Sampson says. "I'm starting to think the 'honeymoon' phase wore off a while ago. What do you think, Penelope?"

I shrug my shoulders, wondering if I looked too far

into him holding my hand for a few seconds on the trail. "Maybe it's nothing, maybe it's something. You should probably just talk to her. I'm sure you'll figure it out."

Sampson nods his head. "Maybe you're right. The problem is, she won't talk to me. I don't know what to do. It feels like everything I do or say is wrong."

"Women," Ben says.

"Woah there," I say, taking offense. "Watch it, I'm a *women*."

"Sorry," he says laughing. "I guess you're just not like the girls we hang out with."

"Sounds like you're just not hanging out with the right girls," I suggest.

Neither of them say a word, they just exchange a dumbfounded expression.

"That's what I thought," I say smugly. "Good luck with that."

Due to my slow hiking, I end up being the last person on the bus. Ben chose to take the back end of the group on the way down, which made me walk a little faster so I would feel less embarrassed. When you're only five feet tall with short legs, it's hard to keep up with everyone else, especially your friend who has legs as long as a supermodel.

There's only one seat left on the bus when I get inside. Everyone else is sitting two to three campers per seat. Sampson looks up from his clipboard and smiles at me from the front seat. He scoots over to the window and lets me slide in next to him.

"Did you do roll call?" asks Ben, sliding in next to me, sandwiching me between him and Sampson. This would be any teenage girl's dream right now, sitting between two cute college boys. That's the last thing I want to think about because all three of us are drenched in sweat.

I watch as Sampson finds my name and Ben's on the list and checks it off. "Yup, you two were the last."

Ben pats the bus driver's seat and tells him we're good to go. We back out of the gravel lot and head back toward the main loop. The ride is bumpy and I try my best to not let my pale, sweaty, sunburnt legs rub against Sampson's or Ben's. I spot a group of three tiny hairs on my knee cap, scolding myself for not taking more time to shave with any kind of accuracy.

Ben turns around and starts singing an old camp song that I know by heart. The campers join in at once, and Ben stops, looking proud of himself.

"Hey," Sampson says, bumping his leg against mine, the three leg hairs feel like they're standing at attention. My stomach turns in excitement and my cheeks flush. "You okay?"

I look up at him and smile. "Yeah, just thinking."

"Do you feel like a loser sitting up here with us?" he jokes.

"No! Of course not, who else would I sit with? My best friend is preoccupied," I nod back toward the end of the bus.

"I can get him to move if you want. I can make up some rule about boys not being allowed to sit with girls."

But then I can't sit by you, I want to tell him.

"It's fine, trust me," I say to reassure Sampson.

Ben and the rest of the group that came with us are on the third verse of the Goldilocks song when I finally join in, and it finally feels like the camp I have always known and loved. I wish I could enjoy being one of the younger kids again, where I don't have to worry about having a crush on one of the guys, or my friend choosing different things than me, or even so I just wouldn't worry about what other people think of me.

Sampson smiles and starts singing the song with the rest of us. We go through song after song and I eventually let my knee fall against his without worrying about the repercussions. Finally, I can relax.

ELEVEN

"Rise and shine, girlies. It's field day," I say in a sing-song voice. The girls start stretching their arms, some of them rolling over and covering their heads, shielding their eyes from the light. When Kelsey rolls out of bed and looks at me, her eyes practically bug out of her head when she sees I've painted my face blue and white like in Braveheart.

Viv starts handing out sealed envelopes to each of the campers, and I bring out the bag of blue and red bandanas, the type that resemble ones on reality shows to indicate what team you're on. You can wear them either as tops, bandanas, skirts or just around your wrist or neck.

"These are your assignments. We've sealed up fifty bandanas for the red team and fifty for the blue team. The teams are selected at random," Viv tells us. "You can sit with whomever you want to for the meals today, but remember, they might be a good ally or bad enemy. Choose wisely."

"Open your envelopes up and then come to me for your team color. We have some extra paint if you guys want to wear your team color in warrior paint," I announce.

"Are we allowed to swap teams?" asks Chelle.

"Yes," I say as Viv says no. "But once we leave the cabin, you can't change after that. It's only fair."

"What color did you get?" I ask Kelsey when she climbs down the bunk and starts searching through her luggage.

125

"Red, I don't even have anything to match this stupid bandana!"

"Here," I say, reaching into my bag and finding my white and red tank top I was never planning on wearing. "You can borrow this."

"Don't you need this?" she asks me, confused.

"Nope, you're on your own today. I'm on the blue team."

"Well this day is going to suck," she says, looking across the room at Viv who's wearing two vertical stripes of red across her face.

I nudge her on the shoulder. "Come on, let's go do your makeup, this might be the only time I can actually do it for you instead of you doing mine."

She smiles and follows me into the bathroom, along with some other girls that want face paint.

"Soldier, I hope you're hydrated," a booming male voice rings out. It's Sampson, and when I turn around he's wearing a blue bandana around his head where his normal daisy headband is, and he has two finger swipes of blue paint below his eyes like he's ready to play a game of football.

I slide over on the bench for him to join me and take a sip of my water. "Thought for sure I would have to feel bad for kicking your butt today," I tell him.

He smiles and blushes. "You almost did. I had to bribe a kid for his blue bandana. Told him I'd give him an extra granola bar at snack time. By the way, your trash talking is on point."

"Greedy spawn," I joke. "Why'd you switch? Viv's on red."

"You know why," he whispers sweetly, like he's hoping he didn't bribe the kid for nothing. "Besides, I kind of like keeping Viv on her toes. It's kind of entertaining."

I smile and take a gulp of my water.

"Looks like Lain is interacting with the enemy," he points out, nodding his head toward a table filled with red enemies.

I look over to where he's sitting next to Kelsey. Boy do they have it bad for each other. She doesn't look happy at all though, probably because Lain ended up on our team which means she won't get too much time with him today. Viv is talking her ear off and Kelsey is just picking at the chipped white paint on the table.

"No," I tell him. "They'll be on our side, trust me. We'll just have to bring her to the good side during capture the flag. It's possible to kidnap other players, right?"

The rest of breakfast flows too easily; Sampson and I eat and talk to the other people at the table. I get to know a few of the new campers and talk to some of the older ones about their own college plans. Sampson allows his knee to occasionally bump into mine and since no one else can see it, I return every knee bump and watch as he smiles. If this is how it'll be next year when I'm working here, everything will be perfect. It's like all the drama that's happened between us is finally over and we can be ourselves.

Ben comes by with a stack of mail, handing out a few letters from home to the younger kids and bills to some of the counselors.

"Here's one for you," Ben says and at first I don't respond because I never get mail here anymore. "Penelope, for you."

I turn and take the envelope from him. It's a big envelope but the return label is from my parents.

"This is weird and a little embarrassing," I say, opening the manila envelope.

Inside is a sticky note from my parents that says to call them with the news and that's when I see that there's another envelope in there from Maryville College. I freeze immediately and can't seem to bring myself to open it.

Sampson nudges me. "You know what they say about big envelopes…"

"What do they say?" I ask him quietly.

"Open it and you'll find out."

I slide my finger and pull apart the opening. There's a huge stack of papers and the only thing I see is one word in bold lettering.

Congratulations!

"I got in…" I whisper, not believing what I'm holding in my hands. I'm up from the bench and so is Sampson, he gives me a hug and then I'm running over to Kelsey.

"Kelsey! I got into Maryville!"

We're both up and jumping around and I hear someone start to dismiss everyone from breakfast. I need to gather up my campers, but I'm too excited.

I look down at the letter and start reading the rest out loud. "Congratulations! You've been accepted to the fall semester at Maryville College! You must attend one of the following orientation dates before August…"

"That's so awesome!" Kelsey yells.

I can hardly contain my emotion. "I thought I sent my application in way too late, I thought I might have to wait until the spring semester to start. Holy crap, this is the best news ever. I need to call my parents," I say, still slightly frazzled by this news.

The whole camp has already cleared the dining hall.

It's just me, Kelsey, Sampson left to celebrate. Viv is already outside lining our cabin up, missing Kelsey and calling after her with her shrill voice.

Viv comes back inside and clears her throat, obviously trying to move things along. Still, she tries to congratulate me in her own backhanded way. "You can use the phone in the kitchen if you want, since service is total crap here. we'll all wait outside for you." She emphasizes the *all* part and looks at Sampson when she says it.

"I can wait on her," Sampson chimes in, almost egging her on. "I don't need anyone from the red team trying to brainwash one of my soldiers. Josh is still out there, have him help with the campers."

Viv play smacks him and I have to bite my tongue so I don't hit her back with much more force. She agrees though, and her and Kelsey leave the dining hall. My friend gives me two thumbs up behind Viv's back.

Sampson walks with me to the kitchen and the whole staff is in another room eating their own meal.

I dial my home number quickly, and my mom picks up on the third ring.

"Mom, it's me, Penelope. I got your letter. Maryville accepted me. I start next fall."

"That's so wonderful!" she says and I hear her yell the news to my dad. "We're so proud of you honey!"

They're both together… that must be good news too. I thought with the way I left things this weekend they'd go back to their separate ways.

"I'm so excited, I can't believe they accepted me and for the fall already. Looks like I don't have to be worried about being behind."

"Of course, are you still going to finish camp out this summer? You'll have so much to do, trying to get stuff together for your dorm and getting ready for classes."

I look over at Sampson and he smiles back. I never thought about not being able to finish my summer at camp. "Of course I'm going to finish the summer up, you didn't raise a quitter," I say and I hear my dad in the background shout something along the lines of 'that's my girl'.

"Besides," I charge ahead, "finishing my summer out here means I'll have some pocket change to buy stuff I'll need for college, like my books and everything. I just need to figure out how to get 25% of my tuition down in August. I don't think I will be able to swing that on my paychecks."

"We'll figure it out when you get home next time. For now, enjoy your day and remember that we're very proud of you."

"Thanks mom, love you," I tell her. "Tell dad I love him too. I hope you guys are doing okay."

She says 'I love you' back and then I hang up. Sampson stands up and gives me another hug.

"Congrats, again," he says, holding me tightly.

"Thanks," I say back, taking a moment to breathe in his scent. I know this is one of those moments that I'll be able to look back on and remember the scent, how his arms felt wrapped around my torso, how it felt to put my head against his chest and feel his heart racing.

He pulls back and without me even thinking, I stand up on my tippy toes and kiss him lightly on the lips. It was an innocent first kiss; it could be regarded as friendly if someone questioned it.

When I pull back, his face is blank and I feel like an idiot for thinking it was okay to make the first move.

"Sorry," I tell him, and then start babbling on like an idiot. "I just didn't know if I would ever have the chance to kiss you. This might have been my only opportunity."

He shakes his head. "No, it's fine. I... actually wanted you to."

And then his lips are back on mine and *he* is kissing *me*. I hold onto his tie-dyed shirt and pull him closer, but before I can get a better grip, we hear the dining hall door squeak open.

"I shouldn't have done that..." Sampson says, regret in his voice.

"Sampson, Penelope?" Viv's voice calls. "You guys ready? The games are starting!"

She turns the corner and we have just enough time for me to pretend like I'm just now hanging up the phone and for Sampson to smooth his shirt out.

"Yeah, just hung up with my mom," I lie. I slide the letter into my backpack for safekeeping and walk past Sampson and Viv. I need air. I walk as quickly as I can to get out of that room, my sneakers squeaking on the floor. Kelsey's outside the mess hall waiting with the other girls and I grab her arm and pull her along with me, heading for the intramural fields.

"Come on girls, let's go meet for the first game," I say, and they start to follow with Sampson and Viv trailing behind us.

"What's up?" she asks in a whisper. I hear Viv and Sampson talking behind us, gravel crunching under all of our shoes.

"Let's just say... things got a little more intense. I might have just ruined everything."

Both scores are tied up after dinner, and the final score

depends on who wins the final event of the day: Capture the Flag. I've never been on the winning team in the past, but with how well my day is going, I'm hoping this will be my year. Even though all the campers know everyone wins (according to the camp director who insists it's not about competition but about team work), the older kids still keep score. *You're all winners*, we're required to say, it's so cheesy, but most of camp is no different.

Our blue team splits up into ten groups of five people in order to cover as much ground as possible. There weren't enough counselors to go around so they stuck the older teens and CITs, with some of the younger kids. I could tell that Sampson didn't want to split up, we have to talk about what happened, but I couldn't miss an opportunity like this. I can get the feel of what it'll be like if I can be a counselor next summer. For me, this is training.

My group has decided to cover the area around the art building, dining hall and welcome center since I have mostly younger kids. Of course, the flag isn't going to be around here though, that would be too easy. Everyone knows you hide your flag somewhere near a trail or far away from the starting point of the game. Last year, they hid it in some firewood that we'd be using for the next fire talk.

Every year we start at the flagpole, which is right in the middle of camp, and this year was no different.

I'm wasting time until the rest of our group returns when I feel one of the little girls pull on my shirt.

"Penel-o-pee?" she says, hardly able to get my name out from all the syllables. "I need to use the bathroom, really, really bad." She's standing with her legs crossed and a terrified expression on her face.

"Okay, let's all go take a bathroom break," I announce to the four other younger kids in my group. The girl holds my hand as I lead all of them to the welcome center to use the bathroom. Some of them say they don't need to go, but I convince them anyways, saying things might get rowdy soon. We don't want any accidents. I haven't had to clean any accidents up yet this summer, and I don't want to start.

I wait outside the restrooms and look at the pictures of various camp groups that have visited over the years. I find one from the first year I attended and smile at how much I have grown up since then. I must have just been like these younger campers, clinging to the older kids and counselors because I was slightly mortified of being away from home. Now, I can't wait to move here and start my college courses.

"Penel-o-pee... someone dropped their cloth in the bathroom," says the little girl, I believe her name is Sophia. She's in one of the other cabins.

I turn and see that she's holding a small piece of red fabric. I have to take a minute to realize that it's the other team's flag.

"Where did you find this?" I kneel down to ask her in my softest voice, trying to cover my excitement.

"In the bathroom, it was under the sink," she tells me. "I couldn't reach the paper towels, so I used that to wipe my hands."

I hold the flag between my index finger and thumb, hoping she could at least reach the soap and water, then pull her in for a hug and she squeals with excitement. "Guess what you just did!"

"What?" she asks with the cutest and biggest grin I have ever seen.

"You won the game for us, but you can't tell anyone! We need to go find our team leader and tell them to walkie talkie everyone that we've won, but we have to hurry."

She agrees and I stuff the flag in my backpack because

I know it's easier for the other team to 'steal' a younger player, it happened to me once during my very first year here. I gather up my group and start heading for the old cabin where the main field is, close to Mr. and Mrs. Garreth's house. I know most of the group will probably be there searching for the flag and I hope I can get everyone to it before our flag is found.

It's eerily quiet on the gravel road leading to the cabin, and I consider just turning around, but I continue on. I keep the group together, imagining this as a test before my interview with Camp Arthur.

Here are four kids, keep them safe and if you do, we'll hire you. If they die, you die.

I can so do this.

I can already see the field and I watch as a few people run around, blue and red mingling, searching hard for a flag, one of which will not be there. As I'm about to round the corner of the old cabin, Ben jumps in front of me. I can't tell if he's switched teams, but he quickly pulls out his blue bandana and the little kids cheer and crowd around him to give fist bumps and high fives. Ben is a God amongst these kids, a great role model.

"Do you have a walkie talkie?" I ask him.

His eyes get huge. "Yeah, why? Is someone hurt?"

"We found the other team's flag," I whisper to him.

He smiles and presses the button to speak. "Blue team wins! Penelope's gang found the red flag."

Ben claps me on the back and I smile.

"It wasn't me," I tell him. "This little one found it on our bathroom break."

He kneels down and gives her a high five. I pull out the red teams flag and give it to her to wave around while we take our victory march back to the flagpole. Ben carries the little girl on his shoulders and some of our team starts coming out of the woods to join us in our celebration, chanting *Go Blue* as we walk.

I tear up a little bit, feeling silly for getting so emotional over a camp game. The thing is, even though we separated into teams, we all still worked together to make the memories. And that's the beauty of camp, it may change, but you'll always have memories to last a lifetime. It won't be just me having these great memories, it'll be all these kids, though they'll all have a different view of it, we'll still be connected by our time together.

TWELVE

"Ten minutes until lights out," I say as the final evening shower finishes. It's been a long day. Half of the girls are already drifting asleep in their bunks, exhausted from the camp games. I'm honestly still a bit wired, and my lips still tingle from the kiss. No matter how much I try to clear my mind, my thoughts keep jumping back and forth from Sampson to Maryville and all the preparations I need to make before my first semester.

I go into the spare room to check my phone for any messages. There's a missed call and a text from Janine that was sent in five different parts. I don't read it, but I do unplug my phone and put it in the pocket of my hoodie.

All the girls have settled into their bunks and Viv is also laying down, flipping through a Cosmo magazine. I shudder at the cover topics. That's not something any of these kids should see.

The New Way to Brighten Teeth-- Hint, Your Boyfriend Will be Thrilled.

Please, let that not be what I think it is.

"I need to go make a phone call," I lean down to tell her. "I'll be back in thirty minutes or so."

"Good luck finding enough service to make a call," Viv says, not taking her eyes off the magazine. "Be quiet when you come back."

I head out through the back door, taking the key with me so I can get back in that way. I turn on my small flash-light that hardly lights up the walkway and head toward the picnic shelter where I know for a fact I can get steady phone service.

Sitting down on the steps of the shelter, I take a deep breath in and find Janine's number in my phone. Sure enough, she's up and she answers on the fourth ring.

"Why haven't you answered any of my calls?" she demands at once. Her words seem to slur a little. She must be at another party drinking. I sigh. She never did this stuff when we were in high school.

"I've been working," I say sternly. "I don't have service half the time and I never carry my phone on me."

"It's been like four days and you haven't even tried to contact me!"

"Same goes to you, Janine," I say. "You could have called or texted. I've been going through so much…"

"I've been waiting for you to call and apologize, you left the party--."

I cut her off immediately. "You've been waiting for an apology? For what? Don't you remember how you treated me?"

"You acted like a total narc in front of my friends!" she squeals into the phone. "And then you just left?"

"Are you kidding me?" I ask. "Janine, the way you behaved that night, I don't even know who you are anymore. One minute we're the same person, and the next you're trying to be this college party girl."

"Maybe we don't know each other at all, you acted like such a prude."

"Because I wasn't going to screw some guy I just met?" I ask, my flashlight shaking in my hand.

"Maybe It would have done you some good and gotten that stick out of your butt."

I take another deep breath in and try to bite my tongue. When did Janine get so hateful?

"I'm done," I say simply.

"Done? What do you mean, done?" she asks.

"I'm just done with us, Janine. I had the best day ever today, and you were the only person I wanted to share everything with, but I feel like you don't even care about me anymore. I'm just done."

I press the 'end call' button on my phone and rest my head on my knees. How can ending a friendship feel like a breakup? I always knew Janine and I were polar opposites, but I thought that's what made us great friends. It gave us something to always talk about, and we were never bored. Our friendship survived all the other summers while I was at Camp Arthur, why couldn't it survive this summer?

"Hey," a voice comes from in front of me and I jump, my flashlight beam lighting up Sampson's face. He squints his eyes and raises his hand to cover his eyes.

I turn the light off. "What are you doing out here?"

"Currently, trying to regain my eyesight," he says.

"Sorry," I say as I place my flashlight down on the ground next to me.

He comes over and sits down, turning his off also. "It's okay. So what are you doing out here?"

"I asked you first," I tease.

"I was sitting outside at my cabin," he says, nodding toward the cabin. "Saw a flashlight, followed it over. Was making sure you weren't a camper."

"Good call," I say, bumping my knee against his. Instead of bumping his back like earlier, he scoots an inch or so away from me. "I just needed to make a phone call."

"I overheard," he says softly. "Everything okay?"

I shake my head and stare down at my feet. "Not really. Janine finally called and I just can't stand it anymore. She's a completely different person."

"People change," Sampson says.

"Yeah, it just sucks."

"All part of growing up, I guess."

We're both quiet, I lean back on my elbows and stare at the stars. It's not the most comfortable position, but I'm relaxing a little now that I've got my mind off of Janine.

"I think we should talk," Sampson says.

My heart speeds up and I feel like I'm going to vomit. Nothing good ever comes out of those words, or so I hear. I try to not look visibly shaken, and I thank God that it's almost pitch black or Sampson would be able to see my shaken face clearly.

"What's up?" I ask, my perfectly perfect day being stripped from me with every conversation I have.

"About earlier," he says. "In the mess hall. I shouldn't have let that happen."

"I'm sorry," I say. "I was just so excited and happy…"

"I know, but I shouldn't have given you the wrong idea."

"Don't worry about it," I say, standing up. Trying to get some space between the two of us. "It won't happen again, right?"

"Right," he says, but doesn't sound sure of himself. "I hope you're okay. I know you're going through a lot right now. I just want to be there for you, as a friend."

I smile. "I mean, I'm running low on friends so any I have is pretty helpful."

He still looks sad, like it's causing him physical pain to have this conversation.

"I should get back, it's a decent walk from here to my cabin," I say, turning my light back on.

"Do you want me to walk you?" he asks, standing up and turning on his flashlight also.

I shake my head and turn away. "Nah, I'll be fine. I just

need the time to myself. It's been a rollercoaster of a day. I'll see you tomorrow!"

"Penelope," Sampson says, but I keep walking. "I'm sorry."

"I'm not yours to worry about, Sampson," I reply. I can't bear to stay here and have him look at me with those eyes full of pity.

My day went from fantastic to 'I just want to give up on life' in a matter of hours. The only thing left to go wrong is if I got a call from my mom saying her and dad were signing divorce papers tomorrow.

THIRTEEN

"Morgan! Walk, don't run," I plead as we head toward the weekly campfire. "There are tree roots everywhere, you could trip and fall."

"You're not my mom, you can't tell me what to do," she says, turning around to stick her tongue out at me.

"I'm in charge of you for the summer, so you need to listen to me."

The other girls snicker behind us. Most of them are being more cautious of every step they take on the path. Kelsey finally got a clue and traded out her flip flops for some tennis shoes.

"Why won't you dish out what's going on between you and Kenny," Kelsey asks.

"I have told you, nothing is going on with us," I say. "And I've also told you that I'm not even allowed to tell you about any counselor to counselor relations."

"So, what you're saying is, you might be with Kenny but you can't say anything."

"What? No," I say, shaking my head. "Why do you care if we're together or not? You have Lain's attention finally, worry about him."

"Come on, Penelope," she whispers. "You know how it was when you were a camper. Any insight into a coun-selor's life outside of camp was fun drama to hear about."

"I'm not saying a word," I say. "You're not using our friendship to get some rumors spread. I can't confirm or deny anything."

"You suck." Kelsey states, crossing her arms over her chest.

I walk passed Kelsey and tugged gently on Morgan's backpack to get her to stop goofing off on the trail. "Slow down, seriously. You need to watch where you're going."

"You're not the boss of me," Morgan says, turning around to stick her tongue out at me.

"Technically, I am," I say, looking toward Viv for some back up but she just ignores us. "Hey, I have an idea. Why don't you just show us one of your pirouette things? You're always dancing."

I'm hoping this will slow her down and take some of her energy out.

We've come to a stop, the whole cabin, at one of the openings in the woods that leads to a section we occasionally use for team building exercises. There's a four by four that makes a type of balance beam connected to a platform and it repeats itself three more times before returning to the original platform and beam.

"Okay," Morgan says excitedly, walking over to the platform as if it's a tiny stage. She bows to her small audience before she turns into a spin, her arms above her head. The problem is, the platform isn't slick enough, so she doesn't spin like she does on the smooth cement floor of our cabin. Instead of hopping off, she talks onto the beam, balancing, trying to show off in any way possible.

"Alright, come on, Morgan. We've got to go," I urge her.

"Look, I can do this with my eyes closed, it's so easy," she says.

I walk over to her and demand that she get down from there, trying to use my best authoritative voice in the process, channeling my inner teacher or mom tone. "Morgan, I mean it. Let's go."

I must startle her because instead of her right foot footing the plank, it slips and she falls in the ground. Her ankle scratching against the wood in the process. My eyes go wide with worry.

"Ahh!" screams Morgan as she hits the dirt hard. "Oww!"

She screams in agony. Viv's radio squawks alive as someone's voice comes over it. "Sampson to Viv, everything okay with cabin six?"

Her screams must have been loud enough to hear or Sampson must have been close behind us.

I'm at Morgan's side as Viv sends a 'Code J-Law' over the walkie talkie along with our location.

"I think her leg might be broken," I say, tentatively touching it where it's already starting to swell as the other girls crowd around to look. "Girls, give her some room."

The girls back up about a foot, and Morgan screams in pain again.

"Yeah, I don't think her foot should look like that," says Olive. "It's definitely not strained, that looks broken."

"Broken?" cries Morgan through a violent sob. "It can't be broken, my mom will be so mad! I have competition in August!"

"Shh, we don't know for sure," I say, trying to keep her calm. "Don't move, help should be on the way."

Three minutes later, Sampson, Mr. Garreth and one of the nurses arrive to help. Mr. Garreth tells Viv to go ahead and take the rest of the girls to the bonfire.

"What happened?" Mr. Garreth asks me as the nurse looks Morgan over, I can hear gravel crunching under the tires of a vehicle.

"I told her not to be running along the trail," I say. "And then a minute or two later she slipped and then tripped over her feet."

He turns to Morgan. "You need to listen when a counselor gives you directions. We're going to load you into the camp van, okay? You're going to need to go to the ER."

Two more people from the nurse staff pull up in the van and park it, coming down the hill with a set of crutches. Mr. Garreth goes to grab her emergency contact information from his office as the nurses pull her up onto one foot and help her with the crutches. She's a bit wobbly on them, but the nurses are spotting her on her left and right side and behind her, saying encouraging words as she goes up the hill.

"Viv, you coming with us?" Asks one of the nurses.

Before Viv can respond Morgan asks for me to ride with her, I follow them into the car, one of the nurses comes with us, the other two staying behind.

Sampson climbs into the passenger seat and pulls his seatbelt on before the nurse puts the van in drive.

"What are you doing?" I ask him, but it's not like he can get out now, we're moving.

"Coming with you, you might need help," when I don't say anything he continues. "Put your seatbelts on, don't need any more injuries today."

I pull Morgan's seatbelt over because she's still moaning in pain, and then lean back to buckle my own. This is not how I thought today would go.

It's broken.

Morgan whimpered into Sampson's shoulder the entire time they were putting on the cast. She begged for a pink cast, but they were out so she had to settle for purple. Afterwards, I let her call her mom and dad while we drove back to camp. Thankfully, she had stopped crying by that time. Mr. Garreth had called her parents right after we left, and I'm pretty sure they're furious right now. I'm not sure if it's because their vacation was cut short or their daughter was injured.

As Sampson drove us back to camp, she gushed on how she couldn't wait for everyone to sign her cast. I sat in silence, terrified of what the repercussions were going to be since she was under my watch when the accident happened.

Sampson had spoken to her parents while we were in the ER, giving them updates on what was broken, how bad it was, and so on. His father told Morgan's parents not to worry about the hospital bill, that Camp Arthur's insurance policy would pay for it. Morgan's parents were still unhappy.

They demanded that her things be packed by tomorrow afternoon because they are driving down first thing in the morning to pick her up. I didn't speak to them myself, but I was around for every phone call, and I could hear her parents shouting in the background.

"It's going to be okay," Sampson says. "Kids are fragile, accidents happen. Let's be honest, you told her not to do something and she went against you."

"It's still stupid. I don't think they respect me enough to stop. Maybe I'm too young to be working at camp."

"Come on, Penelope," he whispers. "Don't say that. Every year parents drop their kids off at camp with counselors your age. You just need to find your inner 'teacher' voice or something. Most of the kids do respect you, they look up to you."

"It's easier for you though, you're older and you don't

look like a child like me. Come on, half of them are taller than me!"

"Half of them are taller than my mom," he points out.

I just shake my head and stare out the window as we pass farm after farm.

Morgan hangs up the phone and hands it back to me. "Man, my mom is pissed."

"Language," Sampson says sternly.

"You think Casanova will sign my cast?" she asks, her voice high pitched.

"Who's Casanova?" Sampson smiles.

"We nicknamed some of the guy counselors. Viv hangs out with Casanova a lot."

"Penelope, who's Casanova?" Sampson asks. I'm sure Morgan doesn't realize the damage she has done. She's already back to talking a mile a minute about who she wants to sign her cast first.

"You know how kids are," I say, ignoring the question. "They think something is everything when it's actually nothing at all."

"Penelope, friends don't lie."

I turn to look at him, he's trying hard to keep his eyes on the road. "I can't be the one to tell you."

He shakes his head and turns down the driveway for camp. As we park, a golf cart is already at the welcome center waiting for us. Sampson helps Morgan out and I grab her crutches and keep a close eye on her to make sure she doesn't fall on the way over to the cart so we can get back to the cabin.

Sampson drives us back, the lights of the cart flashing against the gravel and woods, and he parks us right out front of our cabin. A few of the girls are sitting outside at the picnic table waiting for us, and they jump up and scramble to help Morgan into the cabin.

As I'm about to get off the cart, Sampson grabs my forearm gently.

"Why won't you tell me what's going on?" he asks.

"I told you," I whisper. "It's not my secret to tell. Talk to your girlfriend. Leave me out of it, please."

Speak of the devil.

Viv comes out to greet Sampson with a huge kiss. I shake my head and go into the cabin. I don't know what's worse, Viv cheating on Sampson, or me not telling him about it like I should have a long time ago.

"I think that's the last of it," I say, helping Morgan pack up her belongings. "Do you have anything in the bathroom?"

Morgan shakes her head. She's been lying on her bunk all morning after breakfast. We were excused from morning activities since she's leaving today. She wasn't able to move around and get her stuff, so I've been looking through all the clothes on the floor and trying to find all the ones with her initials on them.

How are these girls so messy?

"I can't believe they're making me go home," Morgan says, tears in her eyes. "They sent me to camp so they would be alone for the summer, why would they even want me home?"

"I'm sure it's not that way," I say. "Besides, your leg can't heal if you're here at camp. They just want you to get better."

She sits up, slowly swinging her leg over to place it on the floor. I look at all the signatures she's already procured between our return last night and breakfast this morning. It's now covered in so much black sharpie you can hardly make out any of the names.

"You think they'll let me come back next summer?" she asks.

I zip up her suitcase. "I don't know. That's between you and your parents."

Standing up, I go to check the bathroom one more time to make sure none of her items are in there and when I come back, she's up on her crutches.

"Ready?" I ask.

"Yeah," she says. "Penelope, I'm *so* sorry I didn't listen to you."

I smile at her and grab the suitcase. "It's okay, we learn from our mistakes."

Mr. Garreth is already outside waiting for us on his golf cart. He helps me load up her suitcase as she sits down gingerly in the passenger seat. I take the back seat and make sure her luggage doesn't fall off. We meet Morgan's parents at the welcome center in Mr. Garreth's office.

Morgan and I wait in the lobby on the old couches like we're sitting outside of the principal's office, while Mr. Garreth talks to Morgan's parents. I feel like I'm in trouble for something I didn't do.

After thirty long minutes, Mr. Garreth finally comes out, but it's only because he wants me to come in and speak with the three of them. I hand Morgan some string for friendship bracelets that I keep inside my backpack so she has something to do. Who knows how much longer this meeting is going to go.

Mr. Garreth introduces me to Morgan's parents, and I shake both of their hands. They don't look pleased at all. I'd rather be swimming in the dirty Ohio river right now than be sitting in this small office with these people.

"How could you let this happen?" Morgan's mom asks. "I was told she was under your 'watchful' eye."

"Ma'am, I'm so sorry this happened. I told her to stop running," I say with a shaky voice.

"So, you're saying this is my daughter's fault?" she asks.

"No, I'm not saying that. Accidents happen..."

"Yeah, like hiring you," she says, spit flying out of her mouth with her words. "Mr. Garreth, I'm not sure what kind of camp you're running here, but what makes you think a seventeen year old girl is capable of taking care of children?"

If she were a text emoji, she'd be a combination of the one with a red face and the other with smoke coming out of its nose.

"I assure you, Mrs. Meyers," Mr. Garreth says. "Penelope is one of our best and she's in training. It was an accident, nothing intended."

"Training? Are you kidding me?" Mrs. Meyers laughs and raises her voice. "You let someone in *training* take care of my little girl?"

"That's how we prepare our employees for the following summer, by training them for a full season. Penelope handled the situation as our handbook says to handle an injury, and in my opinion, I think she handled it wonderfully. She never left your daughter's side."

"This is ridiculous, let's go," Mrs. Meyers says.

Mr. Meyers finally stands. "You'll be hearing from our lawyer. I would advise you train your employees better."

Mr. Garreth hurries to show them out the door and I stay put in his office. I don't want to watch Morgan leave, and I certainly don't want to encounter her parents ever again. Perhaps most of all, I don't want to lose my job because of not being able to prevent a kid from doing something stupid.

Sampson's dad returns a few minutes later and instead of sitting down at his desk, he sits in the chair next to me and rubs his hand on my back soothingly, like my dad does when I'm not feeling well.

"I don't want you to worry about them," he tells me. "You did exactly what we trained you to do. If they try to contact you or any lawyer gives you a call, you let me know and don't speak to them. Besides, this is what the liability waiver is for, when a camper gets hurt."

"It was an accident," I say again, trying my best not to cry. "Why don't they get that?"

"Some people are set in their own ways. We'll get through this. Why don't you go grab some lunch and take it easy the rest of the day? I'll cover your activities. It'll do me some good to see what you guys go through on a daily basis."

He gives me a reassuring smile and I leave his office like a dog with my tail between my legs, defeated. As I'm about ready to leave the welcome center, I notice a piece of paper with my string on it.

I go to retrieve the string and see that Morgan managed to make a bracelet while I was in the meeting. I unfold the piece of paper and in messy little girl handwriting, Morgan says she is sorry and that she's thankful for the month of summer camp fun that she did get to have.

When I hear Mr. Garreth start to lock up his office, I skitter into the women's restroom and lock myself inside.

Finally, I let myself cry.

FOURTEEN

Mr. Garreth excused me from the big rafting trip the following day. I told him I wasn't up for it and he completely understood. I also decided to sleep in the room separate from my campers last night. Viv didn't give me hell for it either, which surprised me. I'm not even sure why I feel so guilty for Morgan's accident. It's not like I could have prevented it. I guess I just let her mom get under my skin.

I listened to them all wake up with excitement, getting their bathing suits on and preparing for their camp outing, and talking about who wanted to be in a raft with whom. At one point I heard a tiny knock on my door and Kelsey whisper my name before they all left, but I made no effort to get up to open the door or even respond.

Once I hear the door to the cabin finally shut, I lay in bed for an hour, just staring at the ceiling. My phone vibrates on the dresser and I don't drag myself out of bed until it vibrates for the fourth time.

The first three texts are from Kenny, the fourth from Sampson.

"How could you leave me alone?"

"Seriously, these girls are going to eat me alive. What happened, raft buddy?"

"Penelope, are you okay?"

"I'm not mad at you," says the text from Sampson. "I just think I deserve the truth."

I text back a simple sorry to both of them, knowing

they won't be able to respond anyway. They should already be at the raft facility gearing up. I head to the bathroom, only being excited that I won't have to time my shower since everyone is gone and I'm not sharing the room with ten other girls.

It feels good to just stand under the shower head even though the water pressure is limited and the 'hot water' is more like room temperature than anything. I wash off and take my time getting dressed for the day. I slide my sandals on and head back to grab my phone. No more missed texts.

I snag one of the protein bars we stash in the closet and put on my backpack, not knowing where I'm going, just wanting some fresh air and some 'me time'. I take the back loop of camp and end up at the old log cabin. I remember when I was younger they used to bring us out here and tell ghost stories about how the camp ended up owning the cabin and moving it onto the land, before they owned it, it was part of the Underground Railroad. Supposedly, at night, you can hear the lost souls humming an old song.

My first year here, I almost left in tears because of the ghost stories. As it turns out, the cabin was never actually lived in, not even part of the Underground Railroad, it was just an actual model size cabin to show what it was like years ago to fit a family into a one room cabin. Ghost free zone.

Yet, it still creeps me out as I walk by it. It feels like someone's watching when I pass by. Gravel crunches under tires, and I turn to see a dusty Rav4 heading down the road toward me.

It slows to a stop and the Mrs. Garreth rolls down the window.

She smiles at me and I step closer to the car, the AC blowing full blast inside.

"Hey, Molly," I say with a wave.

"Where you headed, sweetie?" she asks.

I shrug my shoulders and put my hands in my pockets. "Honestly, I don't know."

"Hop in," she says. "I have some ice cream in the trunk, we can sneak some before Sam gets back."

Ice cream sounds pretty good. I get in the car and accept her company with an open mind.

"I heard about what happened. We don't have to talk about it if you don't want to," Mrs. Garreth says, pushing a bowl full of chocolate chip ice cream toward me.

I put a spoon full of it into my mouth and give myself time to formulate a response. "It's not just that. This summer isn't anything that I planned on it being. It's been kind of awful if I'm being honest. This is supposed to be the best summer of my life, right? The summer before I become and adult and start college is supposed to be awesome."

"Sampson told me about your parents," she says. "I'm sorry that's happening."

"Again, it's not just that."

"What else is there?" she asks, standing at the counter eating her own bowl of ice cream.

I hesitate. I can't tell her the truth. I can't tell her that I've known her son's girlfriend has been cheating on him since the beginning of camp.

"If you knew something bad that a friend of yours

should know, would you tell them? Even if it would probably hurt them badly?" I ask.

Instead of immediately saying yes like I think she will, she thinks through it. I can practically see the wheels in her head turning it over and over.

"I think keeping it in would be worse, but I understand not wanting to hurt the person. Obviously there are a lot of variables, but honey, you've got to stop trying to fix everyone. I've noticed you losing that light in your eyes this summer."

"You have?" I ask.

"I'm a mother, Penelope," she smiles. "Of course I notice. You're wearing yourself too thin, you're too young to be solving everyone's problems. Let them figure it out."

"I... it's complicated..." I say, a tear falling down my cheek. I can't tell her about Viv's infidelity to her son. "I don't know what to do."

She comes over and grabs my ice cream. "Let's do what every normal human does when they need a mental health day. Let's binge watch those crappy daytime talk shows and kill this ice cream."

"Mom, you here?"

Shit!

Looks like everyone has returned from the rafting trip and Sampson decided to come home for a little bit. I must have fallen asleep on the couch watching an afternoon cooking show. The TV has been turned off and I hear Mrs. Garreth shush Sampson from the kitchen. I don't dare open my eyes.

When most animals feel attacked, they play dead--well, possums mostly. Me, currently. Or at least pretending that I'm a heavy sleeper.

"We have a guest," Molly says, and I imagine her pointing her finger toward me on the couch, covered in a blanket. "We had a little bit of a girl's day."

I hear a bar stool being pulled from the counter. It must be Sampson sitting down as he asks, "Did she talk to you about anything?"

"She seems to have a lot of stuff going on personally, honey. I wouldn't take it to heart."

"I just don't understand why she keeps shutting me out. One minute we're best friends and the next she's ignoring me."

There's a pause.

"Don't look at me like that," he continues. "We're just friends."

"Sampson, I see the way you look at that girl in there and honestly, it's not the way you look at..."

"Not the way I look at what, mom? My girlfriend?" He asks. "I don't--"

They're both quiet for a moment, but I don't risk opening my eyes.

"Fine," he says finally. "Maybe you're right. What if I do like her? I'm with Viv, I have to work the rest of the summer with both of them."

And that's why you don't mix business with pleasure.

I let out a fake cough and stretch out on the leather couch, trying to make as much subtle noise as possible instead of just getting up and leaving. I stand up slowly and head to the kitchen to grab my backpack, pretending like I heard nothing.

"Oh, hey," I say to Sampson. "How was the rafting trip?"

He gives me a small smile. "Fun, everyone missed you though. Sophia especially."

And you?

"There's always next year," I say to him and then turn to Mrs. Garreth. "Thank you for letting me crash on your couch and watch your cable. You have no idea how much I needed that. It's nice to occasionally reconnect with the real world."

"Anytime, sweetie," she says, coming over to wrap me up in a hug. "You're always welcome. It's nice to have another lady around."

I nod and smile. "I better get back. I'll see ya."

As I'm walking out the front door, Sampson catches up to me and opens it for me, but also comes out, closing the door behind us. "Can I talk to you?"

"I really don't feel like it…" I say, brushing a stray piece of hair out of my eyes.

"You haven't felt like it, I just need to know that we're okay," he says.

"And if we're not?" *Did I just say that?*

"Then I'll do anything to fix it. I know you're not telling me something and it's putting a strain on our friendship."

I shake my head and start to walk away but turn around to face him again. "Just remember that I'm not the bad guy."

"Then who is? That's all I need to know. Please."

I glance inside, seeing Mrs. Garreth walking by the front door. "Not here. I'll tell you tomorrow, at the sleepover. Once all the kids are asleep, we'll talk then. Okay?"

"Okay," he says, some tension leaving his shoulders.

"Just promise you won't be mad at me."

"I promise," he says.

FIFTEEN

It's pouring outside.

The weather report says it's going to rain all day, which means all outdoor activities are cancelled until the rain is over. I was supposed to be doing the clay wall hike today, which is usually a blast for the campers because they use the clay we find as 'war paint', but now I'm supposed to report to the nature center after breakfast. I'm scheduled to work there with another counselor and then after lunch switch off and do sing along time with most of the younger kids.

I hate the nature center, but only because of all the creepy crawlers in there. If they were left in their cages and tanks, it wouldn't be so bad. It's when the campers start handling them that I get a little bit uneasy. Snakes, mice, tarantula, salamanders, iguana, why can't we just have a nature center filled with kittens? That's therapeutic, right?

I eagerly volunteer to dispense hand sanitizer and constantly remind the campers to keep their hands moist with the water bottle when handling the salamander.

If one of them drops the snake though, I'm out of here.

Sophia squeaks as the snake tries to slither up her arm. It's a small one, but still terrifying to me.

She hands it off to me but I shake my head. "Pass it on to Daisy, please."

"You don't want to hold it, Miss Penelope?" she asks.

"Nope, I'm fine. Thank you though."

"Alright, kids," says Ben, putting away one of the snakes. "We have five minutes left in here, then we have to head to our next activity for the day. Get your raincoats on and meet Penelope at the door when you're ready to go."

I nod at him and tell him a silent 'thank you' with my lips. There's no way I will put all these animals away. Especially the snakes.

"How'd you get stuck coming to the nature center?" he asks, putting a rat away in its cage next to me, I slide away a little bit.

Ben, Dora and five of the other staff members are the ones who handle the Nature Center on a daily basis, they each switch off on a different days. Most of the animals don't need that much attention, just a check on their food and water supply.

"I think Viv has it out of me," I tease. "She seems to assign me to all the things she doesn't want to do."

"Let's be honest, she has it out for everyone," he says.

I laugh. "How do you handle her? Give me some tips. I mean, she's your best friend's girlfriend. I'm sure you have to be around her a lot."

"Let's just say I don't see him much now. I thought us working together would mean seeing each other more often, but not so much. She has him wrapped around her finger."

"Sorry," I offer.

He just shrugs and smiles.

"Alright, time to line up," I say clapping my hands. "First one in line gets to pick a song for us to sing on the way to the art center."

That kicks the campers into gear. They all start scrambling to get their umbrellas and rain gear ready, two of the girls almost knock each other over trying to get into line first.

"Alright," I say, kneeling down in front of Sophia, our new line leader. "What camp song are we singing?"

"The ant rain song!" she squeals.

A few of the boys groan but line up anyway.

"How fitting!" I say. "Shall we?"

As I open the door for them to head out, Sophia starts singing. "The ants go marching one by one."

The rest of the campers join in, "Hoorah, hoorah!"

Ben heads to the front of the line and gives me a high five as he passes by. "Good job, partner."

"You okay?" Kelsey asks as she comes to lie down next to me on my bunk. "You haven't seemed yourself."

I shrug my shoulders and stare at the bottom of the bunk above me. "I can't discuss it with you, sorry."

She sighs. "I hate that you have to hold all of this in just because you're a CIT now. We never have to keep things to ourselves."

Most of the girls are either reading or napping in their beds, and half of them have headphones on, listening to their iPods. Viv has decided to call dibs on our shared space for today. Who knows what she's doing in there while I handle feet off the floor time. I should probably tell the girls they're not supposed to have electronics, but I just don't care, they've gotten this far along.

"Come on, tell me," Kelsey whispers. "It'll stay between the two of us."

"I think…" I say, but stall on my words.

"You think…" Kelsey says, leaning in closer to hear me.

I turn to look at her. "I think I've fallen for Sampson, but it's just so complicated."

"You like who you like," she says simply, as if it should all make sense.

"He's with Viv, but... I don't think she likes him as much as a girlfriend should. And then there's Kenny. He's been so nice to me, not like he used to be."

Kelsey nods. "He used to be such a pain in the ass, remember how annoying he was?"

"Oh, believe me, I do. But honestly, other than you, he feels like the only friend I've had this summer."

"Maybe you should give him a chance then. Test the waters."

I shrug. "But that's not fair to him since I think I'm falling for Sampson."

"I know, but think about it, he's too stuck up Viv's butt to realize how amazing you are. You need to keep your space from him, start giving your attention to Kenny. At least he'll return the favor."

"But don't you think it's weird? We grew up with him."

"And we grew up with Lain too, but look at us! Happy as can be."

I roll my eyes. "I wish I were as carefree as you."

She leans her head on my shoulder. "Don't worry, you'll find your happiness one day. Be patient."

"Can I take my pookie bear?" Daisy asks from her bunk.

"Ugh, don't take that nasty thing to show off in front of camp," grunts Ronnie, one of the older girls.

Tonight is the camp sleepover where we round up all the campers and everyone sleeps in the welcome center. We play PG movies all night and have some board games set up. At dinner we filled all the kids up on garlic bread and spaghetti in the hopes that they'll crash from the carbs.

"Ronnie, be nice," I chide. "Daisy can take her stuffed animal if she wants. Worry about packing up your sleeping bag and pillow."

"God, I hope the boys all wear clean socks," Kelsey says, leaning on the floor to roll up her bag. "Last year, David McKenzie's feet were so gross! My head was at his feet all night. He kicked me once in his sleep, or maybe he wasn't sleeping…"

I chuckle and toss her pillow at her. "Sucks to be you. I get to sleep on the outer perimeter since I'm a CIT."

"Lucky," the five other older girls say in unison.

"Why isn't everyone ready yet?" Viv comes in from the door that leads outside. She said she had some errands to run.

"We have five minutes before we need to be ready," I say as I look up at her. "Your lipstick is smudged."

"Can I speak with you in the hall?" Viv asks.

I nod and Kelsey starts helping the other girls roll up their sleeping bags.

"You," Viv says pointing her finger at me. "You need to mind your own business."

"What are you talking about?" I ask.

"You think you're so cute and sweet and innocent, but I see right through you."

"Viv, what the heck? I was just letting you know that you're lipstick was smudged. Thought you might want to fix it."

"You've had it out for me since day one, trying to turn Sampson against me."

"I've had it out for you? You're the one who has been down my throat all summer. Sampson is yours, just leave me alone," I fire back.

"Whatever," she says, flipping her hair as she walks away. "You're going to get eaten alive in college. Grow a backbone."

Viv slams the door to the bathroom shut and when I turn around, Kelsey is standing behind me, eyes wide.

"What the heck was that about?" she asks, holding her pillow to her chest.

"I have no clue. She's freaking insane."

"Everyone is ready, should we just go without her?" Kelsey asks.

"Yeah, I think Viv needs sometime to herself. She is not a happy camper."

All of the girls are already lined up at the door with their pajamas and sandals on and the sight is so ridiculous it makes me smile.

"Good job guys!" I say. "Maybe we'll get first dibs on bedtime snacks tonight!"

Daisy claps. "Oh, please tell me it's candy!"

I laugh. "If it's not, I'll sneak some back the next time I have a day off."

"Promise?" the girls all ask at the same time.

"I promise."

I'm in the middle of playing Go Fish with Kelsey and some of the younger girls when I glance at the door and see Sampson staring at me. He jerks his head, trying to get me to come to the lobby and talk to him, but I shake my head. He mouths the word 'please' and I choose to ignore him again.

"Don't you need a bathroom break?" Kelsey asks. "I can stay here and sub in."

"No, I'm fine," I tell her.

She stares at me. "Go."

I roll my eyes and pull myself up from the floor, walking through the maze of pillows, sleeping bags and campers already conked out for the night. Sampson isn't at the door where he was standing when he tried to get my attention. I almost turn back to return to my game.

"Over here," I hear him say from around the corner.

I go over to him, but make sure to keep my distance, a good five feet should do.

"What? Are we not friends anymore?" he asks.

"We are, if you want to be," I say, crossing my arms over my chest. Feeling very insecure in my Hello Kitty pajama pants and white tee.

He's wearing a pair of orange and garnet sweatpants with the Maryville mascot on them and his grey shirt stretches across his chest. I want to reach out and hug him so I can feel the soft cotton on my cheek, but I keep the five feet distance.

"I do, but you're being super weird."

"No, I'm not," I protest. "I'm…"

I hear a giggle coming from inside the boys' restroom, but it's not a boy's giggle, it's a girl's voice. When Sampson starts to argue with the fact that I'm being weird, I instantly shush him.

"Did you hear that?" I ask, pointing to the boys' bathroom.

"These kids, seriously. You turn your head for one minute and they go frolicking behind your back," he says, pushing the door open. I come behind him to see the culprits.

"Are you kidding me?" Sampson yells. I can't see who he's looking at because he's so tall. When he suddenly turns to leave, I finally get a good look.

Casanova and Viv, caught in the act.

Her tank top is on the floor, his hands are on her bare stomach. Viv stares at me with vengeance in her eyes and then slides off the sink, pushing by Casanova.

"Sampson, wait," she says as she shoves me to the side. "It meant nothing."

"It sure as hell looked like it meant something," he hisses through his teeth, trying not to make a scene. "How long has this been going on?"

When Viv doesn't say anything, Sampson squeezes his fist.

"How long, Viv?" He says.

"Does it matter how long?" she asks. I think that was the worst response she could have given. She could have said anything else - awhile, a few months, *anything*, but she didn't.

"I thought you loved me," Sampson says and my heart breaks for him.

Casanova just grins as he adjusts his sweat pants and heads back into the sleepover What an asshole.

"Come on, we're young. We don't know what love is," Viv answers.

Sampson just shakes his head. Viv takes that as her cue to go back into the slumber party too. There's no way to fix the damage. Sampson stands there not saying a word, not making a move to go punch Casanova in the face or to storm out.

"Sampson," I start to say.

"Don't," he bites off. "You knew about this?"

I nod my head, afraid to say the wrong words.

"And you didn't tell me? This is the secret you wouldn't tell me? How long have you known about this?"

I swallow. "Since the first day I got here. I caught them in the cabin. She threatened me, and I didn't know she was cheating at the time."

"You didn't think it would be a good idea to tell me?"

"She threatened me, Sampson," I say, throwing up my defenses. "She threatened to get me fired. This has been my dream job, I couldn't…"

"I thought we were friends," Sampson says, shaking his head. "You know, the only thing worse than a cheater is a liar."

He walks away and I chuckle. "I'm not going to feel bad, Sampson. What if I told you? Would you have believed me? No, because in your eyes, Viv could do no wrong. Don't act like you're innocent too…"

"What's that supposed to mean?" he asks.

"Nothing, whatever. I need to get back to my campers."

As I start to walk back in, Sampson pulls on my arm. "Tell me what you mean by that."

My lower lip quivers and I back up against the wall. "How stupid can you be? Were we ever just friends?"

"I thought we were… I'm sorry if you misread any of my actions…"

I'm not going to cry in front of him. I will not cry in front of him.

"Let me go, Sampson," I growl, not looking him in the eyes.

"Geez," says Kenny from the door. "Does no one watch the campers anymore? Everything okay out here?"

"It's fine, Kenny," I say, pushing Sampson aside. "I just

needed some air. So many kids in one room smells gross after a while."

"I'll make sure all the guys wear deodorant next time," he teases. "Sampson, the movie just ended, do we have any more?"

"Yeah," Sampson says. "I'll grab some more from my dad's office."

Sampson heads off to the office and I walk toward Kenny. He holds the door open for me and grabs my hand.

"You okay?" he asks, his voice low. "He didn't hurt you or anything?"

"No, yes, I'm okay. No he didn't hurt me," I say. "Thanks for checking on me, Kenny."

"No problem, I do believe you have a Go Fish game to get back to. I think I saw Daisy peeking at your cards."

I smile at Kenny and head back to my game, but it looks like a few of the girls have ventured over to their sleeping bags to go to bed. Kelsey is up talking to Lain, but when she sees me she stands up and we meet at our sleeping bags. I sit down and pull my pillow into my lap.

"That didn't look pleasant," she says, pulling her bee pillow pet into her lap. "Viv has been fuming in the corner over there."

"You know, I thought people got more mature when they go to college," I say. "But I've experienced more drama this summer than I feel like I've had through my four years in high school."

"Preach girl," Kelsey says, trying to calm my mood. "I'm sure everyone will get over it soon."

I nod and breathe in deeply. "Now that the truth is out there. I'm sure now it will blow over quickly."

"Now," Kelsey says smiling. "Onto more important matters, let's talk about the dance tomorrow."

We both giggle and Kelsey lies down in her sleeping

bag, calling it a night. I check in one more time with the rest of my campers and set my alarm to go off around six in the morning, that way some of the girls can get their morning showers before breakfast. Before I close my eyes, I glance around the room once more and see Sampson sitting with a few of the boys, playing cards. He's looking at me when I spot him, but quickly looks away.

It's time to start concentrating more on making myself happy. I can't try to be something he wants, and I can't keep walking on eggshells around Viv. This may be my last summer here.

SIXTEEN

"Look," Viv confronts me in our private room the next day. "I honestly can't stand looking at your face. I want to punch you every time I see you because you pretend like you're so innocent. I'm going to talk to Mr. Garreth today and get a new CIT."

"What?" I ask, pulling out a clean pair of shorts and a t-shirt to wear for the day.

She rolls her eyes at me. "Clearly, you're not cut out to work here."

"What are you talking about 'I'm not cut out to work here'? I've been around for these girls more than you have. While you've been out traipsing with who knows who, I've been working."

"It's my word against yours," she says, reminding me where I stand.

"You know," I say. "You're not Sampson's girlfriend anymore, you don't get special treatment after the things you've done."

"Oh, honey," she smiles and places her hand on my shoulder gently. "You think we broke up? I'll have you know we made up after you went to bed. He came crawling back to me, just like he always does. Like he always will."

"I don't believe you," I say, grabbing my nametag and toiletry kit. "Sampson has more dignity than to go back to you after you cheated on him."

She puts her hands up in the air, "Okay, you got me.

We haven't gotten back together yet, but we will. We always do."

"I heard you're going to the dance with Kenny," Kelsey says, putting on some blush. She has her makeup all over the sink, some of it opened and leaving flecks of powder on the side of the porcelain.

"Everyone is going to the dance," I clarify, flossing the remains of corn from dinner that are still stuck in my teeth. I can hardly see myself in the mirror because she's taking up so much of it. "And I'm not sure where this Kenny thing came from."

She puts on her bright red lipstick looking like a Taylor Swift impersonator, treating the dance as if it's a legitimate high school homecoming or the VMAs. "Daisy and Sophia seem to think Kenny is your prince charming. What do you think you-know-who will say?"

I shrug my shoulders, toss the floss in the trash, and tighten my braids. "I'm not sure what gave them that impression, and you-know-who isn't talking to me now. But I shouldn't be discussing any of this with you. You're a camper."

"I'm still your friend though, and you need to talk to someone. I feel like you're not as happy as you have been previous summers. What's going on with you?"

I close the bathroom door and lean my back against it. "It just feels like I had such high expectations for this summer and it's just been a total disaster. I've gotten distracted from what I wanted, and now I have no idea what my future holds."

"That's a bit dramatic," she says as she cleans up her makeup and stuffs it back into the bag. It barely zips shut. "You need to find a way to take your life back under control. Grab it by the balls."

"Don't say balls," I say rolling my eyes. "There are little girls in the other room."

She turns and places her hands on my shoulders. "It's going to be okay. Screw Sampson for not seeing what a catch you are and letting Viv control him. Screw your parents for not seeing what a big mistake they're making. Live your life and be the badass chick I know you can be."

"I've never been a badass," I say defeated.

"It's never too late to figure out how to be."

She turns me to look into the mirror and undoes my braids, running her fingers through my hair, trying to pull out the knots. I stare into my eyes reflected in the mirror.

"You can do this, you can be anyone you want to be. Don't let them win, don't let any of them make you feel inferior," she says.

I nod and meet her gaze in the mirror. "Thanks for the pep talk, Kels. I needed that."

"Hey, Kenny," I say when I find him filling up his water bottle with 'bug juice'. They call the red Kool-Aid that because of all the bugs it attracts if you don't put it in a sealed container. "What's up?"

"Oh hey," he says, turning around with a surprised expression on his face. "I didn't think you'd actually show up."

"Kenny, it's a camp event," I say, rolling my eyes and

grabbing myself a cup to fill with water. "We all have to show up."

"You know what I meant. I didn't think you would show up and want to hang out with me. You've been pretty distant lately."

"About that," I say, feeling ashamed. "I'm sorry. I should have told you what was going on."

"Something still going on at home with your parents?" he asks.

"How'd you know?"

His face flushes. "I saw you calling Sampson that night, and he told me you were having some trouble back home. Is it getting better at all?"

We both go over to sit on one of the hay bales and watch the kids run around while the music is on full blast. This is probably the best idea, get all the energy out of them right before bedtime, no wonder schools give younger kids recess time.

"It's okay I guess. I call home about once a week to check in with my parents. Things are still up in the air."

He nods and takes a sip of his drink, the red staining his lips. "You doing okay yourself? With the whole Morgan situation?"

"Yeah, it's so annoying," I say shaking my head. "I told her not to run. I did everything possible and it still happened and I never left her side at the hospital. Yet, her parents are ticked."

"Kids are fragile," Kenny says. "She could have been walking in her own house and had that happen. It's not your fault."

"I know, but right now I feel like everything is my fault."

"It'll get better," he says. "Trust me."

"I'm kind of running low on trusting people," I admit to him. "It's hard for me to believe anything anymore."

And it is. Not only have I lied to Sampson about Viv, but I've been lied to by Janine and my parents. What's the point in letting another person in, if they're just going to do the same? I just need to keep my eye on the prize: finish up camp, start college, begin the rest of my life. No distractions.

SEVENTEEN

JULY

"Come on in, Penelope," Mr. Garreth says when I knock on his door. He's cleaning up his desk from some paperwork that looks very daunting.

"Sorry, I'm early," I say awkwardly.

"You're fine, have a seat," he says, motioning to one of the giant leather chairs. I feel like I'm sitting in the principal's office. "I was just finishing up some paperwork for camp expansion."

"Are you buying more property?" I ask.

"Trying to," he says. "We're wanting to get some more land in order to build some cabins for more employees and campers. I'd like to keep Camp Arthur growing."

"That's awesome, I'd love to see that too!"

Mr. Garreth smiles and pulls my file out of his desk drawer like he does every time we have a meeting, which is about once a week if possible. This meeting seems scarier than the others, especially after Morgan's accident.

"How have you been, Penelope?" he starts, poising his pen over the file.

"I've been okay," I answer with a shrug, trying not to think about what he might write down. "Been better, but doing alright."

"I see you'll be going to orientation soon," he says. "Are you excited for a break from camp?"

I shake my head. "No and yes. I love it here, but I am

173

excited to get my classes for the fall. I'm nervous though, it'll be my first time on campus without my parents."

"How are your mom and dad?"

Shrugging my shoulders, I start to dread this small talk. Can't we just get down to business? "They're okay. I'd rather hear how I'm doing according to your notes. I know I probably lost some points from what happened the other day with my camper…"

Mr. Garreth sits my file down and closes the folder. "We haven't heard anything from the lawyers, but I just want you to know it wasn't your fault. It was an accident, if anything, they'll probably threaten to sue us and then we will blacktop a few trails as a compromise."

"But the whole point of a trail is the dirt and the muck, the downed trees and stumps, right?"

He nods. "I know, but they *are* a safety concern. Camp isn't like it used to be, parents just seem to send their kids here so they don't have to find a babysitter in the summer."

"That's a shame."

"Indeed it is," he says. "I also have heard from some other counselors that you're having a hard time with Viv. Is this true?"

I don't want to admit it, but I can't lie to my boss. "Yeah, she's been kind of aggressive toward me since day one."

"Yeah, I was afraid of that," he says running a hand through his hair. "Don't tell anyone this, but I probably shouldn't have let Sampson talk me into hiring her. I knew it would be a bad idea."

"Then why did you?" I ask, hoping not to sound too blunt with my question.

"Sampson knows how to twist my arm," he sighs. "I'm going to have a talk with Viv, while you're away this weekend of course. She can't be scaring off one of my best CITs."

"I'm one of the best?" I ask.

He nods. "I see how well you do with the younger girls. They're crazy about you. I wish I could employ ten more versions of you. And from how well you work with your other co-workers, aside from Viv, I can see how hard you're trying."

"Thank you for noticing," I say. "I'm loving my cabin. These girls have been pretty great."

"Well, keep up the work. Only a few more weeks."

"You sound like you can't wait," I say with a smile.

He returns the smile. "Oh, my job never ends. I have to keep this place up and running even through the winter."

"Really?" I ask. "You don't have campers then."

"Nope, but we have some companies that want to come in and do team building activities. We also rent out some of the smaller cabins for family getaways. That's one of the ways we stay in business. We don't charge day camper families, most of those campers come from broken homes, so that's a big loss of money. We make it back in the winter and spring and with our full time campers."

"Huh," I say. "Who knew?"

"I'm not just the goofy guy that comes out occasionally to make sure you're always singing or have a smile on your face," he laughs. "I have to constantly be on my toes, year around."

My watch alarm goes off, signaling that I need to meet my campers for their next activity. "Well, I have to go. I need to get over to the lake."

"I'll take ya," he says pushing himself back from his desk and grabbing his golf cart keys. "Let's go. I can't keep myself out of the beautiful sun all day."

"Let's go," I agree.

"Penelope!" Daisy squeals. "Will you paddle boat with me and Sophia?"

Mr. Garreth dropped me off at the lake and when I made it over to the dock, Daisy and Sophia were the only two sitting there in life jackets waiting patiently for their turn. Everyone else was either fishing or already out in a paddle boat or canoe.

"Why yes I can," I say. "But we're going to need another person to even things out."

"I'll find someone!" Sophia says, running off to where everyone is fishing. I grab a lifejacket in my size and check Daisy's to make sure she has it on properly.

"Are you having a good day?" I ask her, pulling one of the straps a little tighter.

She nods and smiles. "Yup. I got to go on the big swing!"

The big swing is just what it sounds like, but inside one of our giant sheds where you're pulled to the top and swing back and forth, strapped in like a zipline. It's fairly new, most of the kids love it.

"You did?" I say, making my eyes light up. "You weren't scared?"

She shakes her head. "Of course not, there's nothing to be afraid of at camp! It was so much fun! I want to come back next year and do it again!"

"Well I'm glad to hear that! Maybe I can try it too."

"Will you come back next year and go on it with me?" she asks.

I smile at her and pinch her cheek softly. "I will try my best to come back, just so I can go on the big swing."

I stand up from my kneeling position and she wraps her arms around my legs, hugging me tightly, or at least trying to. Her lifejacket makes it a little hard to get her small arms to hug.

"Found someone!" Sophia cheers, pulling Kenny by his hand with her.

"Heard you need a fourth person," Kenny says smiling. "Now if only we had a paddle boat."

"Mr. Kenny," Daisy says pointing her finger to the side of the lake. "There's one right there!"

"Well, look at that!" I say. "Our chariot awaits."

The four of us walk over to the paddle boat and Kenny pushes it back into the water, through the cattails and other plants.

"I'll just boat it over to the dock, you guys can get on over there," he says. "It'll be easier, I don't want you ladies getting dirty."

We do as Kenny says, both of the girls holding my hands as we go to the dock.

"Mr. Kenny is such a gentle-man," Daisy says dreamily.

"It's 'gentleman'," Sophia corrects. "I had that word in a spelling bee. One word."

"Did you get it right?" Daisy asks.

Sophia shakes her head. "No, I spelled 'gentlemen' not 'man'."

"Ladies," Sampson says as he drifts up to the dock. I sit down and steady the paddle boat with my feet and help the girls on one at a time to the back of the boat. Once they're situated, I climb on board at one of the pedal seats.

"Everyone ready?" Kenny asks.

"Yeah!" the three of us cheer.

I push us away from the dock and Kenny and I start pedaling the boat, trying our best to avoid fishing lines.

The girls chatter in the back, pointing at the tadpoles and dragonflies at the surface of the water.

"Miss. Penelope," Sophia says. "What are those two bugs doing?"

I turn to look at where she's pointing. Two dragonflies are connected and sitting on the side of our boat. I can't actually tell them what they're doing. I won't be the one to tell them about the birds and the bees or in this case, the dragonflies.

"Umm," I say, not knowing what lie I can make up.

Kenny turns and sees what the girls are watching and laughs. "Penelope, what are those dragonflies doing? I've never seen something like that before."

He's screwing with me. He has this huge smug smile on his face, and he's screwing with me.

"I think they're just chilling out," I say. "They're trying to be friends."

"Friends?" Kenny asks. "You sure about that?"

"Pretty sure," I say.

Daisy swats at them to go away. "Get out of here, go be friends somewhere else. Our boat is full."

Kenny and I both burst into a fit of laughter, so bad that my stomach aches from laughing so hard. Daisy and Sophia probably think we're out of our minds. Eventually, Kenny and I regain control and take two more trips around the lake. We listen as Daisy and Sophia chat about their friends back home and what they're doing when camp is over.

"Alright girls," I say. "You guys ready to go in? We need to get back to land."

"Aww, do we have to?" they plead.

"Afraid so," Kenny says. "We have about an hour until pool time."

"Fine," Daisy says. "Maybe we can hang out at pool time too. Kenny, will you hang out with us at pool time?"

"If you're inviting me, I can," Kenny says.

We come to a stop at the dock and Kenny gets out to tie us off. He then helps the girls out, followed by me. I tell the little ones to go take their lifejackets to the shed and gather up the rest of their cabin mates.

"Hey," Kenny says as I'm about to go put my lifejacket up and retrieve my backpack. "You busy this weekend? I have Friday off and scored some tickets to a concert, thought we could go."

"Oh man," I say. "I totally would but I have my orientation this weekend. I'll be gone Friday until Sunday."

"That sucks, maybe next time then?"

"Yeah, sure," I say. "Have fun though, let me know how it goes."

"Totally," he says, but I can tell he's a bit let down.

"Maybe someone else here can get the weekend off and go with you," I suggest.

If it wasn't for my weekend visit to Maryville, I would take Kenny up on the concert immediately. I have nothing left to lose.

EIGHTEEN

"Welcome Class of 2021 to Maryville college!" reads the banner leading to the quad. I approach the check-in table and give them my first and last name. The bored orientation leader gives me a welcome packet along with an oversized Go Scots! shirt that I'll only be able to wear when I'm sleeping. They were out of smalls and only had large and XXL left.

I head to the performing arts center for the official welcoming committee. The president of the school gives a fifteen-minute speech on what the school means to him and how he hopes we enjoy our time here. The guy sitting at the end of my row is already snoring, and I wonder how long he'll last in school, or why he's even here in the first place.

Various organizations around campus join the president on stage discussing Greek life, spiritual organizations, clubs, and so on. Snoring Guy only wakes up when he hears someone in the art club mention that they have pizza every Friday at their meetings.

"Alright," says the head of admissions after a few hours of orientation. "On the corner of your name tag you'll see a small sticker. This will tell you which group you need to follow for your personalized campus tour. Green follow me, blue will follow our English department representative, orange will follow mathematics…"

The woman goes on, stating all the colors and majors, and all the incoming students start getting up to follow their designated person. I join in with the psychology group of twenty other future Scots and try my best not to look like a horrified freshman. I manage to put on a decent smile as my right leg bounces uncontrollably, my nervous twitch.

Our leader starts counting us and looks down at her clipboard to check something. "Alright, looks like we the right amount of people. I will call you by last name just to make sure we're all in the right place before we begin."

All but one person was in the right place, so we swap them out for our missing student who went to the sociology and anthropology group. We all shuffle out of the auditorium and quietly walk to our first stop on the tour, the student center known as Bartlett Hall that houses a cafe, the bookstore, post office, and more. We quickly finish up there and move onto the library in Thaw Hall, and I stare around in awe at the amount of books. It's not the library I imagined, the stereotypical college movie library with dark and dingy with floor to ceiling shelves, but it does look like a good research environment.

By the time we finish up at the main cafeteria, I'm turned completely backwards and wish I could go on two or three more tours. If I'm being honest, I forgot where I was thirty minutes into the tour.

"Alright," our tour guide says as we stand in front of a long, four story building. "This is Carnegie Hall, one of the student housing buildings you'll have the option in staying in at one point or another during your schooling. Tonight, you'll be staying here, pair up with someone in the group and I'll hand out keys once you have a buddy.

"And before you think about it," she goes on. "Same sex only, we're not matchmakers."

Everyone in my group quickly pairs up to room together for the weekend, and I'm the odd one out. Once everyone else gets their keys and heads to their rooms, I approach our tour guide.

"Looks like I'm last," I say. "Should I just wait for an assignment?"

She shakes her head and hands me the last key. "Lucky you, you get the room to yourself. I didn't want to say there was one single room because people usually fight over it. You fine with your own room?"

I nod. "Sure. Sounds good."

"Alrighty, I'll see you at tomorrow morning's meeting. Enjoy your night."

"Wait," I ask as she begins to walk away, already starting a text on her phone. "That's it, we have to stay in our rooms until tomorrow morning?"

I glance down at my watch and it's only 3 o'clock, we'd just be headed to the pool after 'feet off the floor' time if I were at camp.

She laughs. "No, you're free to explore campus, go off campus, hang out in the residence halls. Whatever, that's part of the experience. There is a summer RA on duty. If you need anything, he'll be at the front desk."

"Okay," I say, staring at my key. "Thanks."

All this freedom is blowing my mind. Is it a smart idea to just set us free for the evening? I guess they have the sink or swim mindset.

I pick up my overnight bag at the front desk and head to the third floor, room 310. Laughter comes from one of the other rooms, and I note that the walls are paper thin. I drop my bag and pull my sleeping bag out to put on the bed. It's not much different from the bunks back at camp. There's a few more inches on the mattress and they look a little less worn, but that's about it. I sit up on the bed and stare at the bare, off-white walls and fluorescent lighting.

With a bookshelf full of books and some of my stuff from home, this place might become habitable.

Wait, technically I am a student. School starts in four weeks. I registered for my first semester classes this morning.

I'm officially a college student.

I sit on my bunk, staring out the window for who knows how long before I startle at a knock on my door. When I open it, there's four girls standing, dressed very differently from earlier. Their tops are cut lower and their skirts are shorter.

"Hey," I say. "What's up?"

"We wanted to invite you out," says one of the girls. "We're heading to an Irish Pub off campus."

"I don't think I'm dressed for a bar..." I say, feeling stupid for not bringing something nicer. All I had was camp shirts and gym shorts, and the only pair of jeans that I'm currently wearing.

"Oh shush," says another girl. "Just come with us, the more the merrier."

"Okay," I say as I turn to grab my backpack and my room key. "I'm ready."

"Do you need that big backpack? Just grab your purse," suggests the first girl.

"I actually haven't used a purse all summer," I say, shutting the door behind me and locking it. "I've been working at a summer camp nearby, so my bag has held my life in it all summer."

We all start walking down the hall and one of the other girls gets excited over that fact, grabbing me by my forearm, her eyes bugging out. I gently pull my arm out of her grasp.

"That's so cool, minimalism is so in right now," she says. "I envy you, I have no clue how I'll be able to fit all my clothes and shoes into one of those tiny closets. I wonder how much a storage facility costs."

We head out to the parking lot and load into one of the girls' cars. I cram myself into the middle since I'm the shortest of the bunch. The girls all discuss more about how cool the minimalist movement is and how awesome tiny houses are, but they could never get rid of their clothes. They all agree that they have dresses in their closets that they haven't worn since middle school dances.

"What about you?" asks the girl driving. "How do you think you'll manage getting your stuff into your dorm?"

"I'm not sure," I say staring at my hands. "I planned on only bringing necessities, but I might have to bring everything. My parents…"

"Go ahead," says one of the girls sitting next to me. "We're great talkers but even better listeners."

"My parents are possibly going through a divorce," I blurt out. "I don't know if they'll sell their house or what. My whole life is up in the air right now."

"That's so shitty," says the girl driving. "I'm sorry to hear that."

"Maybe we can get a townie to buy you a beer," suggests the girl in the passenger seat. "Guys love girls with emotional issues… or so I hear…"

"Carla," scolds the driver. "That's a bit rude."

"Sorry," Carla says, turning around to look at me with a shrug of her shoulders. "I don't have a filter."

I smile. "You're fine, just means you're more likely to tell me the cold hard truth. I think more people need that."

We pull to a stop and all climb out of the car. I follow the girls in and we get a table next to the bar. I, personally, would have chosen a table in the corner, but I can tell these girls like attention. We get some water and a giant plate of nachos, the nachos compliments of a guy sitting at the bar wearing a camo hat and worn out jeans. I'm not under-dressed at all.

Carla blows a kiss to the guy and we all load up our individual plates with some nachos.

"How do you do that?" I ask Carla.

"Do what?" she asks, smiling.

"I don't know, get a guy's attention so easily?" I suggest. "Or feel comfortable enough to flirt?"

"I'm not here to impress anyone," she says. "They're here to impress me. Once you get that drilled into your head, it becomes easy. They're the ones who have something to lose."

Me, Carla, and the driver, Hayley, exchange stories. I thought for sure these girls would be total ditzes or bimbos, but they're actually smart. Carla spent most of her summer backpacking through Europe. She's fresh off the plane from Germany. I found out she's already fluent in German and half fluent in French. She plans on taking some Japanese after her freshmen year.

Hayley wants to become a dietician one day and comes from a family of doctors and nurses. Yet here I am, trying to still decide what I want to do with my life. I can't work at camp forever - I've barely survived this summer.

"Penelope?" says a voice behind me.

"Oh, girl. Who is that?" Carla asks. I can practically see drool running down her chin.

I turn around and see him and quickly turn back around. "Shit, that's Sampson."

"Well, Sampson is coming over this way," Hayley says. "Want me to tell him to beat it?"

I shake my head. "No, I'm fine. He's just a co-worker."

Sampson greets our table and I blush as all the girls say hello in unison like some sort of planned sorority greeting. They all have the same silly grin as Carla's. All except

Hayley, who seems to be gaging my reaction. She seems like someone I need to keep as a friend, no doubt. She just seems sincere, possibly because I've been around Viv all summer, but I just feel like Hayley and I have clicked as friends already.

"Sampson," I start. "What are you doing here?"

"I was dropping off a paper for my summer class," he says. "I come here all the time for a drink after class."

"Oh, well, you want to pull a seat up?" I ask. "We're just eating appetizers. We didn't want to be stuck in the dorm all night."

"No, I was actually just picking up an order to go, I have a meeting with my study group. We have a final next week."

"Oh, okay." I say.

"You want to meet me in about two hours?" he asks. "I can show you around campus."

"No thanks, we already went on our tour," I reply. Someone kicks me under the table and when I glare at them, they mouth the word 'Go'. "On second thought, yeah. I'd love to get another tour. Honestly, I've already forgotten where half the buildings are."

"Still remember where the library is?" he asks and I nod. "Meet me there, say around eight? That work for you?"

"Yeah, yes." I answer.

"I'll see you there," he says. "Ladies, enjoy your food."

After he gets his to go and exits the pub, all the girls eyes' are on me.

"Hubba-hubba, talk about campus hottie," Carla says and the other girls giggle. "You never told us you already had a boyfriend."

"He's not my boyfriend," I say. "It's complicated and

messy. He probably only wants to talk about the fact that I ruined his relationship."

"You're a homewrecker?" Carla says, slapping her hand on the table. "I didn't see that one coming, you look so shy and innocent! I guess they do say it's always the quiet ones."

"She can't be a homewrecker, she looks too innocent," Hayley says to Carla before turning back to me. "Do you want to talk about it?"

And to my surprise, I do want to talk about it. I tell them the whole story. Viv cheating on him with Casanova and me being afraid to tell him and all the in between details just come spilling out. I don't care if this is just the kind of gossip these girls feed on, and I don't care if I sound like I'm whining. I haven't been able to tell anyone the whole story, not Kelsey, not my mom, not Janine who I haven't heard from since the party incident. The girls listen, all of them, and they offer mixed reactions.

One tells me that I should stand him up for being a jerk last week when the truth came out. Another tells me that I should give him a chance. Carla thinks that I should hook up with someone else in the bar and see how that makes him feel, but there's no way I'm going down her route.

"What do you think?" I ask Hayley who hasn't said a word.

"I'm honestly not sure," she says, taking a sip of her water. "I mean, he seemed nice enough. You said it's been a few days since you last spoke, maybe he's cooled off. And without his ex around, maybe you can talk and finally have a normal conversation."

"Maybe," I say. "I just want things to be normal between us, but I don't think they ever were."

"One thing is for sure," Carla says as she finishes off our plate of nachos.

"What's that?" I ask.

"We need to get you a cute outfit," she says pointing to my t-shirt. "Make him regret not realizing what a keeper you are."

We pay our check and head back to the dorm, and I manage to get out of wearing a skirt. The girls settle on a cute black top and let me keep my jeans on. Hayley does my makeup, and I'm too embarrassed to admit that this is the first time I've been dolled up since senior prom.

"Alright," says Carla, putting the cap on her eyeliner about an hour after the makeover began. "My masterpiece is finished."

It's just me, Carla and Hayley now. The other girls went down to the lobby to hang out with some other people from orientation. Hayley gives me a thumbs up and I look into the mirror.

"Wow," I tell Carla. "You made me look like I haven't been getting attacked by mosquitoes and the sun all summer."

"Isn't it amazing what some concealer and blush can do?" Carla says, sitting down on the desk chair and opening a magazine.

"Well, I better get going," I say, checking my watch. "Wish me luck."

"Do something I would do!" Carla says with a sinister smile.

"We'll see you at breakfast tomorrow?" Hayley asks.

"Yeah," I say, surprised by the invite, considering she seems like she would be the 'mean girl' type. "Sure, I'll see you there."

"Good luck!" They say in unison as I leave their room, and head out to the library.

Sampson is packing up his books when I get to the library. I take in a deep breath and walk over as quickly as possible. The library is pretty empty, with only the librarian behind the desk and two more tables occupied with study groups.

"Sampson," I say when I get to his table. One of his study buddies starts packing his stuff up too. "Hey."

"Hey, Penelope," he says with a smile. "We just finished up. This is Robert, one of my classmates."

"Hi," I say sheepishly to Robert. "Summer class, huh?"

"Yeah, they kind of suck," he says. "Sadly, it's a required class."

"Yeah, that does suck."

Robert zips up his backpack. "Well Sampson, I'll see you for the final. Good luck. Nice meeting you, Penelope. I've heard a lot about you from Sampson here," he says with a smile.

I want to ask what he's heard about me, but I just smile and wave instead. At least I know he's not embarrassed to be seen with me. I find a sliver of hope from Robert's words.

Sampson loads his backpack onto his shoulders and then turns to me. "Do you have curfew or anything?"

I shake my head. "Nope, I just have to be at my morning meetings. Do you have to get back to camp soon?"

"Nope, not until the morning."

We stand there for a little bit, and I'm not sure what I'm supposed to say. Maybe, *hey, now that you're single, we should go out.* Or so, *I've kind of had a crush on you all summer.*

189

Maybe it's best to say nothing at all.

Sampson nods toward the door. "You want to see some of my favorite places on campus?"

"Uh, yeah, sure. I'm up for whatever."

Sampson doesn't show me all his favorite spots though. He does show me one spot. We end up sneaking to the rooftop of one of the buildings. Part of me is terrified of getting caught and being expelled from Maryville before I even start, but the other part of me would follow Sampson *almost* anywhere.

"Holy crap, this view…" I say quietly but with enthusiasm. "Would be awesome if it wasn't dark out already. Maybe sunrise or sunset?"

"Alright, so I didn't think about the time of day we were coming up here," he says, putting his hands up in a surrender. "But the view is amazing during the day, and you can kind of see the mountains. It's even more pretty in the winter."

"Well, I look forward to seeing that," I say.

"Are you excited to start college here?" he asks.

"Yeah, nervous though," I say. "What if I'm not cut out for it?"

"You'll be fine," he says softly. "Everyone makes college out to be a huge deal and a life changer, but it's not. Don't be nervous."

His words make me feel a little better, but I'm still not sure what to say. A few days ago he wasn't even speaking to me, so I didn't have to worry about coming up with something to talk about.

"Hey," he says, drawing my attention back to him. "You okay?"

I nod and cross my arms over my chest. "Are you?"

"I'll be okay," he says. "And I'm not mad at you. I was at first, but I understand now why you kept it from me."

"Are you sure about that?" I ask, raising one of my eyebrows. There are multiple reasons why I lied to Sampson, and I'm curious to know why he thinks I did.

"I know Viv's kind of snobby…"

"Kind of!" I say raising my voice without meaning to.

We both listen, waiting to hear campus police bust us for being up here, but they don't come.

"Okay, she is snobby, and possessive and rude…"

"And just an overall bad human being, not just a bad girlfriend," I chime in.

"She is, isn't she?" he says, rubbing the back of his neck.

I nod. "She is, and I'm not sure if I should feel bad for her more or you."

"Ouch," he says. "Kick a man while he's down."

"Sampson," I say, dropping my arms to my side, wanting to wrap my hands around his neck and shake him until he sees Viv for who she really is. "She cheated on you, she threatened me, she lied to you, she's a bully. I wanted to tell you what they did behind your back, multiple times, but she scared the living hell out of me.

"All I've ever wanted since I was a first year camper was to work at Camp Arthur. This year I finally had the opportunity for that and Viv took the dream from me. I won't let her keep bullying me though. When I get back Monday, I'm going to talk to your dad, and I'm going to tell him what happened. If he wants me to leave, I'll leave, but I'm not going down without a fight."

"I understand," he says, kicking a pebble across the roof. "And if he asks me about it, I'll tell him too. It's just embarrassing."

"What's embarrassing?" I ask.

"Being so mesmerized that I didn't see what was actually going on. I mean, I saw the signs. I just chose to ignore them. I thought having Viv even if she was cheating, was better than not having her at all."

"Love makes us do crazy things." I suggest, but I honestly don't know. I've never been in love.

"I don't think it was love, I think I may have been scared of her like you are."

"That's silly!" I say, throwing my arms up. "Why would you be afraid of her?"

"I don't know, everyone- most everyone loves her and she's the life of the party. I thought she would blackmail me or something. It's stupid. Forget I even said that."

"Yeah, it's stupid!" I agree. "Sampson, you can do so much better than her. You're so good at your job, working with the kids and you're so cute! You're smart and you have a fantastic, fun personality!"

"Did you say I was cute?" he asks, making my cheeks blush.

"What, no!" I say. "Wait, that's all you heard out of all that? That's not even the point. The point is, you leaving Viv made you a better person. You never needed her, and maybe one day she'll realize that you may have been the best thing she ever had, but by then, you'll have moved on."

"You think I'm cute," he teases. I start laughing, imagining the scene from Rudolph where Clarice says he's cute.

"Whatever," I say. "Let's go before we get caught up here. The last thing I need is to be known as the girl who got kicked out of college during orientation."

"But it would make a good story to tell the kids one day, right?"

"Whatever you say, Sampson."

Sampson walks me to the front of the dorm. He checks his watch and I check mine. It's already almost midnight. He yawns, and I try my best to not yawn with him. We stand there awkwardly, but I'm not sure what happens now. I could say goodbye and walk inside, then wait to see him back at camp where we'll pretend this never happened. I could hug him and tell him that I don't think I'm going to go back to camp. I could cut things short and put Camp Arthur in my past.

"I should probably get going," Sampson says as another yawn slips out. "I think I'm going to call my buddy, there's no way I'm going to make it back to camp when I'm this tired."

"Yeah, I'm already exhausted, though I'll probably be up at five thirty or six. Yay, camp schedules."

"Yeah, I agree."

"You could stay here…" I say. "I mean, I don't have a roommate tonight. I wouldn't want you to fall asleep at the wheel and wreck."

Sampson looks at me to object. "You sure that's a good idea? I wouldn't want you to feel uncomfortable. My buddy doesn't live too far from here, I can go."

I try my best not to sound nervous, to sound calm and adult-like when my stomach is doing flips. "Yeah, it won't be a big deal. You can take the floor!"

He rolls his eyes but smiles. "Well aren't you a great hostess?"

"Come on," I say, jerking my head to the front door. "If we don't get in there soon, we'll both end up falling asleep in the courtyard."

Sampson quietly follows me in the building. Thank God the front desk person is currently away. I'm pretty sure we're not breaking any rules but I would rather not be known as the incoming freshmen who brought a boy back to her room during orientation. I don't know how I'd explain bringing an upperclassman back here. We head up the stairs and walk past my newly acquired friends' rooms where I hear some music playing and muffled voices.

If they walked out right now, I'm sure they'd get a kick out of this. Carla would probably give me a thumbs up.

"Here we are," I say, sticking my key in the lock and opening the door. "It's not much, but I plan on pulling up the carpet and adding a disco ball where the light is."

Sampson laughs and drops his backpack off at the desk.

"I'm going to run to the restroom quick," I say, grabbing my toiletry kit and pajamas. "I'll be back in a few minutes."

"Take your time," he says.

I smile and close the door behind me. The shared bathroom is empty, so I don't have to have a public freak out over the fact there's a guy in my room. At home, I was never allowed to go to my room with a guy, not that I even had someone to bring home though.

I splash some water on my face and put some toothpaste on my toothbrush. It takes three times for me to run the toothbrush under the water without losing the paste. I'm a mess of nervousness and anxiety. I put my hair up in a ponytail and try to get all the makeup off without a wipe or washcloth. Clearly, I did not come prepared.

"Hey you!" says a voice behind me. When I look in the mirror, Hayley is reflected. "How'd it go with your boy?"

Does she know?

"It went okay," I say.

"Just okay," she asks, leaning against the sink next to me. "He wasn't a jerk, was he?"

"No, no," I say, zipping up my toiletry bag. "We actually talked things out, and I think he finally understands how mentally unhealthy his girlfriend was for him."

"Good, I'm glad to hear that. How do you think things will be the next time you see him?"

In two minutes, I don't know. Maybe it'll be super awkward and he'll realize what a loser I am?

"I'm hoping for the best," I say. "But we'll see."

NINETEEN

"I can't believe I fell asleep on you last night," Sampson says, sitting on the empty desk. "I'm so sorry."

"You're fine," I say as I roll up my sleeping bag. "Get sleep while you can, right? Camp seems to take a lot of energy out of counselors."

When I walked back into my room last night, Sampson had fallen asleep on the floor. Since I had an extra blanket, I draped it across him. Part of me was relieved he fell asleep before I got back since it saved me from a potentially awkward conversation. I tiptoed across the room and climbed into bed, for a while just listening to his breathing, along with the muffled voices down the hall. I was thankful to have my own room.

"You're telling me," he says. "Last week, one of the little boys in my cabin kept waking me up at 3 in the morning saying he heard a wolf in the cabin. *In* the cabin! Not outside, but somehow the wolf made his way in the cabin. I didn't know they knew how to pull doors open."

I laugh. "How'd you handle that?"

He sighs. "I told him there wasn't a wolf in the cabin, but if there was, the stench of his bunk mate's dirty laundry would scare it away. Wolf's hate dirty laundry as much as I hate it."

"Good to know." I check my watch and it's time for me to head out. "I better get going, I have to be at breakfast and then report for another meeting."

"Can I walk you? To breakfast?"

"Really?" I ask, putting on my backpack and grabbing my sleeping bag and pillow to drop off in the lobby for pick up later.

"Yeah, why not?"

"Sure," I agree. "Shall we?"

It's not a long walk to the cafeteria from the dorm I was staying in, but it's the perfect amount of bonus alone time with Sampson. I feel like I might have made some progress in fixing what was wrong between the two of us. I hope this is just a sneak peek of what it'll be like when I'm officially attending school.

"Thanks for... walking me," I say as we come to a stop in front of the cafeteria entrance. I get a whiff of bacon as someone opens the door and passes by us. My stomach rumbles with hunger, this is the latest I've eaten all summer.

"Yeah, I'll see you back at camp later on. Have a safe drive back."

"You too," I say. "Thanks for keeping me company."

We do that awkward thing where we're not sure if we should shake hands, hug, high-five, or just walk away. We laugh after attempting the hug and just wave bye before I turn to go into the cafeteria.

I'm spooning some eggs onto my plate when someone comes behind me and pinches my sides. "You dog, you."

I startle and drop the scrambled egg spoon on the floor. I pick it up and hand it over to the cook before greeting Carla, my face red with embarrassment. "You scared the crap out of me."

"Sorry, you'll get used to it trust me," she says as she picks up a piece of bacon with her bare hands and puts it in her mouth in one bite. "I just saw Sampson and you out front."

"Yeah," I say. "He walked me here."

"Yeah?" she asks. "Did he stay on campus last night?"

"Yes," I say, not wanting to lie.

"In the dorms?"

"Yep."

Her eyes bug out. "With you in your room?"

We're approaching the table where Hayley and a few other people are sitting. "Shh, I don't want the whole campus to know," I tell her, my voice low.

"You're my idol now. I can't believe it, you snagged a college guy," Carla gushes. "School hasn't even started and you're already hooking up with frat guys."

"First off, nothing happened. Second, I knew him before this weekend."

"Thirdly?" Carla asks, arching a perfectly shaped eyebrow at me.

"Thirdly," I say. "We're just friends."

She shakes her head. "No, I think you two like each other."

Hayley and I say good morning when I sit my plate down, and Carla is right next to me, waiting for a response. I just smile and pick up my fork so I can start eating.

"Someone's happy this morning," Hayley says, putting a spoonful of cereal in her mouth.

"She was out--" Carla starts to say, but I cut her off.

"I was out late last night, Sampson was showing me around campus again," I interrupt.

If it were just me, Carla, and Hayley, I would probably tell them all the details of last night, but we have six people that are looking in my direction. I don't want everyone knowing my business.

"That's awesome!" Hayley says. "What do you think happens next?"

I shrug my shoulders. "No idea. I'm just playing it by ear."

"You'll have to keep in touch and let me know how things go," she says and we exchange numbers. "Text me anytime."

"Are you two living on campus?" I ask, mostly because I want to get off of the topic of Sampson.

"We're actually getting an apartment together off campus, but in walking distance," Hayley says. "We're going to sign the papers once orientation is over."

"Did you guys know each other before?" I ask, taking a bite of my food.

Carla nods. "We go way back, back to pre-school."

"That'll be nice," I say, "knowing who you'll be rooming with for at least a year."

"Are you staying in a dorm?" Kelsey asks me.

"Yep, I figure it'll be easier and then once I get settled into Maryville, I can check apartments out my second year or something. I wanted to get the whole freshmen year experience in, nothing like having a terrible roommate to make you miss home," Hayley and Carla exchange a look and then I stumble over my words. "You know, a room-mate you never met before, a stranger."

"Oh, maybe we could eventually get a bigger apart-ment and all room together!" Carla says with excitement. "Rent would possibly be cheaper."

"Yeah, that would be awesome," I say. "I'll keep that in mind."

One of the orientation leaders arrives in the cafeteria and lets us know it's time to head to our morning meetings. We all get up to throw our trash away and I smile, realizing this is the first time I've felt like part of a group of friends all summer.

"You're back! You're back! I missed you so much," squeals Daisy, running up to me and hugging me tightly.

"Well, I missed you too!" I say, rubbing my hand in her hair and messing it up. She immediately pulls away and tries to untangle her blonde locks.

Dora comes up to me with an exhausted look on her face. "Hey Pen, Mr. Garreth needs to see you in his office. I'll take the girls to arts and crafts with my cabin."

"What's up?" I ask her, my voice a whisper.

"Let's just say, it was an interesting weekend…" she says and then adds, "Good luck."

I met with Mr. Garreth less than a week ago, it's not time for our next meeting yet. What could we possibly need to talk about just yet? I walk as quickly as I can over to his office, dread hanging over me like a storm cloud. Did something happen at home? Did something happen with one of my campers?

I'm out of breath when I finally get into the welcome center, and I catch the sound of two male voices coming from Mr. Garreth's office, himself… and… Sampson?

I knock on his door and walk in when he motions for me to take a seat across from his desk. Sampson's sitting in one of the chairs and I expect him to get up and leave, but he doesn't. In fact, he doesn't appear to be going anywhere. Mr. Garreth extends his arm in the direction of the empty seat next to Sampson once again, and I sit down as he hangs up his phone. A smile on his face. This meeting can't be bad then, right?

"How was your weekend?" Mr. Garreth asks, tapping his pen on the desk.

Did Sampson tell him we ran into each other at Maryville? Did he tell him about our sleepover?

"It was good," I say, glancing from Sampson to his dad. "I'm all scheduled for the fall."

"Fantastic," Mr. Garreth replies, and I'm hoping that means this is a good meeting. "Did you just get back?"

"Yeah, Dora told me you needed me, so I came right over. What's up?"

"Well, Sampson and I had a talk," Mr. Garreth begins.

My heart falls into my stomach, and the storm cloud from moments ago lets out a lightning strike. What did they talk about? Would Sampson actually tell him about our night together? Nothing happened! Or did he tell him about the feud between me and Viv? Did they get back together in the last few hours and now Viv is convincing Sampson to get me fired?

"You've had a bad summer, haven't you?" Mr. Garreth asks.

"What do you mean?" I ask skeptically.

He puts his pen down. "Penelope, it's okay. He explained to me what happened between you and Viv, how you felt like you were being threatened to keep a secret in order to keep your job. I don't want someone here that's going to bully."

"So…" I say, not following.

"We've let Vivian go. She packed up her things last night and received her final check. She won't be allowed back on Camp Arthur property."

"She's been fired?" I ask. "What does this mean for me?"

"Well, I'm hoping you'll finish the summer out, we only have a week and a half left."

"Of course I'll stay," I say. "But what about my training? Who's going to help me?"

"I've asked one of the day camp counselors to work with you for the final week with campers. She'll be staying with us to help you in the evenings, but from seven in the morning until six at night, you'll be on your own. It shouldn't be too bad. You'll have other counselors to help you."

Sampson nods along. "And it's only for a week. If you need any help, let us know. Me and Ben especially. We're here for you."

Mr. Garreth's phone rings and he excuses himself to answer it, taking his conversation into the lobby.

I turn to Sampson, who seems to not know where he should be looking, or what he should be doing.

"Did you tell your dad about Josh too? About Viv going behind your back with him?" I ask, my eyes wide.

Sampson shakes his head. "I couldn't do that. I was honestly embarrassed, I still am. I don't want to admit to my dad my girlfriend cheated on me."

"You're just going to let him get away with it?" I whisper. How could Sampson possibly be okay with Josh keeping his job here?

"One day he'll pay for what he did," Sampson says. "I'm a strong believer in karma. It'll come back on him. And I only have to see his face for less than a month anyway. Then he's gone."

I nod my head and relax back into my chair. I didn't give Sampson enough credit. If it was me, I'd be seeking revenge on both Viv and Josh.

Sampson clears his throat. "So, are you okay? With finishing camp, that is? I don't want you to feel uncomfortable."

"Why would I be uncomfortable? With Viv gone, camp should finally be enjoyable again."

He shakes his head. "I get that, but I meant with us. I mean, I was kind of a jerk to you when I found out. You didn't have to let me sleepover last night, you should have kicked me to the curb for the way I reacted. Instead of being mad at Viv, I was mad at you. You were just trying to help."

"You were," I agree, "but it doesn't change the fact I should have told you sooner. Viv honestly just scared me, that probably sounds stupid, but she did. I don't know what you…"

"Saw in her?" he asks, finishing my sentence for me.

I blush and nod. "No offense."

"None taken, I guess I thought she could eventually go back to the old Viv I knew, before she became popular amongst her sisters. People change right?"

"Sometimes for the worst, obviously."

"Just promise me the next time I refuse to believe something that's so painfully true, you'll knock some sense into me."

"Only if you promise me you won't let there be a next time."

"Deal," he says and reaches out to shake my hand. I accept to agreement just as we hear his father's footsteps coming down the hall, ending his conversation.

"Sorry about that, you two," Mr. Garreth says, sitting his phone back on his desk. "You're dismissed unless you have any questions."

"I'm good," Sampson nods, and I nod my head in agreement.

"Alright, I'll see you guys later on at dinner," Mr. Garreth says.

"So," I say when we step outside the building into the sunlight. "What happens now?"

"We go to our pre-lunch activities," Sampson says,

placing a hand over his forehead to block the sun from his eyes.

"No, I meant…" I begin to say, but maybe all of it was in my head, all of the sweet things he has said. "Never mind."

Maybe I looked too far into Sampson and the signals I thought he was sending all summer. He probably did only like me as a friend. Who am I kidding? He just broke up with his girlfriend, the last thing I want to happen is to become a rebound summer girl.

"What's up, Penelope?" Sampson asks.

I shake my head. "Nothing, I just want to make sure you enjoy your new found freedom! You're a free man now, no more Viv the fire breathing girlfriend nipping at your feet! Congrats!"

Sampson smiles and my heart melts. "Thanks! Is it bad I'm kind of over it already?"

"Nah, it's probably your brain going through the stages of grief."

"Feels like I breezed right through them, I'm pretty sure I'm already on acceptance."

I return his smile and nod my head toward the art building. "I better get going, I don't want Dora to panic from having so many girls to take care of."

"Kay, I'll see you later on."

I wave and walk away, ignoring the voice in the back of my head—the voice telling me now's my time. Viv's gone, it's okay to be the rebound. I don't want to be that girl though, the one that spent months of her life trying to convince a guy she was worthy of his attention and affection. I'm not going to grovel at his feet, begging him to be my boyfriend. I'll let him come to me. He'll realize I'm a catch one day, it'll happen when it happens.

You're not supposed to rush a good thing. So I won't.

TWENTY

"You okay?" Dora asks as I walk into the art building. The girls are working on pillowcases they'll be tie dying later on. They're doodling on the pillowcases, some writing their names in large print, others writing their favorite thing about Camp Arthur and trying to illustrate the activity.

"I'm okay," I tell her, leaning against the counter in the back of the room. "I assume you know what went down?"

Dora shrugs. "Bits and pieces, mostly gossip. Some people are saying you got Viv fired because you and Sampson have a baby on the way."

I stare at her blankly, my jaw dropping.

"Of course, that's one of the rumors," she says. "You don't seem like the type of person who would go about stealing a girl's boyfriend and getting pregnant by him."

"Well, I would hope I don't."

"Do you want to talk about what actually happened?" She asks.

I sigh and take a deep breath. "It's honestly stupid, remember Casanova-- err Josh? Well, Viv and Josh were hooking up all summer and I caught them. Viv threatened that if I told Sampson, I could kiss Camp Arthur goodbye, so I kept it a secret."

She nods. "And you told…"

I shake my head. "Nope, Sampson caught them in the act, at the sleepover."

"Oh, shit," she whispers. "That's why he was moping around for a few days."

"It would appear so," I say. "I came clean to Sampson, told him about Viv's threats and I guess he told his dad. Mr. Garreth doesn't appreciate bullies, so he fired Viv."

"Huh," Dora says. "I haven't heard that one floating around in the rumor mill."

"Ah, because it's not a rumor," I say. "Be sure to spread it though. I'd rather the truth be out there. I don't want to be known as a homewrecker."

"You and Sam aren't getting together?"

I shake my head. "No, not at all."

Kelsey waves me over to join her and Sophia, Daisy and one of Dora's campers. I join them and notice Sophia has taken a liking to Kelsey, she's trying to copy everything Kelsey is drawing on her pillowcase, which is just a bunch of daisies and swirls.

"That's so good," I say, complementing Sophia.

"I wonder where she got the idea from," Kelsey says sarcastically.

I kick her leg under the table and she yelps.

"I mean," Kelsey begins to correct herself. "It's so pretty! You're so good at drawing flowers!"

Sophia beams. "You think so?

Kelsey and I both nod and Daisy leans over on the table to admire Sophia's attempt at drawing daisies.

"Daisy," Sophia says. "You're so lucky, I wish I was in your cabin. Then I could hang out with you guys all the time."

"Come back next year!" Daisy exclaims. "We could be bunk buddies!"

"Are you coming back next year?" Sophia asks Kelsey, looking at her with hopeful eyes.

Kelsey is coloring one of the flowerhead on one of her flowers. "I don't think so kiddo, I'll be old next year."

"Old?" Gasps the girls. "You're only 10."

Kelsey laughs. "Hate to break it to you kiddo's but I'm 16, I'll be too old to be a camper next year."

Daisy turns to Sophia and tries to whisper her question but we can still hear her. "Did you know she was *that* old?"

"Hey," Kelsey says, faking offense. "Why you gotta be mean? I'm not old, old."

The two young campers exchange a look with each other but don't respond to Kelsey, they just go back to doodling with their sharpies on their pillowcases.

"Don't get too offended," I tell Kelsey. "If you're old, I'm senile."

"I guess the grass isn't always greener," she says, finishing up her pillowcase. "So, do you need to talk about what happened while you were gone?"

"Not right now," I say, watching Sophia, Daisy and the other younger camper draw.

"When you're ready, I'm here to listen," Kelsey says. "I know there's a rule about keeping stuff to yourself, but you are my friend. I'm here to help."

I nod. "So, how are you and Lain doing? Only a few days left, what happens next?"

She sighs and rests her chin on her hands, leaning on the table. "Honestly, probably nothing. I like keeping him as my summer crush. Who knows who he is outside of camp? I like the idea of just remembering him as is."

"I get that," I say. "You don't want to ruin a good thing."

"Exactly, maybe one day we'll cross paths at college or something, maybe not. I'm not going to force anything. Besides, I still have one year of high school left, I will not let a long-distance relationship keep me from enjoying my final year."

I smirk at her. "You think things through, don't you?"

"More than you know, Pen. More than you know."

"Have you met the girl who will be helping with our cabin?"

Kelsey nods. "She's a total witch with a B."

My heart starts racing, I can't go through another Viv who is power hungry and enjoys belittling others. Kelsey smiles and hugs me tight.

"I'm kidding," she says. "She's actually super nice, we met her last night. She let us have a 'spa night' and brought some activity books for the younger girls. Her name is Winnie, it's short for something."

"I love Winnie!" Daisy says, sitting up in her seat and presenting her nails to me. "Look, she did my nails. She made them say I love camp."

I look at her nails, and sure enough they do say I love camp, instead of the world love, there's a cute little heart. Daisy continues gushing over Winnie and I smile and listen to her story, she seems to have won my campers over.

"She's not mean like, Viv," Daisy says in a whisper. "She's not coming back, right?"

I'm not sure what to say, so I just nod my head. "Well, I can't wait to meet Winnie! Alright, finish up your pillow-cases, it's time to get lunch and we're on duty to do the table settings."

"Aww man," Daisy says. "I hate doing table settings."

"Well, you should clean up your bunk a little," I say. "You know the rule, if you win the clean cabin for the day award, you don't have to set up and clean up the mess hall that day."

"We'll win tomorrow," Daisy says. "I promise to clean all the cabin tonight!"

"We'll see about that," Kelsey says. "I found one of your stinky socks under my bed this morning. You got a lot to clean."

"My stocks aren't stinky!" Daisy protests.

I burst in a fit of laughter. "Okay, okay. Let's get this place back to the way we found it. I hear we're having chicken nuggets for lunch. That's your favorite, right Daisy?"

"Yes!" She says and starts putting away her markers.

I grab their pillowcases and go around to the rest of the tables to collect theirs. Tomorrow morning we're tie-dying them so they'll be ready to take home when camp is over. Once they're finished drying, we'll have a day when fellow campers sign them like a yearbook for camp. It's been a tradition for years.

"Pen," Kelsey says. "I made one for you too. I know this was one of your favorite things to do."

I turn to look and she's holding up the pillowcase. It reads HOME across the center and it looks like the girls in my cabin have already signed it. I smile and take it from her, holding it up and reading some of the cute little notes they scribbled out as my girls crowd around.

"You guys, this is so sweet," I say. "I'll have to take this with me when I start school."

The girls embrace me in a group hug, and a small tear trickles down my cheek. The first happy tear I've cried all summer. This is my home again.

Winnie is amazing. Anyone is amazing compared to what Viv has put me through this summer, but Winnie is awesome. Even though Winnie is more used to the day campers, she already seems like a great counselor for the overnight campers. She shook my hand the second she walked in the cabin and told me how excited she was to be helping out.

"Do you have any plans for tonight?" she asks.

"Actually," I say, "I was thinking we could take the girls out for a surprise. I found these old Chinese lanterns in the back of the closet, and I thought it would be fun to send them up and lay out under the stars. I thought it would be a fun bonding time for the girls before camp is over."

"That sounds awesome," she says. "Should I tell them to get their shoes on?"

I nod. "I'll grab some spare blankets and the box of lanterns. Think you can find some matches?"

"Sure thing."

We gather up our supplies and the girls are all beaming with excitement. We never did fun stuff with Viv in charge; she was always complaining about the bugs at night and the fact we were constantly doing things throughout the day. I take a moment to call Mr. Garreth and let him know our cabin is going on a small night walk and doing a bonding activity.

He gives the okay and tells me what a cool idea the Chinese lanterns are. I'm not sure if he's approving it because he feels sorry about what happened with Viv, or if he actually thinks it's a fun idea. Either way, I'm excited to finally do something fun and memorable with my cabin.

"Time to line up," I tell the girls. "Did everyone put on some bug spray?"

I get a few sleepy nods and some excited 'yeahs' from the girls as they all make their way to the door. Winnie comes to the back of the line, holding some blankets and nods at me.

"Alright," I say. "We need to stay quiet, most of camp is already asleep. Let's head out."

"Where are we going?" asks Chelle as we walk up the trail, my flashlight beam guiding our way.

"It's a secret," I say. "It'll be fun. I promise."

"It better," Olive says. "My book was just getting to a cool part. Now I will spend all night wondering if the goblins won."

"You're such a nerd," Brittney says.

"Am not!" Olive shouts back.

"Are too! All you've done this summer is read," Brittney counters.

"Girls," I hiss as I stop the group. "Stop picking on each other, no more bullying. We only have a few days left of camp, be nice to each other."

If it wasn't dark, I'd say both girls would be blushing and avoiding eye contact with me. They both apologize, to me and to each other, and then we start to walk again, heading for the center of camp.

The intramural field is only hit by a few lights, none that will prevent us from seeing the stars, but enough so Winnie and I can light the lanterns. I lay the blankets out for the girls to lay down on, their heads meeting in a circle. Winnie and I pull out some lanterns and start assembling them.

"Alright, I'll call you up one at a time, and you can come up and make a wish, then we'll send your lantern off into the sky," I say.

"Do we have to say the wish out loud?" Daisy asks, sitting up from the circle to look at me.

"Nope, you can keep it to yourself or tell us," I say. "Do you want to go first?"

"Yeah, yeah, yeah!" she shouts, getting up from the group and coming over to me. I hold the lantern and Winnie prepares the match. Daisy closes her eyes tightly and whispers a wish to the lantern as Winnie uses the flame to light it.

Instead of the lantern being carried up into the air like it's supposed to, the flame quickly goes out and it falls back to the ground.

"Well that didn't quite work how it was supposed to," I say, bending down to find some instructions for them, but the box doesn't contain anything helpful.

"Maybe it's not windy enough," Winnie suggests.

I shake my head. "No, I don't think it has anything to do with wind."

"Does this mean my wish isn't going to come true?" Daisy says, anxiety in her voice.

"No, let's just try another one," I say. "That one might just be defective."

We do the process all over again and Daisy makes her wish, but the lantern just sinks.

"Maybe it's her wish," Brittney suggests and the other girls giggle. "She's probably wishing for something impossible."

"Am not!" Daisy protests.

"Why don't you go lay down with the rest of the girls," Winnie says to Daisy. "Penelope and I will try to get these working."

Daisy reluctantly goes over and lays down, staring up at the stars. The girls talk and giggle amongst themselves as Winnie and I try lantern after lantern, but none of them float into the air like they're supposed to.

Finally on the last one, as we're about to give up, it goes into the air with ease. The girls all clap and cheer and I tell them all to make a quick wish, as cheesy as it is.

Winnie and I go to join the girls, and they make room for us to squish between them and watch the lantern venture away into the night.

"Alright, ladies," I say. "How about we go around in a circle and say what our favorite thing we did at camp this year was? I'll go first. Mine was watching all of you come out of your shells this year. Kelsey?"

"I liked going on the hike we did with some of the guys," Kelsey says. "That was a ton of fun."

"Doing the ropes course was my favorite thing," Chelle says. "This was the first year I actually did all of the course. I usually chicken out."

"I liked the food!" Daisy says. "Mom hardly ever lets me eat chicken nuggets and tater tots. She says processed foods are bad for your figure."

I, along with all the other girls, laugh, my pudgy belly shaking. Clearly, I've had too many chicken nuggets myself. I probably should have paid more attention to my campers' dietary restrictions, but what Daisy's mom doesn't know won't hurt her. It's not like she had an allergy.

The girls continue sharing their favorite things about camp and talking about all their inside jokes. I stare up at the stars, watching as a plane way above us moves gently across the sky, it's blinking lights showing the way.

"How about you, Pen," Kelsey says, bumping my shoulder. "What was *really* your favorite part about this summer?"

I think for a moment, listening to the crickets chirp. "Right now," I say simply, "I want to remember camp at this moment—this moment is one of the best I've had, not just this summer, but probably every summer I've been here."

And it is. This summer wasn't ideal at all with all the drama that has occurred. Looking back though, I'm glad I worked here instead of sitting at home for three months waiting for school to begin. I did meet some nice people, Dora, Ben, Sampson, Kenny and Winnie.

I wouldn't want to relive this summer, but I would never wish it didn't happen. This summer was one of those times that shapes you and makes you who you're supposed to be.

TWENTY ONE

AUGUST

"Can you believe it's the last day?" Dora asks me, our feet swishing back and forth in the pool water. The campers are all splashing about, enjoying one final day in the sun. There's a large group under the gigantic mushroom fountain hiding from the sun, giggling as they push each other under the falling water.

I shake my head. "I honestly can't. I kind of wish we had at least another month."

"Another month with all the rugrats?" Ben asks as he sits down between me and Dora. I notice Dora blush when Ben looks at her and then at me.

"Okay," I confess. "Another month with half of them, the other half has me ready to lose my mind."

"There ya go," Ben says smiling. "What about you, Dora? Are you glad camp's done?"

"Well, it's not done. We still have a week of clean up."

Ben drops his head back to look at the sky. "Don't remind me! I hate clean up week. Why does it last a week?"

"Hmm," I say. "Probably because this place has been inhabited by hundreds of people all summer who haven't been the best neat freaks and have made a ton of messes."

"Don't be logical," Ben says looking at me from the corner of his eye. "No one likes logical."

He smiles though and slides himself into the pool, shivering a little as he goes.

"Cold?" Dora asks him.

His teeth chatter. "Not at all, why don't you join me, Dora?"

"No thanks," she says. "I'd rather not freeze my buns off."

"What if I want to freeze your buns off?"

Dora's blush deepens, and I smile, wondering what took Ben so long to show interest in Dora. Could it possibly be the fact he did it the right way, became friends with her all summer, and waited until his job was almost finished in order to start things?

"What's that supposed to mean?" she asks, but Ben doesn't respond. "Why are you looking at me like that? Don't you dare... Benjamin... stop..."

Before Dora can get up and walk away, Ben has one hand around each of her calves and pulls her into the pool. I'm glad she doesn't resist him, because if she were to fall on the concrete and scrape her skin, that would be a mess. The hard cement scraping across her body, I shudder at the thought as Dora flops into the pool, not graceful at all. She chokes on some water and rubs some water out of her eyes.

"You're such a jerk," she says, but her voice doesn't appear to actually mean it. "What if I didn't know how to swim?"

"I've seen you swim all summer," Ben says with a laugh. "I knew you could swim."

"That's beside the point," she says.

Standing up, I smile and shake my head, leaving them to their first lover's quarrel. I go over to one of the lawn chairs where my backpack is and lay down. Instead of pulling a book out like I would normally do, I just enjoy the sights and sounds of pool time. Kelsey, to my surprise, is actually hanging out with some of the girls in our cabin instead of Lain. Daisy is holding onto Sampson's back in the water, refusing to let go. She sees me and waves, which causes Sampson to also look in my direction.

I smile and wave back to them, relaxing into my chair more, leaning back and closing my eyes. If the sun wasn't so bright, I could fall asleep to the sounds of Camp Arthur.

"Hey," says a soft voice.

I squint one eye open and look up to see Sampson, water dripping down his skin. I used to feel nervous and ashamed when I looked at him, but now I feel fine, like any girl would feel looking at someone they like, even just as a friend, giddy but trying to stay cool.

"Hey stranger," I say, patting the chair next to me for him to sit down. We haven't talked since Viv has been gone. I've been keeping busy with my cabin girls and enjoying the final days with them. Sampson has also seemed to avoid me at all costs. The one time I tried to talk to him, he looked at me and walked away before I could approach him.

"Hey you," he says. "What's up?"

"Not much," I say as I rest my head against the lawn chair again. "Just hanging in there."

"Everything okay?" he asks. "Are you excited that the summer's almost over?"

"Nah, I'm not ready to go home."

"You only have a week or two back home, right?"

I nod my head. "Right, but I don't want to go back at all."

"Your parents?"

I breath in. I've only spoken to my parents a few times this summer because I've been so busy. Every time I've managed to call them, they're never together. I'm thinking they're not going to work it out. "Things aren't looking good."

"Sorry," Sampson says. "It'll get better."

I smile, but shake my head. "I don't think it will. I kind of wish they'd just go ahead and file for divorce, rip off that metaphorical bandage so we can move on. At least I'd have a week to get over it before I start school."

When I look at Sampson he's nodding, but not meeting my gaze. Maybe I shouldn't have said that, but I don't have anyone else to discuss this kind of stuff with. Things with Janine had never been fixed, Kelsey is my camper, and I don't know Winnie well. Sampson has been my friend this summer, my go-to person.

"Sampson," I say, not looking at him. "If you could do this summer over, would you change anything?"

Out of the corner of my eye, I see him look at me and then look out at the pool. "I don't know, would you?"

I look at him and nod my head. "Yeah, I'd change a lot."

He returns my gaze and nods. "If there was something I could do to fix that, you'd tell me, right?"

"You can't fix something that's already happened," I say. "It's all done. I guess that's where the expression 'I've made my bed and now I have to sleep in it' comes from. I can't change this summer."

He nods. "I'm sorry you were brought into this mess."

I chuckle. "Which one? My parents, or you and Viv?"

"Both?" he suggests. "I can't fix your parents, but I'll find a way to make things better with us, I promise."

I pull my knees up to my chest and rest my head on them, looking at Sampson. "You can't make those types of promises, besides, there is no 'us'."

"But Viv's not…"

I shake my head in protest. "You just broke up with

your girlfriend, Sampson. I will not be a rebound. I need you to take some time on your own. The worst thing someone can do after a breakup is jump into another relationship."

Sampson's shoulders fall and he turns away from me. "There's nothing I can do to change your mind, is there?"

"What I need right now is a friend. If you can be my friend, that's all I need right now."

He breathes deeply and his muscles relax. "I can do that. I can be your friend."

"Shall we start over then?" I suggest.

He smiles and reaches his hand over to me. "Hi, I'm Sampson. You are?"

"Penelope," I say, shaking his hand and holding onto it for a little too long. "Nice to meet you."

The second our hands part, I feel a piece of myself go missing, and I desperately want to hold his again, but I keep my composure. This might not be as easy as I wanted it to be, and I urge my heart to calm down as it speeds up its beat.

"Alright girls," I say clapping my hands and sitting down on the cold cement floor of the cabin, crisscross-applesauce style. "Come join me."

"What about feet off the floor time?" Daisy asks, pulling her blanket with her and sitting next to me.

"We're going to do a little cabin activity today since you guys leave tomorrow," I explain.

Winnie comes in with a few sheets of paper and some

markers, sitting them in the middle of the circle that all the girls are forming as they join us.

"Once, when I was a camper," I begin to say to the girls once everyone is sitting down, "I had a counselor who came up with this idea, and I wanted to share it with you. What we do is, everyone grabs a piece of paper and writes their name in the center, and then we'll pass to the person on our right and they'll write down something they love about you.

"My counselor called these 'warm and fuzzies' because they're used to make you feel happy. You can save your paper and hang it in your room or your locker and when you're feeling down, you can look at it and remember all the amazing friends you have here at Camp Arthur."

I look over at Kelsey and she smiles. This was one of our favorite things a counselor ever did with us when we were younger, and I always wished more counselors would do them.

Winnie passes around the paper for the girls and they all dive into the box of markers, looking for their favorite color. I write my name on my paper in loopy script and then we begin passing the papers around the circle. The girls take their time thinking of nice things to say to each other, and this is the quietest I've ever heard the cabin. The only thing I can hear is the telltale gliding of markers across paper.

Before I know it, my page reaches me again, and it's covered in the sweetest words I've read, though some of them are hard to make out. All the girls gush over what their fellow cabin mates have written about them. I'm sort of surprised they all seem to enjoy this as much as I did.

"Penelope, can you read mine?" Daisy asks, crawling into my lap. "I don't understand some of the words."

"Sure can," I say as I take her page in my hand. "Here,

Kelsey says that she loves your spunk, kid. Then here, Winnie says she hopes you come back next year because she loves how sweet you are…"

I finish reading her page and then the girls start dispersing, the older girls trying to figure out what they're going to wear to their final dinner and camp fire while the younger girls are struggling to find one more clean pair of socks. Daisy takes her page and runs to put it in her suitcase for safe keeping. I stand and take my own to the storage room, laying it on top of the dresser, next to a picture of Janine and I from senior prom. Huge smiles on our faces, ignoring our dates, hugging each other tightly.

I turn the frame on its face so I don't have to look at it for the rest of camp. It's time to start closing some of the chapters in my life aren't bringing me any happiness. Once I get back home, I will do just that. I will not let other people's opinions control my happiness. For once, I finally feel like I'm growing up.

"Alright campers," Mr. Garreth says as the bonfire burns in front of the stage he is on. "How was your summer?"

The campers all cheer for a good moment, all of them wired from the ice cream social we had after dinner. Now I know why we weren't allowed to give them sugar unless we're given permission, they turn into Gremlins and you can't calm them down from their sugar high.

Once the campers settle down a little, Mr. Garreth continues. "I'm so glad everyone could join us this summer! I know I had a great time getting to know everyone. I hope you guys come back next summer, we already started working on plans for the upcoming year. Raise your hand if you want to come back next year!"

A ton of campers' hands shoot up, along with some of my fellow counselors and CIT's, Kenny, Dora, and Sampson's hands among them. I don't raise my hand and when my eyes meet with Sampson's, his smile falls a little bit.

It's not that I don't want to come back next year, I just don't know where I'm going to be in ten months. For all I know, I could have a better part time job in college, and I feel like it's too early to decide on anything.

"I'm glad to see so many of you had a great time," Mr. Garreth says. "Now, counselors, the campers and I have a little surprise for you. You may or may not remember that day when you had some free time last week, but the campers have put together a little goodbye skit for you."

Mr. Garreth exits stage left and a few of the campers run behind stage to get ready. Four campers come out in Camp Arthur Staff t-shirts and baseball caps on backwards and start a rap about the summer they had and all their favorite activities, mentioning at one point all the 'cute hunnies in their hot swim sunnies'. Once their rap is complete, they exit the stage for a few more campers to come up and perform a skit about what they think counselors do in their spare time.

The other counselors and I burst into a fit of laughter when one of the younger boys pretends to be Sampson with his deep voice and talking about making flower headbands to wear. Sampson blushes and shakes his head. I smile and go back to watching the kids do their songs and skits.

They end it with all the campers gathered on the stage or around it, singing Camp Arthur's main camp song we drill into their heads all summer long.

We join in with them, wrapping our arms around each other and swaying back and forth. Everyone slowly goes back to their seats as we break into *Kumbaya My Lord* to soften the mood. Daisy comes over and sits in my lap, and I rest my chin on her head as we finish the song. I'm pretty sure she's fallen asleep against me by time the singing ends.

Mr. Garreth quietly dismisses us and I can't move. I don't want to wake Daisy up. Winnie gathers up the rest of the girls and Sampson walks by me and leans in.

"I can carry her for you," he whispers.

"You sure?" I ask. "I can wake her up."

He shakes his head and takes her from me. She wraps her legs around his torso and holds tight to his neck, not as asleep as she seemed to be. I follow behind Sampson and see Daisy smiling against his shirt collar.

That little trickster.

I shine my flashlight in front of Sampson so he can see where he's walking in the dark. Our group is a few feet in front of us, all of them whispering to each other, my cabin mingling with his. We reach my cabin and all the girls say their goodbyes to the boys. I take Daisy from Sampson, almost unable to hold her fifty-pound body.

"Do you need me to carry her in?" he asks.

I shake my head and readjust her weight on my hip. "No, I can make it into the cabin. Thanks for helping. Though, I'm pretty sure she could walk."

I tickle her side and she giggles a little bit, but tightens her grip on me.

Sampson smiles at me and I return it. If I didn't have a camper in my arms right now, I'm not sure what would happen. In a movie, this would be the part in the plot where the characters finally get together with a sweet kiss. Soft music would start playing in the background and the camera would pan up from the kissing characters to the night sky, and a shooting star would probably pass across the frame with 'the end' written in white against the darkness. This is where it would end, a happy ending to a drama filled plot.

But this isn't a movie. This isn't the ending.

Sampson clears his throat. "I'll see you bright and early tomorrow. Don't forget to make your camper awards."

"Yeah, you too," I say. "Have a good night."

Sampson smiles and turns around, flicking his wrist in a wave and then shoving his hands into his shorts pockets.

Daisy turns to watch him go too and then looks back to me. "He likes you."

I smile and shake my head. "You're too young to worry about romance and relationships."

Daisy rolls her eyes and I slide her off of me. "I watch Cinderella, I'm not too young for romance."

"Well, excuse me, missy," I say. "Here I thought you were a little girl."

Daisy trots off to the cabin door and before she opens it, she motions for me to bend down to her level.

"You and Mr. Sampson need to just kiss already."

With that, she quickly goes inside and the door slams behind her. A little girl is pretty much telling me to grow some balls and make the next move. To be young and naive again, and not worry about what may or may not happen after a big decision like that...

Before I go back inside, I look up at the stars. There's nothing written in them, and I at least find comforting in a small way. This isn't my ending. It can't end here.

"All packed up?" I ask the girls as I round the corner into the bunk area.

I get a few sad sounding acknowledgements. The younger girls come running toward me and hug me tightly.

"Do we have to go?" they ask in unison.

"Yep," I say. "Summer's coming to an end, it's time to get back to the real world. I'm sure you miss your friends back home."

They both shake their heads. "We'll miss you more."

I smile and pry their hands off of my waist. "You can write me letters, you have my address."

"Can't we stay here with you?" Daisy asks, plopping down on her bare bed, the sheets and pillow already packed away.

"I have to go home too, silly. I have to see my parents and go to school."

The girls pout and I go back into the spare room, grabbing their going away goodie bags I made up from the last time I went into town. When I come back in, my arms full with the bags, and I pass them out to all the girls. They open them practically before they're even out of my hands.

I packed them some candy, a little kit to makes smores at home, and a friendship bracelet I made during some of the nights when I couldn't sleep.

"This is awesome!" Ronnie squeals. "I haven't had candy in so long!"

Kelsey takes her bracelet from the bag and then hands the candy off to the younger girls. She ties the small knotted string and then rolls it onto her wrist and looks up to me with a smile.

Sitting on the edge of her bunk, I wrap my arm around her shoulder and lean my head against hers.

"Are you going to come back next year?" I ask quietly.

She breathes in and lets the air out in a quick burst

along with her words. "I don't think so. I think I'm ending camp on a good note, and I don't want to ruin that."

"Like I did?" I ask, moving away from her and arching an eyebrow.

She shakes her head and bumps my shoulder. "You didn't ruin camp, you just... okay, you might have ruined the way you see camp."

"Yeah, pretty much."

"Look on the bright side though," she says.

"Don't you say it…"

She grins and proceeds to say it anyway. "At least you finally came out of your shell and met a cute counselor that liked you back."

"We're *friends*," I say, putting an emphasis on the friend part.

"No, you're friends with me, Kenny, and Dora. You like Sam and you know it."

"And if I do?"

Kelsey sighs and stands up to put on her backpack. "My dear, dear Penelope, stop being afraid of letting your guard down."

"I'm not," I protest.

She shakes her head. "You are. I've known you for years at camp, where you're supposed to come out of your comfort zone and you're always more resistant than you mean to be."

I let out a sigh and stand up, avoiding bumping my head on the bunk above us. "Let's start moving everyone's bags over to the welcome center. They have to be ready for when the parents get here."

"I'll help the younger girls," Kelsey says as she grabs two of her bags.

"I'll stay here while you and Winnie take trips over with the girls," I say.

Kelsey gathers three of the younger girls and has them follow her out of the cabin with their stuff. Winnie follows behind, looking like a donkey being weighed down by duffels, sleeping bags, and backpacks.

"Remind me not to volunteer for dismissal day next year," Winnie says, already out of breath.

I laugh and shake my head. "You go this trip and then I'll go next."

I run over to hold the door open for her and the girls just in time to hear one of the gators come to a stop. Kenny and Sampson hop off when they put it in park.

"Need some help?" Kenny asks, already taking bags off of Winnie.

"Thank god," she says. "There's no way I would make it. I overestimated what I thought I could carry."

"Ya don't say," Kenny replies as he walks the bags up and tosses them in the back of the cart.

"Is your cabin already done taking their bags?" I ask them.

"Yup," Kenny says. "That's what's so great about boys, they don't pack a bunch of stuff they won't need. We walked them over to the mess hall to prep for lunch and thought we'd help everyone else."

"Thanks for coming," I say. "There's a few more bags in the cabin, should only need two more trips after this haul."

"We're on it," Kenny smiles as him and Sampson load up the last of the bags the girls had and the guy's head off for the welcome center.

"Alright, might as well grab another bag or two," I say. "I'll send you ladies off and then send the rest when the Sampson and Kenny come back."

The girls all complain and go back in the cabin to grab more of their stuff. Thank God Viv isn't here, I imagine she'd pull out her metaphorical whip and be pushing us to get things done in an instant.

Winnie and the girls head in the direction of the welcome center, and I go back in the cabin to start doing some clean up and to make sure nothing's left behind. First I make sure all the remaining bags have names on them and then place them just outside the door for Kenny and Sampson to pick up. Then I go to the cleaning closet to make sure I have enough supplies for tomorrow's cabin cleaning on my own.

"Hey," comes a male voice from behind me.

I jump and slam my hand against my chest when I realize it's only Sampson and he's staring at me with a shy smile. "You scared the crap out of me, Sampson," I say as I close the closet door.

"Sorry," he says, leaning on the wall. "I just wanted to make sure this was the last load you needed me to take over."

"Yeah, should be." I glance around him to the open door but Kenny's not there. "What happened to your help?"

"I sent him to help at the mess hall. Can we sit and talk?"

"I can't, the girls will be back soon and…"

"They're all at the mess hall too. Winnie's watching them."

I sigh and brush past him, not wanting to have whatever conversation he's wanting take place inside the cabin. He follows me out to the picnic table and we both sit down on the top of it, our feet resting on the seat. He leans down, his elbows on his knees.

"What's up, Sampson?" I ask, leaning back on the table, my arms supporting me. I feel a splinter of wood stab my finger, but I ignore it. I'm trying to be cool, calm, and collected.

"I just feel…" he doesn't complete his sentence, and I'm not sure if I even want him to. Instead, he switches his train of thought and changes what he would say. "Are you excited to start school?"

"I guess. Nervous. Please tell me college isn't as intimidating as they make it out to be."

He smiles at me. "It's not, just stay away from Dr. Whyte. He's a crazy guy from Europe who thinks Americans are lazy slobs and will tell you you're worthless and incompetent because his five year old knows six different languages and most students barely communicate in full sentences."

I stare at him, my mouth agape. "You're not helping at all, he sounds awful."

"Well as long as you're not taking any poli-sci courses, you're fine."

"I'll be sure to steer clear of that," I say. We sit in silence, and I know that's not what he wants to talk about. "Sampson, what did you *really* want to talk to me about?"

"Is it that obvious?" he asks, and I nod. "I don't want this to be one of the last times I see you."

"It won't be," I say, and his eyes light up. "You'll see me for the rest of the week. I'm sure we'll be on cleanup duty together sometime this week."

"You know that's not what I meant…"

I breathe in. "Sampson… I like you… a lot…"

"But?" he says.

"We've been over this, I'm not going to be a rebound. I deserve to be courted. I deserve someone who wants to get to know me, all of me, someone whom I can call any time of day to talk to."

"You know I'm that," he pleads. "I'm here for you.

Literally, I was there answering my phone when you were in trouble earlier this summer."

I shake my head. "I know, but I need you to take some time to yourself. You just got out of that mess of a relationship. You need to learn to love yourself again before you can love someone else."

"There's no changing your mind about this, is there?"

I look him in the eyes. "Not yet, but one day, yes. If you'll still have me. All I ask is that once I leave here, you don't come looking for me. I want us to be like that Serendipity movie, if we meet again, it's meant to be."

He nods and then looks down at his feet. "You know, I didn't think it was possible for someone to have the power to break your heart when they didn't even know they had it."

My heartbeat speeds up and butterflies thrash around in my stomach. Breaking Sampson's heart was the last thing I wanted to do.

I ignore the ache in my own heart and bump my shoulder against his. "Don't you think you're sounding a little over dramatic?"

"Maybe just a little," he says.

I reach for his hand and hold it in mine. It feels strange holding his hand, it feels strange to make such a bold move, but it also feels nice because I can notice him relax a little next to me. His hand is double the size of mine. His nails are trimmed so much that there's no white tip to them, and his finger tips are rough in places, possibly from years of playing a stringed instrument.

He laces our fingers together and I lean my head on his shoulder. How is it possible that this feels so right?

"I could stay here forever, like this," I say, closing my eyes and listening to the nature around us.

"Then stay," he whispers.

"If only," I reply, opening my eyes and lifting my head from his shoulder, but still holding onto his hand. "I have to get back to real life. I can't hide away at camp forever."

"Sure, you can, my parents are doing it, I'm sort of doing it."

I stare at him and roll my eyes. "That's different, you guys live here. I have to go back to my home and try not to worry about the future of my parents' marriage."

"If you need me, you can call, you know that," he says, squeezing my hand.

"I know," I say. "But you're not always going to be around. I can't attach myself to you."

"Why not? What are you so afraid of?"

I shrug my shoulders. "Not being the girl you think I am. It happens all the time, right? Girls get clingy quickly and guys don't like that."

"I *love* clingy," Sampson says. "You have no idea. Clingy is the best."

"You say that," I chuckle. "But I doubt you truly do."

"Hello, look at my last relationship, she wasn't clingy at all and that turned out horribly. Clingy would be a fantastic change."

"Do you want there to be an *us*?" I ask him. "Do you want things to not end?"

"Yes!" he blurts out. "That's what I've been trying to tell you for days now. I want you. Clinginess and all."

"How about we compromise," I suggest.

"And what are the details to this compromise?"

"I'm not planning on dating anyone, I have too much to deal with right now with school starting. Guys are the last thing I need to worry about, but I don't want you to start seeing other girls because I do like you, a lot.

"Let's just say we leave camp and we don't talk to each other, you handle your stuff and I'll handle mine. You can give yourself some time to move on from Viv without moving on with someone else, including me, and then, let's say we run into each other on campus, then we know it's meant to be."

"What happens if we don't run into each other?" he asks softly.

"If we don't run into each other our first semester… then we should both move on."

"You don't want that," he says, probably hearing the sadness in my voice.

"I don't, but maybe that's how it should be."

"So," he says. "Where are the top five places you're sure to be on campus?"

I laugh and pull my hand out of his. "That's cheating, it has to be by chance that you find me."

"At least tell me two of the places."

"Fine," I say rolling my eyes. "My dorm and the library."

"You suck," he says. "Those are a given."

"You asked for two," I say.

As I'm about to get up and leave, Sampson grabs me by the wrist and gently tugs me back to him. I'm standing between his legs and he's looking at my lips intently. I bite my bottom lip, feeling self-conscious. He pushes a fallen strand of my hair behind my ear and before I know it, his breath is mingling with mine.

His lips press gently against mine, and I accidently let out a soft sigh, praying he didn't just hear what he does to me. I've never had a kiss as sweet and amazing as this. It takes all my effort to not wrap my fingers in his hair or pull him closer to me by the lanyard around his neck.

When our lips part, he leans his forehead against mine, and I keep my eyes closed.

"Sorry," he whispers. "The thought of possibly never getting to kiss you again got to me."

"Don't apologize," I say. "We should head to the mess hall though, we need to see our campers off."

He nods and pulls me into a hug. When we break apart, he loads up the gator with the remaining bags and we drive the final items over to the welcome center in silence, but I can still feel the butterflies floating in my stomach from that kiss.

It's going to be a long semester if I don't get to see him again. That was probably the stupidest compromise I have ever made.

TWENTY TWO

Saying goodbye is always the hardest part about camp. This time is a little different for me though, especially since I'm not leaving yet, I'm watching each of my campers leave, and that's a little overwhelming.

The second we finished awarding campers their awards and singing a closing song, the parents started snatching their children and leaving. Clearly, they don't want to stick around too long. The refreshment table is clear of cookies and fruit punch and after just a few minutes, the only things left are a few used cups and tons of crumbs.

I go over to the table and start throwing the empty cups into a bag for recycling. Most of the campers are already gone, at least mine are. A few of them hugged me good-bye, but other than that I think they were all too excited to get back to their virtual worlds in their phones. Most of them had their phones turned on before the closing cere-mony was even finished.

Arms wrap around my waist and I drop the bag as someone rests their chin on my shoulder.

"You didn't think I'd leave without saying goodbye, did you?"

"I was hoping our friendship ran deeper than that," I say as I turn to hug Kelsey.

"Of course it is," she says with a smile and squeezes me tightly once more before pulling me away. "Promise to invite me to some cool parties at college?"

"When you're eighteen," I say, laughing. "Keep in

touch, seriously. I hate when we don't talk once camp is over."

"Me too, I just suck as a social human, I get so caught up in everything."

"In boys, you get caught up in boys and their drama," I correct, and she playfully punches me on the shoulder.

Her parents shout her name and her dad points at his watch.

"Well," she says. "This is it, my last time leaving camp as a camper."

"I hope that means you'll come back next year."

"We'll see," she says.

I grasp my hands together and bribe her the only way that I know will work. "Think about all the guy counselors you'll finally have a chance to flirt with…"

She narrows her eyes at me. "You, my dear, play dirty… and that's why I keep you around!"

"Get out of here," I say, hugging her one more time. "Before your parents have to drag you out of here."

She waves goodbye, and I watch as she heads out of the welcome center with her parents, and then I continue to finish cleaning up. I tie off the bag and take it outside around back to the recycle bin and run into Kenny on the way.

"Hey!" he says, a bit more cheery than usual.

"Hey yourself, all your campers gone?"

He nods. "Yup, just sent off the last few, yours?"

"Same, Kelsey just left."

Kenny takes the bag out of my hand and tosses it up into the large recycling bin and motions for me to walk with him. "Now that everyone's gone, we need to talk."

"Uh oh," I say. "That doesn't sound good at all."

When I look at Kenny, he's blushing. "No, it's nothing, I just need a huge favor, and I think you can help me."

I look at him skeptically, stopping in my steps. "Okay… what is it?"

He shoves his hands in his pockets. "You and Sampson are friends right?"

"I mean, yeah. So are you."

"But he actually likes you…" Kenny says.

I squint my eyes at him and cross my arms over my chest. "Would you just spit it out? What do you need?"

"I need you to convince Sampson to let me have the cabin to myself for the rest of the week!" The words quickly tumble out of his mouth and I'm still wondering what he means.

"I guess I can," I say. "May I ask why?"

"You know Winnie?" When I stare at him like he's an idiot he continues. "Well, of course you do, she helped you with your campers. Well, Winnie and I kind of… like each other and she's been sending me these signals…"

"Signals?" I ask.

"Yeah, signals," he says. "I mean, Jesus, I'm sounding like a scum bag aren't I? Look, she told me if I could arrange to have the cabin to myself, she'd stay at camp for the final days instead of heading home. I like her."

"You're planning on shacking up?" I ask. "And you want me to ask Sampson to allow that? Where's he supposed to stay?"

"I don't know," Kenny says, voice squeaking. "His parents own the camp, he can stay at their place. He could even just set up a tent, I just need him out of our cabin."

"I don't know, Kenny," I say shaking my head. "This seems kind of shitty to do to Sampson. Kicking him out of his cabin."

"I've got it!" Kenny says, a smile branching out across his face. "Invite him to stay with you or go to his parents! Haven't you two wanted some alone time too? I heard his parents are going out on an overnight date, Mr. Garreth's wife got him some tickets to the Knoxville Symphony, so they're just getting a hotel and coming back early tomorrow morning.

"Doesn't the sound of staying in a house with him instead of a mildew smelling cabin sound a lot better? Think of the nice clean shower you won't have to wear sandals in."

I shake my head and turn from him, but he's right. "Fine," I say with no plan at all. "I'll do your dirty work. You owe me though."

Kenny pulls me in a tight hug and bounces up and down. I keep my hands to my side, weirded out by his strange version of saying 'thank you'. "You're the best," he says as he pulls away from me.

"I know, remember that."

Kenny nods and turns around, practically sprinting for his cabin, most likely to clean it up a little. The boys' cabins tend to be pig sties. I turn around, heading for my own cabin to get a head start on clean up. I decide to just go ahead and text Sampson a warning to avoid his cabin at all cost.

"Hey, Kenny needs the cabin to himself tonight. I would get what you need for the next twenty-four hours and go," I text.

He sends back a response right away. "Not *you* and Kenny, right?"

I send back a winky face with a teasingly message. "Why?"

My phones shows that he's typing, but then stops and starts again only to stop once more before settling on responding with a sad face emoji.

Now I feel guilty. I won't play with his emotions like Viv did.

"You have nothing to worry about," I type. "Him and Winnie will be using your cabin to hang out."

"Don't scare me like that," he sends back quickly. "I thought the whole plan on keeping our distance until school was just to make me feel better."

"Not at all," I send back, and then in another text, "Want to help me clean the art building tomorrow? I signed up but no one else is willing."

"Sure, I'll be there. After breakfast?"

"Sounds good."

"Penelope," says a familiar female voice walking behind me as I'm heading up from my cabin to the mess hall. I finished cleaning up my cabin so now I'm starving. I could use a dozen of the chicken nuggets and a plate of tater tots right now.

I turn to see Molly following behind me. "Hey, how are you?" I ask.

"I'm good," she says, coming up and wrapping an arm around my shoulder. "Haven't seen you in a while. How've you been?"

We walk up the hill, her arm still around my shoulder. "I've been doing better, thanks for asking."

"Good, I'm so glad to hear that."

"What brings you to these parts?" I ask, realizing I've never seen her walking around camp.

"I thought I'd go for a little hike. Where are you headed?"

"Dining hall, I'm starving. Been cleaning like a crazy person since the campers left earlier."

"Would you be interested in a homemade meal?" she asks.

"Possibly, you sure I wouldn't be intruding?"

"Of course you wouldn't be," she says and checks her watch. "Why don't you get a snack and then head over at 3, dinner will be ready then, we're eating early because we have a show in the city to catch. I'll even make brownies."

"You know how to bribe a girl, don't you?" I ask with a smile.

"What can I say? I enjoy having you around. I'll see you then?"

"Sure thing," I say as I head up the concrete stairs to the mess hall. "See you then."

Mrs. Garreth waves bye and heads down toward the bridge which leads to the rest of camp. Inside the cafeteria, all the tables are already pushed to one side of the hall, with all the benches on top of them. The dining staff is already getting the room cleaned. There's a few counselors in the meeting room eating some dinner, laughing, and talking. I surprise myself by grabbing an apple and heading in to join them. This is how it should have been all summer. I shouldn't have been so worried about joining my fellow counselors. After all, there's nothing to worry about at Camp Arthur, it's my happy place.

I climb the stairs to the Garreth's house, my heart hammering out of my chest. I feel silly showing up empty handed, like I should be bringing them a bottle of wine or something. I shouldn't be this nervous. I've had dinner with them before, I've had ice cream with Mrs. Garreth, and

I've watched crappy daytime TV with her. What's changed?

Opening the screen door I ring the doorbell and hear Sampson's deep voice coming from inside.

"You expecting someone, mom?" he says, his voice coming closer to the door.

When he opens it, his jaw drops but he quickly smiles. "Hey you, kicked out of your cabin, too?"

I grin at him. "Nope, your mom invited me for dinner." I look him up and down. He's wearing a Maryville t-shirt and grey sweatpants, clearly settled in for the night. "You going to invite me in?"

He moves to let me slide in the doorway and closes it behind me. I turn in time to see him looking me over. I'm glad I decided to put on a red and white sun dress that Winnie gave me from her recent shopping spree. She said it didn't fit her and it was on sale for only ten dollars, so there was no sense in taking it back. It would have cost more money in gas to drive back to the mall.

"You look nice," Sampson manages to say as I slide my white Keds off and drop my backpack next to them. "Hot date tonight?"

I smile. "Just a nice family dinner."

"Well, I feel way underdressed," he says, shoving his hands in his pockets.

"Is that Penelope?" Mrs. Garreth asks, coming around the corner. "Well look at you, that's a pretty dress."

"Laundry day," I lie. "Nothing else to wear."

"Sampson," Molly says. "Why don't you grab Penelope a drink, dinner will be ready in about ten minutes."

"What would you like?" he asks, leading me to the kitchen.

"Water's fine, thanks," I say.

Sampson grabs me a glass from the cabinet and then

grabs the water pitcher from the fridge to fill the glass. He hands it to me and our fingers touch for a brief second. The fun electric flow I get every time he's near me returns.

"Want to go sit outside with me? I think the porch swing is calling your name," he says.

I turn to look at Molly. "Do you need any help, Mrs. Garreth?"

"No, dear," she says waving us away, not even looking up from the veggies she's cutting. "Go enjoy this nice weather. I'll be just fine."

Sampson grabs my hand gently, and I follow him out the front door, barefoot with my glass of water in my other hand. The front porch swing reminds me of the swing from The Notebook on Noah's porch, and I smile at the romantic gesture.

I sit down next to Sampson with the smile still on my face.

"Whatcha smilin' about?" he asks, swinging us back and forth with his legs. My feet don't even reach the ground.

"Nothing," I say, taking a sip of my water. "Just thinking."

"I hope you're thinking about changing your mind on the whole 'serendipity' thing. Not sure how I'm supposed to go who knows how long without talking to you."

"Nope, sorry. Though, you're close to breaking me," I say.

"How's that?"

I nod toward where he's still holding my hand, his thumb rubbing lightly over one of my knuckles. "What can I say? I'm a sucker for the little things in life."

He slowly brings our hands up to his mouth and places a kiss on the back of mine, lingering for a few heartbeats. "How about now?"

I take in a shaky breath. "Sampson Garreth, you'll be the death of me."

"Come here," he says, releasing my hand and motioning for me to move closer.

I'm not sure what I was expecting, maybe for him to pull me in for a kiss or tell me something else in the hopes to get me to change my mind, but he just wraps his arm around my shoulder and holds me as he continues to swing us back and forth.

"Sampson?" I whisper.

"Yeah?"

"You know, I'm pretty sure I've had a crush on you all summer. Now it's your turn to have a crush on me."

I kiss him lightly on the cheek where his beard is getting stubbly just as we hear his mom yell out the open window that dinner is ready.

He smiles. "Let's go in before I try to convince you to be my girlfriend already."

"Thanks for dinner," I tell Mrs. Garreth as I walk out with them to their car. "And thanks for the leftovers."

Mr. and Mrs. Garreth are dressed up nicely for their date night. I feel bad for almost making them late. Mr. Garreth opens her car door and glances nervously at his watch again.

"Oh, make sure you and Sampson finish those brownies," she yells from the car.

Sampson had disappeared right after dinner, but I hear him bounding down the stairs now, a peach in his hand and gym shoes on his feet. "Mom, you're going to give her diabetes." He shouts. "First you let her lick the brownie batter from the bowl, and now another brownie? You don't even offer me extra."

"That's because I like her more," she says with a smile as he jogs over to the car to give her a quick kiss on the cheek.

Mr. Garreth closes her door and waves at us as he climbs behind the wheel and starts the car. Backing up in the yard and heading for the camp entrance.

"Ready to go? I'll walk you back to your cabin." Sampson says, taking a bite out of his fruit, some juice dribbling down his chin before he wipes it away with the back of his hand.

"You don't have to do that," I say.

"Would you just let me be chivalrous?"

"Okay, fine!" I laugh and feign defeat. "To the cabin, Jeeves!"

"You've already won my mother over, you know that right?" He says as he closes the door behind him and I follow him across the field, taking the shortcut to the cabins.

"Maybe she'll adopt me," I tease, trotting a bit ahead of him and dancing, my dress swooshing in the breeze. "I'd love freshly baked sweets every week."

"Don't even joke about that," he says. "She'd probably sign adoption papers if you handed them to her right now."

"Eh, I'm almost eighteen anyway, it's not worth the legal trouble. Don't worry."

We're both quiet for a little bit, and I fall back in step with him.

"Has anyone told you how cute you look in that dress today?" he asks.

"Well," I say, holding my hand up and counting the

people. "Your mom, Kenny, Dora, some guy from the cooking crew…"

"Really?" he asks, and I know he is trying to be cute.

"No, just your mom. I was teasing."

He breathes what I think sounds like a sigh of relief. "Good, I was starting to worry I was going to need to have a talk with some of the guys here. Trying to swoop in and steal you, who do they think they are?"

"I already told you the other day, I'm not interested in dating anyone else. You just have to court me."

"Does walking you back to your cabin count?" he asks as we stop right in front of the door.

I smile and nod. "Look at how well you're already doing. I don't need elaborate things, just actions. It's the little things that matter."

"I can do that," he says, leaning in to give me a hug. "I'll see you tomorrow. Be safe. Lock your door."

"Yes, sir," I say and head down the walkway into my empty cabin. It's tempting to invite him in, I do have extra sheets he could use. Having another sleepover wouldn't be awful. Part of me is nervous about being alone with Winnie gone tonight, but I'll have to get used to being alone once school starts. Who knows what my roommate will be doing at night?

Before I close the door, I watch as Sampson turns back to head toward his parents' house, waving one last night as I turn around and lock myself in for the evening.

It's so quiet, I can hear my heart pattering away in my chest.

TWENTY THREE

"I brought you those brownies," Sampson says as he joins me in the art building the following day. "And some fruit in hopes that it'll even out with the sweets. For every brownie, you have to eat a piece of fruit."

"I hate fruit! Well, most fruit, not apples," I whine, but go over to pop a grape in my mouth.

"See, not so bad," he says. "It's not going to kill you."

"You don't know that," I shoot back. "I could be allergic."

"So, that means you've never tried some fruits, so you don't know if you hate them or like them."

I squint my eyes at him. "It's a texture thing."

"Fair enough, it's here if you want it," he says. "What would you like me to help you with?"

"We need to make sure everything is in the correct containers and put away, then we'll wipe tables off, sweep, and mop."

"Sounds good," he says, following me over to the storage cabinet and pulling all the containers out.

We're both quiet for about an hour, separating ribbon, beads, coloring books, crayons, and markers and other various supplies for crafts. Sampson has his phone out with some indie rock band called Southern Rebirth playing, sitting it on a plastic cup to use as a speaker.

I hum along to the songs, even though I don't know all the words, as I start putting the items back in their correct boxes, and Sampson begins wiping the tables off with disinfectant wipes. Once I have all the containers put away, I grab a broom to sweep, looking up at the handprints again.

"Where's yours?" he asks.

"Hmm," I say, searching. Some of the campers started overlapping handprints this summer so when I find mine, it's covered up. "Ah, here. Looks like it's been outranked."

"Let's fix that," he says, going to the closet and looking for something. He comes back with a gallon of the yellow paint and a pallet.

I follow him to the counter and he pours some paint onto the plastic reusable pallet. I watch as he puts the cap back on the paint and lets it go all over the tray.

"Pick a spot," he says, following me to the wall with the paint. I place my hand in it and then find the clearest spot on the wall to leave my fresh handprint.

Once I'm done, I take the supplies from Sampson. "Your turn," I say with a smile.

He does the same as me and places his hand right next to mine. "There we go. Perfect."

"Not just yet," I tell him. Before I can stop myself, I turn to Sampson and stand on my tippy toes to kiss him on the lips. I place my paint covered hand on his cheek and then slip away. "Now it's perfect."

I look up at him and admire my handiwork, pun intended.

"You think you're so cute, don't you?" he says, taking his yellow finger and marking it on my nose.

I shake my head. "I'm pretty sure you're the one who thinks that I'm cute."

"Point taken," he says, letting me slide away to go wash my hands.

"So, when are you leaving?" he asks, coming up behind

me and playing with a strand of my hair with his hand that's not covered in paint.

"Probably tomorrow afternoon, though I would stay here forever if I could. I'm kind of dreading going back home."

"Your parents still…" he begins, but doesn't seem to know which words to use.

I nod and move away to dry my hands so he can wash his. "Yeah, dad has pretty much moved out, I think. He's probably not moving back in, ever."

"I'm sorry," he says as he scrubs his hands.

"Me too, we'll see what happens…"

The next morning I have one final meeting with Mr. Garreth before I head home. My car is already packed up with my stuff, and I'm amazed how I acquired more items when leaving than when I showed up here, possibly from grabbing extra clothes when I went home for visits. I have the keys to the cabin in my pocket, ready to hand them over to Mr. Garreth.

"Come on in, Penelope," he says when I arrive at his office. His desk is a mess. I assume he has a lot of end of the summer paperwork to go over. "I think I need to consider hiring a file clerk for myself next year. I'm losing my mind with all these papers."

"Your receptionist doesn't file for you?" I ask, raising an eyebrow.

He rolls his eyes. "She's supposed to…"

"Yikes," I say, taking a seat in the only other chair that's not piled up with files. I remember the first day I checked in and how the receptionist didn't seem to care about her job. "Good luck with that."

"Yeah, it's not just you counselors that I have to keep an eye on," he says as he adds another file to his pile, which, at any moment, might just topple over. "So, did you have a good summer for the most part?"

I smile and place the key to the cabin on his desk before I forget and walk off with it. "Yeah, I had a blast with my campers. It was obviously different from being a camper, but I'm so happy I was given the chance to work here this summer."

"I love to hear that," he says with a smile. It amazes me how well Mr. Garreth can switch to a businessman's persona versus Sampson's dad who I've had dinner with a few times this summer. "What are your plans for the rest of the year? You'll be going to Maryville, correct?"

"Yep, I'll be going there, studying, and that's about it," I say with a chuckle.

Mr. Garreth laughs. "I'm sure you'll find a way to have a social life. What about a job? Are you planning on finding something near campus or taking it easy for a semester or two?"

"Honestly?" I ask. "I hadn't thought about it. I know I need a job, but I haven't had the time to look into finding one, and I'm sure the jobs will go fast around there once school begins."

"Well," he says. "I was thinking, I could use someone around here to help me get this stuff organized. I'll need to move a ton of files across camp to the storage unit, and they'll also need organized. You know, camp is only about a forty minute drive from campus... It would only be weekends however, or whenever you can get here. I'm sure you might have certain days where you don't have to go to class."

I nod. "Yeah, I'm free on Thursdays and Fridays actually."

"Four day weekends? Good for you!" he says. "What do you think? Of course, there would be way more things for you to do. I know it doesn't seem like it, but we do try to keep some stuff going at camp year round. I believe I told you, we have some businesses come in for team building weekends and a few church retreats as well."

"Can I think on it?" I ask.

"Of course! I'll shoot you an email tonight with all the information on the job. I'll just need an answer before Friday," he says. "But I'd love for you to take this position. I won't be mentioning it to anyone else. I'd have Sampson do it, but he has his own on campus gig during off season."

"Alright," I say. "I'll let you know as soon as I can, Mr. Garreth."

He stands up and I do also, reaching out to shake his hand. "Good luck with your classes, Penelope," he says with a smile. "Be safe on your drive home."

"Will do," I say. "Thanks for everything."

I exit his office just as his next meeting arrives at his door. Casanova... I imagine that meeting won't be going as well as mine. He gives me a sly grin as he passes me on his way into the office. I hear Mr. Garreth ask him to close the door behind him. Yep, that one isn't going to end pleasantly.

When I make it to my car, the interior is practically burning with heat. I've only driven it once a week this summer and it was usually in the morning or evening. I immediately roll down my windows to let a breeze in when I start the car. I back out of the spot and start heading toward the exit. I can already feel my heart breaking from leaving this place.

I said my goodbyes this morning at breakfast, so I'm

good to go. As I approach the lake, I see a figure sitting on the dock and my heart swells. I know it's Sampson even though I only catch a glimpse of him. I've memorized the back of his head over the last two months, he's still sporting that flower headband.

If I wanted to, if I thought it would make the goodbye easier, I could just continue on, but I know I can't. I need to speak to him one more time. It's silly, it's not like I'm never seeing him again, it's just not knowing when the next time will be that makes me pull over to the side of the road.

I bring my car to a stop on the edge of the gravel road and I turn it off, leaving the windows down. I shut my door and head over to the dock, carefully avoiding some mud. This feels like it's coming full circle from one of our first conversations, I smile at the thought.

"Fancy seeing you here," I say, echoing his words from my first day.

He turns and gives me a smile. "You following me?"

I join him on the dock, sliding close to him, way closer than our first time sitting here together. He reaches for my hand and laces our fingers together.

"Heading out?" he asks, staring at the lake.

"Sadly," I say.

He squeezes my hand a little. "Thank you."

"For what?" I ask with a nervous smile.

He rubs a finger over each of my knuckles. "For this summer, if it weren't for you, I'd probably still be a poor ole' sap following Viv around and letting her treat me like a doormat."

"A very cute doormat," I correct him.

"Seriously, Penelope," he says. "Thank you. You're amazing. You have been such an awesome person this summer, a great friend."

"Wait…" I say. "Is this where you friendzone me, and I find out that you actually never liked me at all? That you were just pretending because you didn't want things to be weird between the two of us?"

"No!" he says defensively. "Hell no, I still like you! Don't you dare think otherwise."

"Okay, good," I say. "Because that would have been awkward. I would have to head back to the office and turn your dad's job offer down immediately."

"What job offer? For next summer?" he asks.

I shake my head. "He didn't tell you?"

"No, you should fill me in," he says, staring at me intently, his eyebrows tugging inward with confusion.

"Your dad wants me to work here some weekends as a file clerk and possibly a person who helps with the team building stuff."

"No way!" Sampson says a huge smile breaking out across his face. "I heard him discussing with mom that he might need someone for the winter, but I didn't hear who he was choosing. Did you accept it?"

"I'll think it over on my drive home. I'm sure he'll tell you my decision."

"Nah, he keeps most of his employees' business to himself. He'll probably tell my mom though, and I'm sure I'll be able to get the scoop from her. That's awesome though, I hope you take it."

"Do you still want me around a bit longer?" I ask.

"A lot a bit longer," he says, leaning in to press his forehead against mine. "But I want you to make this decision for you, no one else."

"I'll keep that in mind," I whisper before pulling away. "I should go though. Walk me to my car?"

He nods and stands up, reaching down to give me a hand, and pulling me up into a hug. Just like before. This time though, I let him hold me longer, savoring his scent, his touch, the feel of his heart beating.

He holds my hand all the way to my car, and even opens the door for me. Before I slide in, he gives me a soft kiss on the forehead and tells me to drive safely.

I turn the car back on and pull away, kicking up some dust from the gravel and finally making it to the exit. When I make my left turn out of camp, the tears start to stream down my face, just like every summer when I leave my home away from home.

There's no way I will turn down the job. I don't need a three-hour car ride to figure that out.

TWENTY FOUR

There's something nice about sleeping in your own bed after being gone for a while. I try my best not to get used to it though. In one more week I'll be sleeping on an uncomfortable plastic extra-long twin bed surrounded by four off-white walls. I hope my roommate is good at decorating. I haven't gotten a call from her, so I have no idea if she's wanting to go with a color scheme or theme.

I open my phone again to read over my e-mail with Mr. Garreth about the job offer. On the way home yesterday when I stopped for gas, I responded to his offer, telling him I would love to do it for him and that I look forward to getting back to camp as soon as he wants me to start.

A knock comes on my door and I stretch out a little and pull the covers up to my chin, snuggling in with no intent on leaving my bed.

"Come in," I say.

My mom opens the door and leans against the frame with a smile. "It's so good to have you home, kiddo."

"It's nice to be home," I say.

She walks over and sits on the edge of my bed. "What do you want to do today? I was thinking I could go buy you some new outfits for school and get you some school supplies and dorm items."

I point to the pile in the corner of my room to two laundry baskets full of laundry detergent, cleaning products and some snacks. "I think I'm good, but I'm starting to feel like you're trying to buy my love."

"Is it working?" she asks, raising an eyebrow.

"Maybe," I say. "Can dad come with us?"

Her smile slips away and she doesn't look at me. "I don't know if that's a good idea…"

"Can I at least see if he wants to get some lunch or dinner tonight?"

We stare each other down for a moment or two before she finally breaks under my gaze. "Fine, but only if we go for ice cream after. Me and you that is; it's been forever since we have gotten ice cream together, and the little shop we like will be closed for the season once you come home for Thanksgiving."

"Deal," I say, jumping up to hug her tightly. "Love you, mom."

"Love you too, dear." She gets up to leave my room, but stops short. "Oh, the mailman dropped off a package for you, did you order something?"

I shake my head. "Not that I know of. I'll check it out after I shower. Is there a return address or anything?"

"It said it was from an address in Maryville, but no name."

"Hmm, maybe it's school sending me something. Just leave it on the kitchen counter, I'll get it. Give me twenty minutes."

"Twenty?" my mom asks loudly. "I thought camp trained you to take five minute showers?"

"They did," I say, getting up to grab some clothes to wear and my toiletries I hadn't unpacked yet. "But I haven't had a good scrub in months. I need to get all this caked on sunblock and bug spray off my skin. I feel like I will smell like camp for another month or two. Just wait until I take my hour long bubble bath tonight."

She smiles and shakes her head, leaving me to detox the camp life out of my body.

I walk down the stairs and my mom is currently brewing herself some coffee when she looks up at me and chuckles.

"You can take the girl out of the camp," she says. "But you clearly can't take the camp out of the girl."

"What?" I ask, and she looks me up and down. "I like this shirt."

I'm pretty sure all of my t-shirts are from Camp Arthur.

"Honey, that shirt is from four years ago. It has a hole in the armpit, trust me, I know. I've tried to throw it away a dozen times now and you keep getting it out of the trash."

"Well, it's a good thing you're taking me shopping. I wouldn't want to show up to college with a bunch of holes in my clothes."

"Smart ass," my mom says, putting a lid on her travel mug. "Open up your package so we can go."

"Okay, bossy pants," I say as I grab a knife from the butcher block and take the package to the table. I inspect the handwriting, but it doesn't give anything away and there's not a name with the unfamiliar address.

Mom peers over my shoulder as I cut through the packaging tape carefully. "The suspense is killing me, seriously, what if it's a head? Didn't you and your dad make me watch that movie where the head was in the box?"

"It was Seven, and I'm pretty sure you fell asleep and

only woke up to see that scene," I say rolling my eyes. "Maybe I should just open it when we get home."

"You'll open that box right now, young lady. It's been here for hours bothering me. It could be time sensitive material... like a severed head."

"I'm pretty sure it would say so on the box if it were perishable," I reply, putting the knife down and opening the box. It looks like a care package of goodies, and I pull them out one at a time.

Inside, there's a Maryville College t-shirt, some Maryville sweatpants, some notepads, pens and pencils, along with a gift card to the coffee shop on campus and a map of the city with some places circled with a marker and a note at the bottom that says 'Welcome', but there's no name signed to it.

"Who do you think it's from?" She asks.

I shrug and put all the stuff back in the box. "No idea, maybe it's from my roommate or something."

"Seems like a generous gift from someone you've never met before, and they even know your sizes."

"Weird," I say. "Oh well, let's head out. I'm ready to spend all of your money on stuff I'll probably never use."

She grabs her purse and mug and pulls me into a side hug. "That's my girl. I knew there was some girlish person-ality trait you had to receive from me in there."

"Don't get used to it," I tell her. "You know I hate shopping for myself."

"Well, just think of it as I'm shopping for you, but you're with me so you can tell me what you want and don't want."

"We better go, the more we discuss shopping, the more I'm starting to regret going with you."

"How about this?" my mom asks, holding up a tacky pink crop top with a pair of high waisted shorts.

"I'm pretty sure the last time I wore pink was when I was four and you were still dressing me. Also, you're my mom, shouldn't you be constantly making sure I cover as much of my skin as possible?"

"That's your dad's job," she says, refusing to put the outfit back. "Will you at least try the shorts on? I think they'd look so cute on you. I haven't seen you wear anything but gym shorts in so long."

"Fine," I say, taking the shorts from her and putting them in our cart that's already full of some items that I know I won't be getting. "But for every item I get that you pick out, I think I should be able to get a clothing item of my choice."

"Deal," she says, searching for more clothes she can dress me in.

"I'm going to take some of this stuff to the dressing room and start trying things on," I tell her, picking out six tops and bottoms.

"Okay, but take pictures of each outfit, I want to be your second opinion."

I leave her in the aisle and pull my phone out when I feel it vibrate once indicating a text message. I unlock my phone and open the message, and my heart speeds up when I see it's from Sampson. I'm tempted to delete it. He knows I wanted to take a breather and just see what happens. I read the message anyway.

"Did you get my package? The tracking number said it was delivered."

The text brings a smile to my face. I never thought Sampson would send me a gift. I stop short of the fitting rooms to send my response. "We're not supposed to be talking. Serendipity, remember?"

"Screw serendipity. So you got the package then?" he sends back right away.

"Thank you," I send and then add onto that, "The package was very thoughtful. What were the places that were circled on the map?"

"The places I plan on taking you on dates when we're reunited," he says not missing a beat.

"Penelope?" says a female voice.

I look up from my phone with a huge smile from what Sampson just said, but when I see that Janine is standing in front of me, my smile fades. I didn't want to run into her.

"Hey," I say, shoving my phone into my pocket. "How are you?"

"I'm fine," she says. I look at her clothes, she's wearing sweats and a hoodie, and I've never seen her dressed so casually. She's usually wearing something like what I'm about to reluctantly try on. "Did you just get back from camp?"

"Yeah, I got back last weekend. I'm shopping with my mom for some school stuff."

She nods and glances down in her cart and I also look down in it, taking note of the items. She quickly tries to bring my attention back to her, but I'm staring at the diapers, newborn onesies, and stretchy jeans.

"Are you excited to start school?" she quickly asks.

"Um, yeah," I say, trying to look at her, but I can't take my eyes off those diapers. "Are you going to a baby shower? Who is expecting?"

Her cheeks blush. "I'm an idiot," she says as a tear streams down her cheek.

I awkwardly walk over and wrap my arm around her shoulder in an effort to comfort the girl who used to be my best friend. "No you're not, what happened?"

"I'm pregnant," she says, looking at me. I gently wipe a tear from her cheek and then pull back.

"How far along? Who's the dad?" I ask, feeling like the second question is rude as hell, but those are the only two I can think to ask. She wasn't 'seeing' anyone the last time I was here. Just the guy from the party.

"I'm so stupid," she says, her hand covering her eyes. I can tell she's still trying to get used to the fact that she's pregnant. "It was one of those college guys from the bonfire we went to. We talked for a week or two after the party and then he invited me over to his place and things got out of hand."

"He didn't…" I say, gently placing my hand on her shoulder.

"Rape me," she finishes, moving her hand and shaking her head. "God no, just knocked me up."

"Shit," I say. "Which guy was it?"

Just as she's about to respond to my question, a familiar face approaches us and wraps his arms around Janine's waist. I can't put a name to the face, but he must be the baby's dad. Who else would show that kind of affection in a store?

"You've met Denny, right?" Janine asks me, trying to extract herself from his groping hands.

Denny. There's the name. The same guy that tried to get my attention at the party. I feel like I'm going to faint or vomit at the sight of him, at the sound of his name, at that stupid smile on his face.

"I think we have met," Denny says, going to extend a handshake to me, but I'm saved by my mother's voice coming from the racks of clothing.

"Penelope, how'd the clothes fit?" she calls.

"I haven't made it to the dressing room yet," I say. "I was talking."

She looks up and sees Janine and comes over to give her a hug. I still haven't told my mom about our huge fight at the beginning of the summer.

"Hi, sweetie," my mom says. "How have you been? I haven't seen you in forever."

"I've been okay," Janine replies, placing her hand on her stomach and then quickly moving it away.

I wonder how many people know that she's pregnant. I hope mom doesn't look in her cart like I did, that might not be the attention Janine is looking for right now.

"You should come over tonight for dinner!" mom says and then looks over at Denny. "You can come too, we're having a final big family dinner before Penelope leaves for college."

"Sorry ma'am, I have to be somewhere tonight," Denny says. "Thanks for the invite though."

Thank God.

"I can come over," Janine says and then looks to me for possible assurance. "If you're sure I won't be intruding on anything."

"You wouldn't," I say with a small smile.

Mom lets Janine know what time to come over and I excuse myself to go try on my new outfits, grateful to be getting away from Denny the sleaze ball. I wonder if Janine remembers he was the main reason I left that bonfire.

I hang up my outfits on the provided hooks in the dressing room and lock myself inside. Instead of jumping right in on trying the clothes on, I pull my phone out and realize I forgot to respond to Sampson. There are two text messages that I missed over the last ten minutes of running into Janine and Denny.

"Did I come on too strong? Was that too cheesy?" asks Sampson in the first text.

I read the second that I received three minutes after the first. "Okay, yikes. I now know what it feels like to be the clingy girl. I'll go jump off a metaphorical bridge now."

I smile and shake my head, typing my response and sending it. "Sorry, I ran into someone at the store. The joys of a small town. And if you're wanting to metaphorically end it all, I recommend and overpass, not a bridge."

"Never leave me hangin' like that, Penelope," he sends back. "You had my heart racing. I'm too young to have a heart attack."

I send back a smile emoji with my next response. "I like my gift, thanks again. I have to go, though. My mother is making me play dress up. And you and I are supposed to be letting fate work its magic."

"Get something nice to wear on our first date," Sampson sends back. "Can't wait to spontaneously run into you on campus."

Is this what liking someone feels like? A constant smile on your face, butterflies in your stomach every time your phone chimes, wondering when you'll see the person again? I have no idea if I will be able to follow my own rule. It's going to take a ton of self-restraint to not call Sampson the second I get to Maryville.

The doorbell rings and I jump up to get it, opening the door I see my dad standing there with a bottle of wine. He smiles and pulls me into a tight hug. I try not to be bothered by the fact that my dad rang the doorbell instead of just walking in. It's not a good sign.

"Hi, Dad," I say, hugging him tightly. "Missed you."

"Missed you too, kid," he says. "How've you been?"

"Good," I say as I close the door behind him. "Are you going to be able to help me move next week?"

"Of course! I wouldn't miss it for the world," he says with a smile and follows me into the kitchen where Mom has been cooking up a storm. "Smells great in here. I brought some wine."

Mom looks up from washing her hands and dries them before taking the bottle from my dad. She thanks him, not making eye contact and then goes over to the oven to check on the meatloaf.

The doorbell rings again. "That must be Janine, I'll get it," I say, excusing myself from my parents awkward interaction with each other. Have they already forgotten what it's like to love each other?

"Hey," I say, opening the door for her.

She holds up a round plastic container. "I brought dessert, your favorite, cheesecake."

"Cool," I reply. "My dad just got here."

I close the door behind her and she leans into whisper to me. "I take it they haven't gotten back together?"

"Nope," I say with a shake of my head. "I'm pretty sure all of his stuff is now moved out. It's not looking good."

"Sorry," Janine says, glancing down at the floor. "Should I be here? I can go."

"No, stay. It'll make it less awkward. They're probably both in there staring at the boiling water for the potatoes."

And sure enough, when Janine and I walk into the

kitchen, they are both staring at the oven as if it's about to explode if they look away.

"Look who showed up, guys," I say to my parents so they'll stop being so quiet.

"Janine," my dad says with a smile. "How have you been?"

"Good," she says. "How have you guys been?"

"Good, good," Dad says, but he doesn't seem to mean it. "It's been weird not seeing you around. What have you been doing all summer?"

I notice Janine's cheeks blush when she replies. "Oh, just hanging out."

"Is dinner almost done, mom?" I ask, trying to save us all from this bizarre conversation we're trying to have. It's like we're all tiptoeing around a divorce and pregnancy.

Just then, the stove timer buzzes and my mom grabs her oven mitts. "Looks like right about now. Can you and Janine set the table, please?"

Janine and I both nod, glad to have something to do. I grab the plates from the cabinets and she grabs the silverware. We've set the table together so many times, so we know the routine by heart.

I set the plates on the table and move my box of goodies from Sampson to the floor in the corner of the room.

"What's in the box?" she asks.

I shake my head and start putting the plates in their spots. "Nothing, just a gift from a camp friend. Something to welcome me to college."

"You're already making friends at school?" she asks, her eyes not meeting mine. Her voice seems sad.

"Yeah, a few. I met some girls at orientation and then a few of my coworkers at camp go to Maryville."

"I'm glad," Janine says, placing the silverware next to the plates. "I'm glad that you're making friends already."

"Me too," I say.

Dad comes and sits four wine glasses at the table and I look at him like he's lost his mind. "Umm, dad... I think you got too many glasses out."

"Don't be silly," he says. "Tonight's a celebration. You're going off to college, we're going to have a toast."

Janine's eyes are huge when I turn to her and apologize. "Just pretend, right?"

"This will be interesting," she says.

Mom and Dad start bringing the food over and sitting it on the table. Janine digs in right away. I'd blame it on her pregnancy cravings, but she's never been shy around my parents.

"How are your parents?" my dad asks Janine as she passes him some food.

"They're okay, hanging in there I guess."

"I'll have to give your mom a call one day," my mother says, pointing her fork at Janine. "I feel like I haven't talked to her in ages."

"She'd like that," Janine says with a smile. "I'll let her know you guys asked about her."

"So, Penelope," my dad begins, raising up his glass once his plate is full of food. "Shall we make a toast?"

I nod and pick up my glass, my mom and Janine also stop and hold up their glasses.

"To Penelope: may you have the brightest future. Your mother and I are so proud of you, and we know you're destined to do amazing things. Good luck on your next adventure in life. To Penelope!"

My mom and Janine say 'to Penelope' in unison and we all clink our glasses. I almost gag when the wine meets my tongue. I haven't had alcohol since that awful first night at camp. I'm not sure if the wine is worse or not. Trying my best, I swallow a small sip and turn to look at Janine who has sat her glass down, a purple drink mustache across her lips. She grabs her napkin and wipes her mouth quickly.

Janine and I are pretty quiet for the rest of dinner. My parents occasionally ask us questions and we answer, but the dinner is more awkward than I thought it would be. Janine and I excuse ourselves after about 45 minutes of discussion, taking our dirty dishes to the sink as we go, but leaving our barely touched wine on the table. I know my mom will probably finish our glasses once dad leaves.

The two of us head outside to the backyard where my old swing set still stands. My parents kept it all these years, but I don't think it'll ever get used again. Mom said they were saving it for 'grandkids', but those won't be coming for a very long time.

We take a seat on the swings side by side but facing each other. I gently push myself back and forth, knowing the set isn't too reliable. When we were kids, we flipped it multiple times because my dad never filled in the concrete around the legs. Janine sits idly, her hands in her lap, staring at the ground.

"What's your plan?" I ask, and then clarify my question. "With the baby, that is."

"Have it, stay here in this crap town for the rest of my life," she says with a sullen expression on her face.

"And the dad? Are you going to stay with Denny?"

"I think the real question is: will he stay with me?" she asks. "He's talking about going back to school, which means I'll be staying here. I know he doesn't want to be a dad."

"He probably should have thought about that before."

"We're both to blame," Janine says, looking up at me.

"I wasn't taking my birth control daily, and he never asked about that kind of stuff."

I shake my head and look down at my shoes, not sure what to say to that. How do you comfort someone like that? Janine and I were in the same health class. We heard the same sex-ed talks year after year in high school. We both knew birth control and which ones were best. There's no excuse...

"You must think I'm a total idiot," Janine says.

I shrug. "Not total…"

She punches me in the arm and I laugh as I rub the spot she hit.

"I just…" I start, not knowing which words to choose. "Why Denny? He was a total creep."

"Honestly?" she asks, raising an eyebrow and looking at me. I nod and she proceeds. "It was stupid. In my head, he was just supposed to be a summer fling. I knew that he had a thing for you. I saw you guys talking at the party. When you and I were fighting, I thought, 'what better way to get back at her than to sleep with the guy she liked?'"

"But I didn't like him, Janine!"

"I kind of figured that out. It was shitty and stupid. Now I will be connected to him for the rest of my life because of this baby."

"So, what are you going to do?" I ask.

She takes in a shaky breath and lets it out slowly "I have no idea. I guess I spend the next seven months or so going through the pregnancy. I'm keeping the baby, and my mom said she'd help me as long as I don't run off with Denny or take her help for granted. I'll find a job after the baby comes. No sense in finding one right now. After that, I have no idea."

"What about school?" I ask.

She chuckles and shakes her head. "You and I both

know I was never book smart. College was never in my cards."

"You don't actually need college, right? I'm sure there's something you can do with a high school education. A monkey could answer phones and work in an office."

"Most jobs are run by robots and automatic recordings," she says. "As long as I don't end up working at the Little Shrimp like my mom when she was my age, I think I'll be doing fine."

I stare up at the stars, but can't make them out like I could when I was at camp. Star gazing was what always made me feel better. I'm not sure if I'm missing camp or if I'm missing Sampson.

"Enough about me," Janine says. "How was camp?"

"God!" I say, shaking my head. "Do you really want to know?"

"Sounds juicy," she says. "I'm all ears."

I catch Janine up on everything that happened at camp. The good, the bad, and the ugly—from the fun stuff I had the chance to do and the things I missed out on because of Viv's attitude. From the rise and fall of Viv and Sampson's relationship, to my realization that I did like Sampson. By the time I finish getting her up to speed on my life, it's pitch black out and the lightning bugs are in full force in the backyard.

To my surprise it actually felt good to catch Janine up on everything that happened this summer when we weren't talking. Though, I now feel a ton of bug bites on my legs, and I know they're going to itch like crazy. Bug spray isn't just for camp.

"Ya know what?" Janine says after my words sink in. "I think I'd rather be knocked up than go through your summer camp drama. Viv sounds worse than me."

"I don't think anyone could top how horrible Viv was," I reply. "I've never met such a hateful human in my life."

"Sampson sounds nice though," she says. "Maybe he can be my baby daddy."

I don't laugh at that.

"I'm kidding," she says. "You must totally be into him."

"I guess so," I say. "You know me though, I don't know how to date. I've always been the awkward friend who was a girl, never the girlfriend."

"That's what a new start is for," Janine says. "You can go to college and be whoever you want to be. You don't have to be the friend, you can be the girlfriend."

"But I'm also going to college to get good grades and a job…" I say in protest.

"But you'll need someone to cuddle when you get stressed out during finals…"

I look at her, shaking my head. "You only have a one-track mind, don't you? Why did you even become my friend?"

She laughs. "What can I say? I've always been boy crazy. Every slut needs the goodie-two-shoes friend to keep her out of trouble."

"I didn't do too good of a job, did I?" I ask, nodding toward her belly that's just starting to show. I have a feeling she'll be one of those fit pregnant girls, like the ones that only gain the weight they're supposed to, but hardly even show any of it, the ones with cute baby bumps that everyone envies.

She reaches out for my hand and holds it in hers. "I made my bed, now I have to sleep in it. This was all me… Well, mostly me. You're going to be a kickass person in the real world, and I hope you don't forget to come and visit your little 'niece' or 'nephew'."

"Of course I will," I say. "I promise. You'll keep me up to date on how things are progressing?"

"All of the dirty details," she says with a wicked grin. "It'll be bonus 'birth control' for you."

I smile and we shake on it.

"I guess I should get going," Janine says as she stands up from the swing. "Mom will start to worry. What other trouble can I get in? It's not like I can get knocked up again!"

I laugh and shake my head, standing up to hug her. I don't feel like we're back to being the friends we were at the beginning of the summer, but I do feel like we're taking a step toward that again. I squeeze her tightly and rub my hand on her back, not wanting to let go.

"Thanks for coming," I tell her as I pull away.

"Of course, thanks for having me," she says. "Good luck with school. You leave tomorrow?"

"Day after tomorrow," I clarify. "I'll be packing up tomorrow, and we leave early Friday morning."

"Safe travels," she says, backing away from me. "And don't do anything I would do!"

I smile and watch her turn to go, remembering those words from when I left for camp.

TWENTY FIVE

As if the drive to campus couldn't be more awkward with my dad, we passed some off campus apartments with bed sheets spray painted to say things like 'Freshmen Daughter Drop Off' and 'Daughter Day Care'.

Dad huffs and shakes his head. "Your dorm is girls only, right?"

"Yeah…" I lie. Anything to make him feel better seems worth it. I wouldn't go for any of those frat guys who wrote those not-so-clever sayings anyway. I hope to God Sampson has never been a part of that scene, and as we pass another frat house, I make sure to look and see if I recognize a guy with shaggy brown hair, but most of them have buzz cuts or super long hair in man buns. Not Sampson.

My dad and I unloaded my dorm stuff into my room in about thirty minutes. There were some RAs who offered to help us, but Dad refused, and I think that's because he wanted to be able to spend more time with me. I didn't have much though. The heaviest items were the mini fridge and microwave. Everything else was easy: bedding, clothes, laundry supplies, and a bulk box of cheerios Mom got me.

I was surprised when dad even offered to stay and help me organize my room. Mom stayed home today, and I think she wanted this to be a father-daughter thing. Besides, she had plans on coming up three weekends from now to check in. Dad made sure to connect my TV and Xbox while I put the fresh sheets and comforter on my bed. Instead of putting the matching pillowcase on my pillow, I reached in my backpack and pulled out the one from camp that the girls in my cabin signed for me, a smile spreading on my face.

Dad even helped me make sure my posters were hung up on the wall straight before pulling me in tight for a hug.

"If you need anything, call me, okay?" he asks, placing a kiss on the top of my head. "Anything, and I'll be here as soon as I can."

"I will," I promise him. "Same to you, Dad."

"When does your roommate get here?" he asks, pulling away and looking at her empty side of the room.

"No idea," I say with a shrug. "Haven't heard anything from her. Might get a new assignment. I know they over-booked the rooms, so there's a waiting list."

"Seems silly to overbook a dorm," he says with a grunt, turning to the door. "Well, I guess this is it."

I smile at him and sort of wish I could see myself through his eyes. Do I look happy, like a girl with her whole life ahead of her, or do I look scared shitless?

"This is it," I say. "I'll see you at Thanksgiving?"

"For sure, kiddo," he says. "Be good. Do good."

"Do *well*," I say, correcting him.

He shakes his head and chuckles. "No, I want you to do well and do good, but try to have some fun too. Don't take life so seriously. You tend to overthink things."

"I'll be fine, Dad."

He puckers his lips and gives an air kiss before opening the door. Just as he steps into the hall, I hear some guy yell at the top of his lungs that the kegs have arrived at Theta House. Dad gives me one more look before he leaves, though he seems a little terrified.

"Call me tonight," he begs, and I nod as he closes the door.

I go over to my bed and climb up, I literally have to climb because it's about four feet off the floor, the beds are not bunks like you would expect to save space in the tiny room. Note to self, I need to go buy a small step stool. I lay down and hold my tie-dyed pillow tightly against my chest. I honestly thought I might automatically feel at home here like I do at camp, since after all, school and Camp Arthur are only a few miles from each other.

I'm not sure what to do with myself.

I close my eyes and try my best not to cave and contact Sampson. I'm a big girl now, and I don't need to be calling him the second I get on campus. Besides, he's probably either not on campus, or he's busy doing his own thing. I just hope that thing isn't luring girls to his frat house with those silly signs offering free beer.

My phone wakes me up with it's annoying vibration. How did I fall asleep? I jump out of bed searching for it, but it stops vibrating before I can locate it. Finally, I find it at the bottom of a bag with dryer sheets and hangers, no idea how it got there.

I don't recognize the phone number but it's local, and they're calling me again.

"Hello?" I ask, putting the phone to my ear, assuming it might be a department here at school calling me.

"What room are you in? We've been trying to find you for an hour now!"

"Who is this?" I ask, furrowing my brow.

"It's your favorite person from camp!" says the male voice. "Now where are you?"

"I'm not telling you my room, I don't even know who you are!"

"It's Kenny!" says the voice as two other people shout their names at him too. "And Ben and Dora. Now stop playing hard to get!"

"Fine, fine, I'm coming. I'm in room 306," I say.

"Perfect. Open the door, we're here."

Sure enough, when I go to my door, they're all standing there with smiles on their faces. Dora jumps into my arms and almost tackles me to the ground. It's so good to see some familiar faces.

"Let's go out, it's time to break you in," Dora says with a smile. "Drinks on Ben!"

Ben laughs. "That's funny, but you do remember I'm just as broke as all of you, right? We worked the same job this summer."

"Fine," Dora says rolling her eyes. "Dessert on you."

"There ya go," he says, lacing his hand in hers.

Kenny and I smile and follow behind the two of them, Ben and Dora swinging their arms back and forth without a care in the world. I'll have to get the story later from Dora on how and when her and Ben finally got together.

Kenny drives us to some bar just outside of town that Ben said never checks IDs. It sounds kind of sketchy, but I tag along anyway, only a little nervous about being caught. What else was I going to do locked up in my dorm alone? Besides, I have the next few months until Christmas break to lock myself in my room and hide from my social life.

Inside, the bar packed with people, and a good percentage of them are wearing Maryville shirts. There's not even a table open for us. This place must have a huge reputation for not carding, because almost everyone has a beer in their hand, and a few of them look just as young as I do.

"Maybe we should find another bar," I suggest, glancing around the room. It feels like the AC is busted.

"Nah, there's got to be a spot here," Ben says, standing on his toes to look through the crowd.

"Penelope!" yells a voice over the blaring nineties country music, some guy singing about a storm. I turn just in time to see Carla running to me.

I almost topple over from the impact of her body colliding with mine, I can smell beer on her breath. "Hey! Good to see you!"

"Come sit with us," she says, already pulling me by the arm. "We already have a table and a bucket of beers."

I motion for my group to follow me and they do. Hayley is at the table that Carla brings me to and she pats the open chair next to her for me to sit down in.

"I have some friends with me," I say into her ear so she can hear over the music. I point to them all and say their names for her. "Ben, Dora, and Kenny. They worked with me at camp."

She waves to them and then leans into me. "Where's Sampson? Is he joining us or did that not…"

I shake my head. "It's a long story. I'll steal some chairs for us."

Kenny and Ben go and search around the bar for some more chairs that other tables aren't using, and after a five-minute hunt we're all sitting around having a drink. I didn't expect it to feel this easy to have a college social life. I never pictured myself with a group of friends sitting at a bar and actually having fun. I can't hear half of what anyone is saying because it's so loud, but I love my life right now.

Before I even know it, the bartender says last call and we get one more bucket of beers, and Ben orders one of every dessert for the table to share. Carla and I share a bowl of ice cream and deep fried cookies while Ben and Dora share some pie, and Kenny and Hayley laugh over a huge piece of chocolate cake.

The bar thins out and we pay our bills, all tossing in enough money to cover everything. We don't worry about splitting it evenly, it doesn't matter because everyone seemed to have a blast. I say goodbye to Carla and Hayley and wait over by Kenny's car.

It's locked, so I lean against the half rusted door.

Dora and Ben walk over, Ben's arm slung around Dora's shoulder.

"Where's Kenny?" I ask once Dora and Ben get over to the car.

They turn to look over at a car a bit further down the lot and I follow their gaze.

Kenny has a huge smile on his face and he hands his cell phone over to Hayley who starts typing something into it, possibly her number. She smiles and hands the phone back before climbing into her car. Kenny even shuts the door for her once she's safely inside.

When he joins us at his car, he still has a huge smile and doesn't say a word as he unlocks the car to get in. Once inside, I buckle up and then stare at him, waiting for an explanation.

He looks at me and shakes his head as he starts the engine. "Don't look at me like that…"

"Are we going to talk about what just happened?" I ask as he backs out and then puts the car in drive, heading back to campus.

"Nothing, I just got your friends number," he says.

"I thought…" I say and then burst into giggles. I must be drunker than I thought.

"Thought what?" he asks, the smile fading from his face.

"What about Winnie?"

Kenny shrugs his shoulders, one hand on the steering wheel. "We're two different people. We hung out all night on our last evening at camp. Texted a few times over the following weeks, but I just wasn't into her and she wasn't into me either."

"What girl would be into you?" Ben asks and then bursts into a fit of laughter.

Kenny glares at him in the rearview window. "Cool it, dude. I'm not afraid to stop this car and kick you out."

"Yeah, yeah," Ben says, shrugging the threat off.

Ben's phone rings a loud, shrill song. I recognize it as the theme song for Futurama.

"Bro! Where are you? I miss you!" he says, answering it.

"Who is it?" Dora asks, leaning into Ben.

"It's Sammy boy," Ben says, and my heart speeds up.

"Sampson?" I ask, the name making my heart sing.

Ben doesn't respond to me, he keeps speaking to his phone. "Yeah, Dora, me, Kenny, and Penelope were just at the bar. We're heading back to campus...

"Yeah, I said Penelope... do you want to talk to her? Okay, well we'll see ya when you get to school. Later."

Ben hangs up, and I turn around in my seat to look at him, my eyes trying to pop out of my head. "What did he say? Did he not want to talk to me?"

Ben gives me a smirk. "He was happy you got out, but he didn't want to talk. Said something 'bout obeying your wishes and planning on running into you on campus."

He didn't want to talk to me?

"Is he meeting up with you guys?" I ask, curiosity and hurt mingling in my voice.

"He actually won't be on campus until Monday. He had some family business to take care of."

That makes me feel a little better I say, and then realize I actually said it out loud.

Dora leans up and puts her hand on my shoulder. "Why don't you just tell him you want to see him?"

I shrug my shoulders and look down at my hands. "I don't know, I thought it would be romantic to just bump into each other out of the blue. I also wanted to give him time to get over Viv."

"I hate Viv!" Ben says from the back seat. "Don't worry about that, Sampson got over her a long time ago, he just never realized it. You're way better than her, so much more chill."

"Uh, thanks?" I ask. "You guys think..."

"He's crazy over you, Penelope!" Dora says, moving back in her seat. "Don't worry your pretty little head over that. We all see how much he wants to be with you."

I nod my head in thanks as we pull into the parking lot of the dorm. And wave goodbye before I head up to my room. As I unlock the door and step in, turning on the light, I'm surrounded by towers of boxes and a pile of clothes on hangers covering the other bed. No roommate though. Normally, the clutter would bother me, but I just shrug out of my shorts, flick the light switch to off, and climb up into my bed.

It feels like I just fell asleep when I bolt upright from the sound of a key in the lock and the door opening, letting in a sliver of light from the hall. A girl comes in and turns on the lights. I quickly put a hand over my eyes to block the light when she notices me.

"Crap, sorry!" she says, the lights going back off in a hurry. She pulls her cellphone out to light her way back to her bed. "I didn't know you were here. I mean, I saw your stuff earlier, but I didn't know if you were coming back tonight."

"You're fine," I say, laying back down and pulling the covers up to my chin. "I didn't know if you were coming back. My name's Penelope. And yours?"

"Grace," she says, coming over to extend her hand for me to shake. She has one of those heavy Tennessee accents I've come to love. "Freshmen majoring in education."

I shake her hand and she goes back over to her bed to hang up her clothes.

"Nice to meet you," I say. "I'd get up and help you out, but I misplaced my pajamas, and I don't think we're close enough to walk around in our underwear just yet."

She laughs and gives up on hanging the clothes, moving them to rest on her desk instead. "It's fine, I'm too tired to deal with this mess. I'll work on it tomorrow."

She climbs into bed, turning on a reading lamp and pulling out a small paperback novel that has a shirtless guy holding a woman in his arms. "Hope you don't mind, I'm going to stay up and read for a little bit. It's part of my night routine."

"It's fine. I'm going to try and sleep. I'll talk to you in the morning."

"Night, Penelope," she says.

I roll over and close my eyes, holding my blankets tight to my chest. "Night, Grace."

TWENTY SIX

SEPTEMBER

I didn't run into Sampson the first week of school, or the second. Not even the third. I find it strange, considering that I had been hanging out at Ben's place with Dora a decent amount on weekends. I was sure Ben and Sampson were close. By my fourth week at school, I gave up looking for him. After all, if I wasn't in class, anytime I saw a guy wearing cargo shorts, a T-shirt, and shaggy hair, I thought it was him. I was driving myself crazy.

I tried hanging out with Kenny and Hayley, but they were usually shut into her apartment with a hair tie on the door handle.

"This is ridiculous," Carla said one day when we were studying in the student center. Well, I was reading and taking notes, she was pouting. "It's my apartment too! She can't just lock me out of there once I go to class for the day. What if I need something?"

"You could always go in there," I suggest. "You have a key."

She stares at me incredulously, but I ignore her. "I can't just go in there, I don't know what they're doing! What if I see Kenny's junk? Gross!"

I laugh. "Maybe you should just talk to Hayley? I'm sure if you explain to her that you need Kenny to be out of the apartment at a certain time, she'd kick him out."

"It's just… don't you think it's ridiculous? He's practically living there. The room isn't that big. I have to listen to him snoring, Penelope."

"I agree," I say as I flip a page in my sociology textbook. I had read the same paragraph about ten times and still have no idea what it said. "But seriously, you just need to have a talk with her."

Carla slumps down deeper into her seat. "I guess you're right. Why couldn't we had been roommates? You're boring and celibate, you'd make the perfect roomie."

I glare at her and then glance back at my textbook. "I'll take that as a compliment. I'm taken though." Thankfully, my roommate is hardly ever around. I'm pretty sure she's moved in with her boyfriend in his off-campus apartment. I only see her once or twice a week when she's stopping by to get a bag of new clothes or something.

"I have to get to my next class," she says after a moment. "Mind if I stay in your room this weekend?"

"I'm actually leaving today after my last class. I start my camp job this weekend."

She pulls her backpack onto her shoulder. "Think you'll see the hot ghost boy?"

Carla and Hayley have taken to nicknaming Sampson 'ghost boy' because I have yet to run into him. Carla thinks I'm being 'ghosted' by him, but Hayley tries to be positive about the situation. I can only pass so many curly-headed guys and drive by so many old blue pickup trucks before I have to realize I'm getting my hopes up for nothing. I won't run into him, at least not on campus.

I heard from Ben that Sampson took an internship at a hospital or clinic and it's taken him away from campus for the most part. I thought he would have told me he had an upcoming internship, but he didn't. He acted like bumping into each other would be the easiest thing. I try to shove the thought away that maybe he was just trying to let me down easy, that he didn't want to be with me.

"Who knows if I'll see him," I say, shoving my book into my backpack and pulling out the current book we're reading in English. "I'm not going to get my hopes up. He's probably busy."

"He's an ass, that's what he is," Carla says. "I'll see you Sunday for friend's dinner then."

"See you there," I say.

Every Sunday since the first week of school, we've been going to Ben's place for dinner. Dora cooks most of it and, the rest of us bring dessert or a side. Sampson has never shown up. I'm not the only one he's been ghosting.

Once I finish my last class of the week, I head straight to my car, excited to get back to camp for a few days. I packed up my car this morning, making sure I wore one of the outfits Mom bought me when we went school shopping. If I will have a higher chance of running into Sampson, I want to look good. I settled on a pair of tan capris and a jean blouse, wanting to look cute for him but jobworthy at the same time.

The drive over to camp isn't too bad. I could totally get used to coming back here every weekend, possibly seeing Sampson, being around his mom and her amazing cooking, working at a place I love.

I pull into camp ten minutes ahead of schedule, so I head down to the welcome center parking lot to meet Mr. Garreth. He and Molly are just coming out of the building. Molly has a huge smile on her face when she sees me.

"Good to see you, sweetie," she says patting me softly on the back and then squeezing my shoulder.

"You too, I've been missing this place," I say as I pull away and shake Mr. Garreth's hand.

"You just missed Sampson!" Molly says, and my heart starts hammering in my chest, trying to break out.

"Did I?" I ask, trying not to sound too disappointed.

"Yeah, he just had to pick up some stuff. He and his fraternity brothers are having a weekend trip. They're staying at a cabin in Gatlinburg for a retreat," she says.

"I tried to talk the guys into having it here," Mr. Garreth says. "Apparently the offer was too late, and they had already paid for the rental cabin."

Molly nudges me and grins. "Now that would have been a weekend, right? Helping around here with a bunch of frat guys your first weekend. I bet your girlfriends would have been jealous."

"That would have been something," I say, and smile thinking about how jealous Carla would be, she would definitely be wanting a summer job here.

"Let's go get you some dinner," Molly says. "I hope you don't mind, but for the weekend, we're going to put you up in our house."

"We had to turn off all the water to the cabins," Mr. Garreth explains. "Everything's being shut off maintenance this weekend."

"Yeah, sure, that's fine. I just don't want to get in your way at all," I say.

"You're fine, hun!" Molly says.

I turn back to head for my car. "I'll meet you guys back there, see you in a bit!"

When Mr. and Mrs. Garreth offered to let me stay with them, I figured it would be in their guest bedroom or maybe the basement, but I was wrong. I follow Mrs. Garreth up the stairs, my duffle bag in hand and enter what I'm told is Sampson's room. Mrs. Garreth's amazing dinner wasn't even enough to distract me from the nervousness I was feeling about sleeping in Sampson's room. I think I might do better in a lone cabin without running water, but it's too late for me to turn back.

"Now," Mrs. Garreth says, picking up a dirty white sock from the ground. "I just washed the sheets so they're fresh. There's a bathroom right across the hall, and it's all yours. I'll leave you to get settled in, and we'll see you in the morning."

I nod and gently sit my bag on the floor next to his desk. It's covered in papers with a dusty desktop computer that he forgot to shut down. I gently bump the desk as I'm trying to lean in to examine his Funko Pop figures when the computer wakes up from its sleep. I must have brushed the mouse.

A smile slips across my face when I see a picture of me and him sitting on the logs showing Daisy how to play the red hands game where one person hovers their hands over the other person's and that person tries to slap the other's hands before they pull away. Sampson and I are both smiling. I have no idea who took the picture, or how Sampson acquired it. Maybe it was a picture taken for the camp website or something.

My heart flutters seeing that Sampson made me his screensaver. I grab my toiletry bag and pajamas and head over to the bathroom to get ready for bed. I don't think I will be able to sleep. The thrill of laying my head where Sampson has slept might be too exciting for me.

I finish up in the bathroom and tip-toe back to his room, closing and locking the door behind me. I climb into the bed with my phone and a book I found on one of his shelves.

Just like earlier with my sociology book, I can't concentrate on my reading. I just keep skimming over the same words, but never actually reading and taking them in. I grab my phone and start a text message to Sampson.

"I'm in your bed right now…" I start to type, but think better of it. If he wanted to hear from me, he would have found time to talk to me over the last four weeks. I'm not going to be the one to crawl to him.

Shutting off my phone, I slip under the covers and try my best to stop thinking about him. Maybe taking this job wasn't a good idea.

EPILOGUE

DECEMBER

My parents are trying one more time to save their marriage. In September they booked a winter cruise for the holiday to try and get back to being in love. Though the two of them being away over Christmas is going to suck, I've had plenty of offers from my friends to come home with them for the holiday.

Luckily, them planning so early gave me the chance to schedule a winter course. I took two sociology classes my first semester, and I figured I would try out a third for the month of December. At least that would give me something to keep me busy while my parents are cruising somewhere warmer and I'm not getting any hours in at Camp Arthur.

Campus is pretty empty and when I checked the online roster, it appears only 30 people will be in my sociology lecture. Being an eight o'clock class didn't help its popularity. Thirty bored souls for the holiday season. No doubt half of them will probably try sleeping through the lecture each day.

Bundling up in my winter coat, boots, scarf, and gloves, I head out into the cold, an inch of snow already blanketing the ground. I glance at my watch and realize I only have five minutes to make it to class. My first day of a miserable winter course I will be late, but maybe the snow has slowed down some other students, or maybe the professor is planning on playing hooky.

I'm almost to the door of the sociology building when a stranger rushes in front of me holding the door open, a cup of coffee steaming in his other hand.

"Thanks," I say and head to the elevators. I'm not walking up four flights of stairs in my winter gear, or I'll end up drenched with sweat sitting through class.

As the stranger and I both stand there waiting for the elevator, I slip off my hood, remove my gloves and place them in my pockets, watching the illuminated numbers say which floor the elevator is currently passing. From the corner of my eye, I see the stranger looking down at his phone, so I take the chance to steal a look. Maybe he's the perfect rebound for me, someone I can cuddle with in this chilly weather. Or possibly just a good study partner. Campus has gotten pretty lonely with everyone gone on winter break.

I practically choke on my tongue when his eyes meet mine and I realize he's not a cute stranger that could be my rebound.

"Penelope?" he says, shoving his phone in his pocket and pulling his beanie off to reveal a fresh haircut, his cute boyish curls replaced with one of those metalcore hairstyles where the sides are shaved and only the hair on top remains, slicked back. Not a man bun at least, thank God.

"Oh my god, Sampson," I stammer, barely believing my eyes.

He pulls me into a tight, warm hug, and I practically melt into his arms even though I'm shaking. The elevator doors open and the two of us walk in side by side. Sampson presses a button and the doors close. I notice we're both going to the same floor. I don't even care that

I'm running late now. It's been three months since I've seen him. Three long months.

"It's about time! Talk about serendipity," he says.

"Yeah, I... I've been working at camp all semester. I thought I'd see you there."

He goes back to his side of the elevator and scratches the back of his head. "Yeah, I've been busy with my internship and classes are getting tough. I had to get a tutor and everything. If I wasn't locked in my apartment studying, I was working."

"Busy man," I say.

"What are you doing here?" he asks as we both get off the elevator. He proceeds to follow me to the door of my classroom. "Not going home for winter break?"

"My parents are going on a vacation in a last ditch effort to save their marriage. I figured I'd just take a class to pass the time."

"Well it's good to hear that they're trying to work things out!"

Sampson is giving me a funny look when I turn around to glance back at him and start making my way into the lecture hall. He follows me in and I stop at the bottom of the stairs leading to the seats.

"Wait," I whisper. "Are you in my class too? What are you doing taking a lower level sociology class?"

When he stops at the desk in the front of the room and opens his bag, I grab a seat in the front row, still shocked that he's in the same room as me after months of not hearing from him.

"Hey guys," he says to the class, and my cheeks burn with embarrassment. "Looks like we'll all be spending the next two weeks together. My name is Sampson and I'll be your TA for this class. Your professor is actually sick with the flu right now, so it'll be me for a few days until he gets better."

My jaw drops. Sampson is going to be my TA for the winter semester?

"Now, I know what some of you are thinking, 'Golly, he's so young and attractive, he can't be smart too'." That gets him some giggles from the other girls. "Well, clearly someone thought I was smart enough to help with this class. Take a syllabus and pass the rest to the row behind you…"

Sampson goes on, proceeding with class rules, the attendance policy, and the units we have to learn every week. Since it is such a short class, most of it is learn at your own pace online. We regroup on Mondays and Thursdays to go over the material together. I try my best to concentrate, but it's always been hard for me to focus around Sampson.

He ends the class a few minutes early, and everyone begins packing up their stuff.

"Penelope, can I see you for a moment?" he asks me with his 'teacher voice', not looking up from a piece of paper he's writing. I blush and a few of the other students look at me, probably wondering how I could already be in trouble.

"Sure," I answer, pulling my backpack over my shoulder as the last student quickly shuffles out of the room.

When I approach the desk, he looks up at me and smiles. "Now what?"

"You tell me," I say, grinning back.

"Well, I'm starving!" he proclaims. "Want to go get lunch? It's on me."

"You think that's okay? With you being my TA and all?"

He finishes putting his stuff in his messenger bag. "I've waited long enough to start courting you, I'm not letting this class get in my way of that."

"Okay," I reply. "But you're buying me a dessert, too!"

He shakes his head. "My mother has created a monster."

I follow him out of the room and back to the elevator where his hand meets mine. The butterflies erupt in my stomach, and I can't help but lean my head against his shoulder.

It's finally happening.

Finally.

Acknowledgments

Firstly: thank you to my husband for always pushing me to finish my novel. There were times that I wanted to strangle you for making me write or edit instead of watching a movie or going out, but *The Last July* is finally finished. Thank you for telling me how amazing it would feel to finally hold my first book in my hands and be able to say I wrote a novel. Thank you for editing my first draft and my second—and not complaining… too much.

Thank you to my mom and dad who have told me I could be whoever I wanted to be from a very young age. I know you're proud of me no matter what, but I'm sure you'll be even more proud since I put my English major to use and finally wrote a book. Thanks for all the amazing summer vacations spent hiking in the Smoky Mountains, and thanks for sending me to summer camp as it made for great inspiration. I love the both of you so much.

Thank you to my English and creative writing teachers from high school through college. You helped shape my writing and taught me so much about life, real and written. It is because of you that I found myself in the pages of novels.

And last but not least, thank you to my granny. I wish I could have finished this novel before you passed on, but I know how proud you would be of me. I may not have inherited your green thumb or artistic skills, but I did get your story telling attribute, and I'm so thankful for that.

About the Author

Breanna Mounce grew up in a small Kentucky town and dreamt about exploring places she had yet to see, real and fictional. She received her BA in English from Northern Kentucky University and currently resides just outside of Cincinnati with her husband, dog, and cats. When not writing, she loves escaping to the mountains, hanging out at concerts, and reading as many books as possible.

You can catch up with her blog full of quirky book tidbits at https://breannareadsberks.wordpress.com/

www.ingramcontent.com/pod-product-compliance
Lightning Source LLC
Chambersburg PA
CBHW060855250626
47159CB00008B/2749